I0563232

Love Between Times

by

Beth Ford

Copyright Notice
This is a work of fiction. Names, characters, places, and incidents are either the product of the author's imagination or are used fictitiously, and any resemblance to actual persons living or dead, business establishments, events, or locales, is entirely coincidental.

Love Between Times

COPYRIGHT © 2024 by Beth Ford

All rights reserved. No part of this book may be used or reproduced in any manner whatsoever without written permission of the author or The Wild Rose Press, Inc. except in the case of brief quotations embodied in critical articles or reviews.
Contact Information: info@thewildrosepress.com

Cover Art by *Kristian Norris*

The Wild Rose Press, Inc.
PO Box 708
Adams Basin, NY 14410-0708
Visit us at www.thewildrosepress.com

Publishing History
First Edition, 2024
Trade Paperback ISBN 978-1-5092-5896-3
Digital ISBN 978-1-5092-5897-0

Published in the United States of America

Chapter 1

Alexandria, Virginia

Each call drove the price up. By the time Ashley left the long, tree-sheltered confines of King Street and battled her way through the ramps onto the Beltway, she had three offers over asking. The excitement loosened the knot of tension in her stomach. At twenty-eight, she was relatively new to real estate, but today's open house proved she could succeed.

With this commission check, she could cover the three partial back payments she owed on her mortgage. And if her boyfriend, Trevor, paid his half this month, she could catch up.

However, his track record on that front was abysmal.

She sighed and rested her elbow on the driver's side door as traffic slowed to a crawl. Her phone rang again. The knot in her stomach clenched as she glanced at the screen and saw it was Trevor. She tapped the button on the steering wheel to answer.

"Weren't you supposed to be home already?" Trevor asked.

"I stayed late because so many people came. I've already gotten some ridiculous offers."

"Where are you now?"

"I just got on the Beltway." A car honked for an extended time somewhere behind her. "I won't be home for another hour probably."

"I told you we needed to talk today."

Ashley scrunched up her nose. *He* was telling *her* they needed to talk? Sometimes men were unbelievable—at least the ones she ended up with. "I'll be there when I can."

Trevor paused. "Yeah, okay."

She hung up without saying goodbye. The blue sedan in front of her ground to a halt again. She glanced in the rearview mirror. Her lipstick was long gone, and mascara smudged across one corner of her eye. She fought the urge to pull her lipstick out of her purse and fix it. She should be allowed to be a mess sometimes, right?

Unease tightened her stomach again as she neared her house. Whatever he wanted to discuss, she knew she had to have her own conversation with Trevor. He had a way of making her lose her nerve whenever she decided to stand up to him. He would remind her of the good times they used to have and, if that didn't work, would make her feel guilty for not supporting his dreams. After she pulled into the driveway next to Trevor's twenty-five-year-old beater, she sat in the car for a moment to gather herself. She fixed her makeup to increase her confidence. The peachy-pink lipstick shade she had selected that morning matched her complexion perfectly. Satisfied, she exited the car with purpose. She would not give in this time.

Inside, Trevor waited at the dining room table, legs crossed while he scrolled through his phone.

"Hey," she said, planting an awkward kiss on his cheek. She set her purse on the kitchen counter, then steadied herself with a deep breath before turning to face him.

"What did you want to talk about?" she asked as nonchalantly as possible.

He pulled out the dining chair closest to him and waited for her to sit. His tight smile didn't extend to the dimple that normally appeared in his right cheek when he teased her.

The hesitation to speak showed he lacked his usual confidence. His dark brown eyes searched her face. She suddenly understood that she had some power in this relationship, too, and she needed to own it. She would let him speak first before she told him of her own decisions. She set her hands primly on her knees, steeling herself.

He set his phone on the table and leaned forward. "You remember my buddy Cooper?"

"No."

Trevor sighed. "Well, you've met him at least twice."

It was hard to track all the artist friends that had passed through their house the last few years. "Which one was he again?"

"The sculptor. From New York."

"Right," she said, even though that vague description didn't help. Was he the one with the giant mole that moved as he talked? If so, she hadn't liked him very much.

"Anyway, he's got a room free in his apartment in Brooklyn. He asked me to come up there to live with him. You could come, too."

"Trevor, you can barely afford to live here. How can you afford to live in New York City?"

"There are more opportunities in New York. Cooper has connections with galleries. Ones that pay the big bucks."

Ashley looked at the painting hung on the wall behind Trevor. It was one of her favorites of his, thick swirls of red and black with just enough blue in it so it didn't feel angry. Trevor was talented, she had always known that. But that didn't mean bills didn't need to be paid. By her, mostly. "I can't just pack up and move right now."

"Why not?"

"Are you really asking me that? You know the situation."

He leaned forward. "Come with me. This is our chance to get out of this hellhole. You're always talking about how you hate the traffic and the people here. So, escape with me."

"Who says New York is going to be any better?"

"What is there to think about? This used to be your dream. We were going to be an artist and a writer in New York, remember?" He stood. From her seat, his 6'3" frame seemed to nearly reach the ceiling. "The problem is you've lost your sense of adventure. You're happy to stay here and sell houses and make money."

"What's wrong with that?"

"You're not even good at it. You're miserable and you refuse to admit it."

Ashley pinched the bridge of her nose and willed herself not to scream in frustration. She let out a shaky breath. "I am good at it. I'm struggling because you haven't paid any rent for the last six months."

"I'm your boyfriend, not your tenant."

"It doesn't matter. We agreed when I bought the house—"

"Have you told your parents you're behind on your

mortgage?" he asked.

Ashley shook her head. They had been so proud when she bought the house. Her mother had been happy that, unlike her, Ashley would never be dependent on a man. Except here Ashley was, flailing because Trevor had put his own dreams ahead of financial stability. Her dad wouldn't be able to resist saying "I told you so." She dreaded telling her parents she had failed. "I don't see what that has to do with anything."

"You know your dad would give you the money. Why not take it?"

"I don't want to rely on him. Especially when I'm not the problem."

"Wow, Ash, that's fucked up. The problem is that you've given up on your dreams."

"One of us had to. There has to be balance between dreams and responsibility."

"Well, not in my world."

"Good luck with that."

She stood. He stared her down, a few inches from her face. She knew he was waiting for her to crumble like she always did. She remembered her resolution in the car. This time she would stand firm.

"I guess I'm leaving without you," he finally said.

"Go right ahead."

"You know what?" He fished in his jeans pocket and pulled out his key ring.

Ashley bit her lip to keep from laughing as he struggled to remove his house key from the loop.

Finally, he got the key loose and brandished it at her. "Here's your key. Good luck with your sad, pathetic, suburban life."

By the time Ashley turned around, he was already

stomping down the driveway. She opened her mouth to call after him, but no words escaped her dry throat.

After his car pulled away with a sputter, silence took over, reverberating around her. The wind went out of her. She had kept her resolve, but it had ended everything. She raised her shaking hands to her face and touched the tears streaming down. She was less relieved than she thought she would be. Instead, he had managed to make her feel small even when she was taking control of her own life. And the confrontation brought her no closer to an answer to her problems. Now there was no Trevor and no hope for any additional rent support at all.

At this thought, righteous anger flared. Who was he to lord his artistic commitment over her, when she had supported it financially all these years? Yes, when they first got together, after Ashley returned to the States from grad school in London five years ago, she had dreamed big with her writing. She had loved Trevor's dedication to his art. But he hadn't grown along with her. He made her be the adult while he stayed a child, and she hated it.

Ashley clattered around the kitchen to give herself something to do. She opened a bottle of wine as she made dinner, but the alcohol didn't quiet her mind. Her thoughts circled around the drain her life was going down. She had worked so hard, and her reward was the loss of her boyfriend—though honestly it was good riddance on that front—and potentially her house.

She considered calling someone for support. But with so much of her attention focused on work and money lately, she had let her friendships lapse. She would hate to be that person who only called when she needed help. There was her mother, of course, but she would probably sympathize too much. Ashley's mom had been reliant on Ashley's dad for the entirety of their marriage and had struggled mightily to support herself after the divorce. When her receptionist job couldn't pay the bills, she had relied on a series of increasingly questionable men to support her and Ashley, but after a time, each one had pulled the rug out from under them. Ashley had promised herself she would never be like that, that she would always be independent. And to hear her mother equate their situations would have Ashley grinding her teeth. But without help, even if she could put the bank off for now, with Trevor gone, she would have to either sell the house or get a roommate pronto to afford the payments.

After dinner, she went upstairs to the spare bedroom, taking a fresh glass of wine with her. She sat at her desk and opened her laptop, navigating to the photos from her time in London. Things had been so easy then, all the possibilities of life before her. She paused at a photo of herself and her friend Yipeng both grinning like crazy in front of the Charles Dickens Museum. Ashley had been elated to stand in the rooms the great man had lived in. It had brought her back to when she was a child reading *A Christmas Carol* and *Oliver Twist*. She had written her master's thesis on Dickens, too, but even that couldn't capture the magic she experienced meeting those characters for the first time.

She set down her wine glass. When was the last time she had even read a book?

She rifled through the bins stacked on the floor of the guest bedroom closet. She pulled out a folder of papers she had written in grad school and flipped through the first few. It transported her back to the small classrooms stuffed with U-shaped tables where all she had to think and talk about was books.

She shut the folder and peered into the bin. A notebook sat freshly exposed. Beneath it, another, and another. She laid them on the floor in front of her and flipped through their pages. None of them were full, but each held the scrawl of her own stories—fantasies she had long since given up in favor of the things she had to do.

Was Trevor right? Had she lost something she had never thought she'd lose? She never thought she would remain permanently in Northern Virginia, and certainly not doing something as boring as selling houses to people with too much money. She had been sure that if she could get settled and secure, then she could focus on her creative side. She downed the remainder of the wine. How long would she have to wait for that to happen?

Tears pricked her eyes again. She slammed the notebook cover down to protect the ink from the fat, wet drops.

Clearly something needed to change. She had to figure out what she really wanted. Otherwise, she would stagnate in some cut-rate apartment, daydreaming and drinking wine alone for the rest of her life. With Trevor gone, she only had to worry about herself. She could take charge and fix this.

Maybe.

When Ashley awoke the next morning, her circumstances felt less catastrophic. She had a touch of a headache from all the wine, but nothing she couldn't push through. She was more determined than ever to salvage her situation and prove herself. She had to focus on what she could gain, not what she had lost.

Ashley went into the office to deal with paperwork

and send the previous day's offers on the townhouse to the Patels. She hadn't settled at her desk before Marilyn, the broker, called for her. Ashley forced a smile and headed to Marilyn's office, closing the door behind her. Marilyn motioned for Ashley to sit. Marilyn was in her late fifties but kept her dyed blonde hair so perfectly styled Ashley was certain she must get a blowout at the salon every morning. The only detriment to her appearance was that she continued to wear the same skirts she had before the coronavirus pandemic, even though they were now a bit tight. To compensate, she wore them fastened high above her waist, which made them all impersonate miniskirts.

Almost as if she had heard Ashley's thoughts, Marilyn tugged at the hem of her skirt. "How are things going with that listing you viewed last week?"

"I gave it to Jayna like you asked," Ashley said, referring to the assistant—and, not coincidentally, Marilyn's niece—that Ashley was supposed to have been mentoring for the last year. When she could be bothered to on top of everything else she had to do, that is. Which, unfortunately, wasn't often, and Marilyn had noticed.

"How is she doing?" When Ashley didn't immediately respond, Marilyn continued. "I know I said make her the primary, but you may still need to help her. Check what she's doing. Give her some advice."

Ashley's heart picked up its pace. She was already losing part of this commission just when she really needed it. And now she had to babysit the person taking it away from her? But the long-term benefit of staying in Marilyn's good graces overrode her short-term concerns. "I'll check in with her right now."

Ashley returned to her desk. She stood resting her fingertips on the smooth wood surface while she took a few deep breaths to steady herself. She would help Jayna, placate Marilyn, and no one would be any the wiser about her own predicament. She picked up a notepad from her desk, then walked over to Jayna.

Jayna perked up as Ashley approached. "I have a couple of questions about that listing you gave me, since I haven't seen it in person." She held a pen at the ready above a legal pad. "Can you tell me—"

Ashley's stomach heaved, last night's wine suddenly making itself known. "Why don't you send me what you've prepared for the listing, and I'll identify how I can help, okay?" She turned and hurried to the bathroom.

When her stomach had settled and she returned to her desk, the email was waiting for her. Jayna had sent the listing to the owner, Deedee, and Deedee wanted some changes. Jayna promised she would work on them that day. Ashley braced herself and clicked through the photos, pushing down her desire to gloat that Jayna couldn't do this without her. The house appeared cheap in the photos, and the clunky language in the writeup didn't sell it.

I'll talk to Deedee and handle this, Ashley wrote back. Ashley had met with Deedee originally, after all. This was her problem to fix. Jayna might get the credit, but Ashley could make sure Marilyn knew the work Ashley had put into it for her.

Ashley finished her paperwork, then got on the road for a couple of showing appointments. Once in the car, Ashley phoned Deedee. She assured her that everything was under control, and that Ashley reinserting herself into the process absolutely did not mean that Jayna didn't know what she was doing. She thought Deedee bought it, or at least was willing to go along with it because it meant she got what she wanted.

Between showings, Ashley called one of her interior design contacts to stage the house, then called in a favor with Shawna, who Ashley had given a lot of business to over the years, to take the pictures for free so the redo costs wouldn't eat into the commission too much. By late afternoon when Ashley pulled back into the office parking lot, she was sure she had saved the day and Jayna would be thrilled.

But as soon as Ashley stepped through the front door, Jayna rushed over, glowering.

"Why is someone named Shawna calling me to coordinate new photos for Deedee's house?"

"She's going to do it for free, don't worry." Ashley navigated around Jayna to set her purse on her desk.

"How dare you go and make all these arrangements behind my back?" Jayna shouted.

Ashley stopped and peered at her. Was this really happening? "I was trying to help. Like I said I would."

"You could have talked to me about what you thought needed to be fixed and then I could have taken care of it. But now I look like I have no clue what the fuck I'm doing and you had to swoop in and save my ass."

Ashley raised one eyebrow, biting back the retort burning in her mouth. Instead, she said, "I was being efficient."

"Bullshit. You were taking over so you could be the lead. And get the big fat check to yourself again. So, you know what? Fuck you. Take the listing. I never want to talk to you again."

A tittering came from the other side of the room, reminding Ashley that the other agents were watching. "Why don't we go in the conference room?" she asked quietly.

"No, I'm done." Jayna turned and stormed outside. A moment later, a car engine started and sped away.

Ashley watched the door in disbelief. After a moment, she slowly turned and walked toward Marilyn's office. Marilyn was already standing, peering like a meercat out her door at the scene.

"What the hell just happened?"

"I don't know. I really was trying to be helpful. And clearly that wasn't appreciated. It never is." Tears pricked Ashley's eyes. She shook her head. She never cried in public. "I'm sorry."

Marilyn's frown softened. "Is everything okay?"

"Yes," she said, then stopped herself. Honesty was probably the best policy here. "I mean, no. I broke up with my boyfriend yesterday, which sounds like a lame excuse when I say it out loud."

"It's not. I'm sorry. You guys were together for a while, right?"

Ashley nodded and wiped at her eyes.

Marilyn came around the desk. "I think what was lacking here was the approach. This is a people business," Marilyn said. "You have to be able to work with other people. Sometimes that requires finesse." She paused and rubbed Ashley's shoulder. "That said, it wasn't appropriate for Jayna to yell at you like that. We can all talk it out tomorrow."

Ashley's head shot up. Suddenly, she knew exactly what she didn't want. "No," she said. "We won't." She cut off Marilyn's sound of surprise. "I'm not happy here, Marilyn. I need to figure out a new path for myself. I have to leave the agency."

"But the clients—"

"I'll brief Jayna. Or you. Whichever will cause the least stress. I just know that something in my life needs to change."

"I guess we should admire you for acknowledging that. We'll be sad for you to go, though."

"Maybe I'll be back. I just need to figure some things out first."

"Take the time you need. We'll be here if you decide to come back." She looked at Ashley with concern. "Will you be okay?"

"Yeah. I'm just going to go."

Ashley packed up her belongings in a daze. She said goodbye to no one as she left, and they made no attempt to acknowledge her. Her bridges here were burning, and she didn't have the strength right now to put the fires out. She had made the right decision, but with no more money coming in, all hope of saving her house evaporated.

In her hurry to leave, her box of office supplies and random cords slipped out of her hands onto the pavement beside her car. She left it there and ran it over with a satisfying crunch as she backed out of her parking space for the last time.

Chapter 2

Wiltshire, England, 1377

The silence of approaching death draped the walls of the house like heavy tapestries. Thomas waited in the small closet at the top of the curved stone staircase. He ran his finger lightly along the wall as he paced the small space, tracing the vines connecting the floral motif painted onto the plaster walls. No voices drifted from his father's bedchamber. From the great hall below came only the occasional sound of the shift of feet or clink of a mug against the wooden table. Throughout the castle, even as the servants' movements up and down the stairs grew more hurried, their footsteps quietened, as if they were being swept up to heaven with their master.

Thomas's mother emerged from the bed chamber. Thomas halted his progress across the room.

"He's asking for you," she said. She set a hand gently on his arm and squeezed.

Thomas nodded and entered the room she had just vacated. He shut the door firmly behind him. Inside, the curtains were pulled tight, giving the room the aspect of midnight rather than midday. A single candle burned on the bedside table. The low fire burning in the hearth against one wall made the room unbearably stuffy in the summer heat. Even with the smoke canopy venting the worst of it outside, wisps of smoke dimmed the room further.

Thomas coughed as he sat in a chair pulled close to the side of the bed. His father had already summoned Thomas's older brother, John, and the estate manager to receive their instructions. Then his mother had had her final goodbye with him. Thomas, of course, was last, of least importance. Thomas would have to say what needed to be said before the priest arrived.

His father had lived with a weak heart for years, and it had caught up with him. He lay propped up in bed, his skin pale, his face slightly puffy. He labored to suck in each breath. The powerful knight Thomas recalled from his childhood was lost, subsumed by this weak body in front of him now. His father's chest rattled as he let out a breath. Thomas crossed himself for good measure against the curse of death.

At first, he thought his father didn't realize he was there, but he eventually turned to Thomas and locked eyes with him. His mind was still there, sharp and ready to cut.

"You know what I'm about to tell you," he said.

Thomas had to lean in to hear him. He did, in fact, know where this conversation would go. He had walked in thinking he would confront his father, finally make a stand, but seeing his father now, about to fade away, there seemed no point. Why argue with a man who wouldn't be here in the morning? Thomas would simply let the words he knew were coming be said.

"It is beyond time you were ordained. You must do your duty to your family and make your way in the world."

His father didn't ask for a promise or a vow. He simply believed that his will would be done. Thomas didn't disabuse him of that notion. He squeezed his father's hand in response.

"When John goes on campaign, you must care for your mother."

"I will."

When no further instructions were forthcoming, Thomas stood and crossed himself again. His father returned to staring at some far away point in the distance, as if Thomas were never there. Thomas walked to the door and paused as he held the handle. "Goodbye, Father," he said quietly, then stepped out of the unbearable room and shut the door firmly behind him.

The relative brightness took a moment to adjust to. His mother was gone. In her place, hovering by the narrow window, stood John's wife, Kathryn. Thomas wasn't the last, then. His sister-in-law ranked below him. The sight of the sunlight illuminating her fair skin took his breath away. He didn't dare say anything to her now, in this heavy moment. Instead, he reached across the small space and touched her elbow lightly with the pad of one finger. She jolted at his touch but quickly settled and smiled when she realized it was him.

He thought back to the last conversation he had had with his father before he had taken to his sickbed. "You must stop mooning over Kathryn after all these years," his father had said. "You always knew it would be this way. You must stop coveting your brother's life."

Now, Thomas shared a barely perceptible nod with her. Nothing ever passed between them except fair words and these occasional glances. But, still, he knew their affection for each other was obvious, even to his father who didn't pay attention to much besides war, politics, the estate, and ale, in that order. Thomas tore his gaze away from Kathryn's green eyes. He walked downstairs and joined his family in silence at the long table in the great hall.

An hour later, the priest had just ascended the stairs to the death chamber when the clamor of an arriving rider arose in the courtyard. John went out to investigate. He returned a moment later with a sheet of curled parchment in his hand. "A messenger from the king," he announced. As he read the page silently, he slowly crossed himself. "The king is dead," he told the others.

The news caused no uproar. The elderly king had held no real sway over the government the last few years. But, still, it was odd to think of a new ruler in his place. For all of Thomas's twenty-five years, and even for the entirety of his mother's lifetime, Edward III had ruled, a constant through the many battles with France and through the Black Death which still left so many villages across the nation emptied.

"The court calls all the nobles to London," John said.

"You can't leave now," their mother said, stepping closer to her eldest son. Her hood was askew, revealing the hairline just above her forehead, but she didn't bother to adjust it.

"Of course not," John said, folding the page and tucking it into his shirt without a glance at his mother. "I'll wait until after the funeral."

His mother pursed her lips and diverted her eyes. "Of course," she said to no one in particular.

Thomas bristled at his brother's use of the singular. "*We'll* go," he said. He would not be left behind at a moment of such import.

Measured footfalls rang down the stone steps. The priest walked slowly into the room. "He has gone to

God." He held the gaze of each occupant of the room in turn, offering silent condolences through the reassuring firmness of his presence.

"Thank you, Father," John said. "Please, refresh yourself before you journey home." He extended an arm toward the table. "I will talk to you before you leave about the payment for masses to be said for his soul."

The priest inclined his head and settled onto the bench along the table where he looked eagerly around for a servant to bring his meal. One of the family hounds padded over from the warmth of the central hearth to the priest's side, ready to accept any scraps.

John, Thomas, and their mother walked toward the stairs. John pulled Thomas back and let their mother go ahead. "You don't have to go to London. As the new baron, I am sufficient to represent our family."

"I want to go," Thomas said. "It will be expected for everyone to appear at court and support the new king."

John watched Thomas for a moment, then sighed. "I don't have the energy to fight with you about this right now. Very well, you can come. But when we return…"

"I know."

"Good." John nodded curtly and took the curving stairs up two at a time.

Thomas followed more slowly. He hadn't needed to remind John about Thomas's new role in the family. Thomas was now the next heir to their father's title. Despite nine years of marriage, John and Kathryn had produced no living child. A son had died at two, a stillborn girl had arrived three years ago, with nothing since then. Should John be killed on campaign in France, Thomas would inherit the family's lands and title. There would be nothing shocking about him appearing at court alongside his brother now.

When Thomas reached the landing, John had already disappeared into their father's bedchamber. Kathryn hovered near the shut door, chewing a thumbnail down to its root. Despite himself, a spark of hope lit his heart that she was waiting for him. But his approach didn't ease her stance.

"Are you all right?" he asked.

She didn't catch his eye as she responded. "Yes, of course."

His hope sputtered out. She was clearly adrift in her own worries that had nothing to do with him. However, he couldn't resist continuing the conversation, like pressing on a sore bruise. "John told you the news?"

She nodded and glanced at the bed chamber door. "The king and your father in the same day. That whole generation is dying off. And who knows what will be here to replace it."

Thomas watched her in profile, remembering how much laughter they had shared as children playing in the woods around her family's estate, where Thomas had spent the years of his squire training. Now, there were lines around the corners of her mouth, a lingering sadness in her eyes. He wondered if he would have made her any happier than John had managed to.

He shook the thoughts off. On this topic, at least, his father was right. He must put the past behind him, gazing only ahead. There was duty, and there were dreams. The one must sometimes give way to the other. "I best go in," he said, and she stepped aside to let him pass.

****

The funeral was held quickly; the death surprised no one, and plans had already been in place. The night before the brothers were to leave for London, Thomas crept across the lawn to the estate's chapel. The heavy door creaked as it swung open, but he was the only one around to hear. He liked the church best like this, when the silence edged out any worries about his future, and no one was around to judge which path he chose for his life.

He stood by his father's tomb. It had been constructed several years before to his father's exact specifications, sitting empty until its planned occupants were ready. One day, it would be his mother's tomb as well. Thomas laid his hand on the cool stone. The effigy of his father showed him in his armor, hearkening back to the long-lost days when his father had fought alongside Edward III in France. All old men yearned to return to their youth. Thomas was in his youth now. What would he do with it?

Stretched out beside his father was an image of his mother, her hands clasped in prayer. One day, she would lie here next to her husband. The thought didn't depress Thomas. He knew they would be together in the hereafter. But it drew his thoughts back to what his father had demanded of him: it was time for Thomas to become a priest. He had always known his destiny lay with the church, though his parents had hedged their bets in case something happened to John and had trained Thomas as a knight as well. And now Thomas felt the possibility of that life he had to relinquish.

He closed his eyes. Somewhere an owl hooted, a gentle, questioning sound. He made no formal prayer but listened to what he could hear between the silences seeping out from the stones. He could sense this last journey with John to London would be a turning point, but what lay around the corner he couldn't quite work out. It didn't feel like it would be a quiet clerical life, but that could be his own stubborn foolishness getting in the way. He knew he had to get out of Wiltshire once before he decided which path his life would take. He had to experience something of the world before he accepted giving it up.

He opened his eyes and regarded the stone form that had replaced his living, breathing father. "I'll do my best," was all he could promise to the ghosts.

****

"To your travels, gentlemen," the brothers' new London friend said at the end of their trip two weeks later. The man clinked glasses with Thomas and John. "May your ale always be strong and your barmaids sweet."

Both brothers sipped from their mugs. "Thomas won't be having the latter for much longer—at least not officially," John said with a wink.

"That's right," the man said as if recalling a long-ago conversation, not one from a mere half an hour ago. Thomas couldn't blame the man, as Thomas couldn't even recall their drinking companion's name. "Our soon-to-be priest," the man continued. He clapped Thomas on the shoulder, then called for another round. When one was not forthcoming, he tripped off to procure it himself.

Thomas scooted to his left along the bench, taking over the vacated seat. Around them, a dozen conversations bubbled in the alcoves throughout the hall. Thomas wished he could join any one of those other than this. "I wish you wouldn't tell everyone we meet that I'm about to be ordained," he said.

"Why not? It's the truth. And you've been putting it

off long enough. It's time for you to go back to Salisbury and meet with the bishop."

Thomas frowned. He searched for a good change of topic. They had left court the day before, and it seemed safe enough to discuss politics among themselves here, with their voices covered by the garrulousness around the rest of the hall. "What do you think of the new young king then?"

John shrugged. "He's a boy. His uncle will run things until his maturity and probably long beyond that." He dropped his voice even lower so that Thomas had to lean in to hear him. "John of Gaunt's the real king, not that child Richard."

Thomas wasn't shocked. Many people had said it since Edward's death. "Is that why you're joining his campaigns in France?" Thomas asked, referring to John of Gaunt's gathering forces.

John reclined against the wall and waved his mug languidly through the air. "I'm going for the glory of myself and my family. Just like you are desperate to do yourself." Seeing this comment had soured the mood again, John drained the rest of his ale. "I'm off to bed, brother. I'll see you in the morning." He stood. "Don't be too loud when you come in. Take your whore somewhere else, if you get one." He grinned and trooped upstairs to the small corner room the brothers had rented for the night.

Thomas scooted to the edge of the bench so he could scan the room from his now-empty alcove. People crisscrossed the hall in search of whatever they needed, be it more ale, a hot supper, or a trip to the outhouse. A smartly dressed young couple entered the building and spoke with the landlord. Thomas wondered if they were newly married and where they were headed to.

More people lived in London than he would have believed existed anywhere. The first few days he found it jarring, but now he relished the anonymity brought by a crowd. Here, he was just a traveler, not the second son of the local lord, the third Baron de la Warr. The unimportant, disposable second son, destined for the church even though he had received a squire's training like his brother. Tonight, with John asleep upstairs, he could be Thomas, a knight, destined for battle like his brother.

His friend returned with three fresh pints of ale. Thomas thought the man's name might be Edward, but maybe he was mixing this man up with the others they had met on their travels the last few weeks. Either way, he accepted the drink gratefully and passed the third on to a new man who appeared beside him, instantly securing another friend for the evening.

A while later, he went outside to relieve himself. Two women plied their trade across the way. He considered his brother's earlier comment about bringing a whore to their room. He felt ambivalent about the prospect. He had enjoyed his fair share of women back home, but tonight he was lamenting something else—the fact that if he went through with his ordination, he would miss out not just on sex but on the companionship of a wife and the legacy of children. Not that he had any woman he wanted to wed, especially now he had vowed to forget Kathryn, but the thought of the possibility closing itself off forever saddened him.

As he watched the women, two men in monk's robes approached them. After a moment's negotiation, the four went into the building. Thomas shook his head. This is what he was joining? An institution full of hypocrites? He knew the Bishop of Salisbury, who would ordain him soon, was rumored to live a lavish lifestyle, as were many others within the church. A priest's life may not deprive Thomas of too many fleeting material pleasures, then. But what was the point if those leading the church didn't live up to the standards they set for themselves and expected of the common people?

Guilt struck him at the mere thought. He crossed himself in penance and hurried back inside.

It was only a few hours before dawn when Thomas made it upstairs to bed. John snored without stirring as Thomas removed his boots and hose. He would regret at least three of those pints in the morning. The day's ride would be rough, and he probably wouldn't make it very far.

He watched his brother sleep. In the morning, John would meet with a ship to take more men across the Channel to protect England's interests in France. And Thomas would head west, back home to Wiltshire to start his career as a canon in the church. He had been promised a parish in the diocese of Lincoln. But a journey fifty or a hundred miles from home was not the same as sailing to a new country.

He pulled back the sheets and slid into bed. While he and his brother had been at court, declaring their fealty to the newly crowned king, Thomas had relished being treated like any other noble, a man of the realm. Once he became a man of the cloth, he would never be treated the same again. He would give anything to go off to war like his brother.

And why shouldn't he? The idea pierced the haze of his thoughts like an expertly loosed arrow. There must be ships leaving for France all the time. Surely, they would need more men after the disastrous campaigns of the last few years. For all his brother's praise of John of Gaunt, the man had not managed to turn the tide in France during his time there. England needed to regain its foothold in that country to prevent the attacks on England's port towns that had become increasingly frequent.

Thomas's father thought too small. He had been worried only about Thomas's future, and no one could blame him for providing for his children. But there were larger forces at work, concerns greater than Thomas's own career. Thomas reminded himself he had promised nothing to his father on his deathbed. Besides, he could always be ordained in the future. He had put it off for so long, what was another few months, or a year? This was what he had to do now if he wanted any scrap of enjoyment out of his life.

By the time the first rays of summer sunlight entered the room, Thomas had decided. He would leave this morning and head off just as his brother expected him to. But he would turn south as soon as he could instead of continuing west. He would find a ship to take him to France or find an English port to help defend in the meantime. He would not be sucked into the church before he had brought glory to himself on the battlefield.

It was his birthright as much as his brother's.

The repercussions within his family would be unpleasant, but he would deal with them when they came. For now, he would pursue what he was sure was his destiny.

Chapter 3

When Ashley returned home after quitting her job, she called her dad. Now that her circumstances had changed, the time for grandstanding was over. She didn't get into the details but simply asked him to come over that weekend. He showed up after lunch on Saturday. His manner was brusque, and he told her he was missing a movie with his wife and stepchildren by being there. "I only have an hour," he said, though movies lasted longer than that. Ashley rolled her eyes as he pulled off the baseball cap he often wore to cover his ever-increasing bald spot.

Ashley had promised herself she would face this conversation with a steely resolve, but as soon as they sat across from each other at the dining room table, tears pricked her eyes.

Her father's gaze softened immediately. "What is it?"

Her tears flowed unstoppably at the unexpected tenderness in his voice. Once she collected herself, she spilled the whole story: quitting her job, Trevor letting her down, and most importantly for her financially minded dad, the mess with her mortgage. For once she appreciated his no-nonsense approach as he immediately plowed ahead into how to rectify the situation. It kept her grounded, and her tears at bay.

He frowned as he shuffled through the late notices

and payment records. Once he reached the bottom of the stack, he looked up at her. "You take after your mother when it comes to finances."

The wind went out of her as if she had been punched in the chest. That was exactly what she had been trying her whole life to avoid. Her father had always been financially responsible, completely in control. She hated that she had disappointed him like this.

"And I suppose there was never a written lease with Trevor to give you legal recourse?"

"No. I thought—" She stopped herself. She didn't know what she had thought. She hadn't expected Trevor to take care of her, like her mother had with her string of boyfriends, but Ashley had expected Trevor to take care of himself. That had been too much to ask, apparently.

Her father gave his head a wide-eyed shake as if he couldn't believe what he heard. Then he gathered himself and looked her full in the face, all business. "You obviously can't afford this house. I said that when you bought it, didn't I?"

It seemed childish for him to say he told her so, but she nodded meekly.

"I don't want this to ruin your credit, so I can give you the money to cover the missed payments." He thumped a forefinger on the table. "But I will only do that if you agree to sell the house. The market has gone up in the last few years, so you may even make money on it."

The ultimatum made sense, though she couldn't quite bring herself to say so. "Then what will I do?" she asked instead.

"Come live with us. Get yourself back on your feet."

"I can't do that."

"Why on earth not? Mandy won't mind. Zoe will leave for college in the fall, so her room will open up."

The thought that it was April and he was thinking she would still be in his house by the fall floored her. She had hoped for a quick fix, a way to escape. But she had backed herself into a corner.

"It's the only long-term solution," he said. "You have to think about your future."

"I have to think about it," she said quietly, leaving it open whether she referred to her future or his proposal.

He stood. "Well, don't think about it too long." He waved one of the pages at her. "Tomorrow's the first, so you're going to be late on another payment."

"I have some money I can put toward it."

"That's not good enough, Ash."

"Let me think about it until tomorrow."

He sighed. "Fine. I've got to go anyway. But understand there is only one option here."

She forced a smile. "Thanks, Dad."

He left without a hug or a goodbye. His baseball cap sat forgotten on the table, but he didn't return to retrieve it. She ran her fingers absentmindedly along the tattered rim, trying to decide what to do.

The next day, before Ashley had mustered the courage to accept her father's offer, Hannah, Ashley's older cousin from her father's side, called from England, where she lived with her husband and daughter. Ashley had spent time with Hannah while studying in London but hadn't talked to her much since. Ashley settled into her favorite armchair in the living room to answer it. There was no way the timing of this phone call was a coincidence.

Ashley said as much to Hannah after they said hello.

"Why can't this just be a friendly phone call?" Hannah asked. Her accent had softened, over her years in the UK, to something not quite English, not quite American.

"You haven't called me since I've been back home."

"To be fair, you haven't called me, either. You have a tendency only to call your family when you need something. You know that, right?"

Ashley was silent. Hannah wasn't entirely wrong, but how was Ashley supposed to respond to such an accusation in the moment?

Hannah continued. "Yeah, truth, cuz. Anyway, your dad did ask me to call you. He told me what a bad spot you're in."

"I wish he wouldn't spread that around. It's not something I'm proud of."

Hannah's tone softened. "I know, but something good will come out of it, I promise. In fact, I'm proud of you for taking control of things. This Trevor fellow sounds like a deadbeat, and I never pictured you as an estate agent. We all just want to help."

"I appreciate that." She didn't know why she had started off so confrontational. She had always liked how little Hannah judged herself and other people.

"In a way, you're in a great position," Hannah said. "You can do whatever you want next. Any thoughts on what that will be?"

Ashley sighed. "I don't know."

Hannah let the silence drag out, forcing Ashley to fill it.

"Honestly, I've been thinking a lot about the time I spent in London. I loved it there."

"You were also a student. It's easy to feel nostalgic."

"True. But…you know I used to write, don't you?"

"I remember. You used to show me the little books you put together when you were a kid. Your drawings were terrible, by the way."

Ashley laughed. "Yeah, I won't attempt any illustrations now. I always thought I'd be a writer, but I haven't put a word on paper in years."

"So what you need is time to focus on that."

"Yeah, maybe."

"I have a proposition then. You know we own a few rental properties. We have two in the same building in Salisbury. You know where that is? One is about to be vacant, and the other we've switched over to a vacation rental. Why don't you spend the summer over here and stay in the empty flat?"

"That sounds expensive," Ashley said, even though her heart picked up pace at the prospect.

"We won't charge you. In fact, you'll be helping us. You can let the guests in and deal with any issues they're having. Answer questions for them about the town. It'll be perfect for you with your real estate background. You just have to promise me that you'll call me to be nosy, not just because you need something."

Ashley agreed. It was an easy promise to make.

Once they hung up, Ashley called her dad and agreed to sell the house and pay him back as soon as she was able. Before she hung up, she said, "Seriously, Dad, thanks. I'm lucky to have you guys."

He just grunted in response, but something in the sound betrayed his affection. She smiled.

She was less sad than she thought she would be as she surveyed the detritus of her life. Sometimes things had to be destroyed to be rebuilt, but she still had a couple of bridges that she hadn't burnt yet. Solid bridges that would take her places.

Ashley determined to move forward to the next phase of her life and think of the past as little as possible. On Monday, she contacted a quick homebuying company so that she wouldn't have to wait months for the sale to happen and she could get to Salisbury as quickly as possible, which was now her only goal. Going that route would also avoid having to list it and offer showings—all things that would remind her of the career she had thrown away. She accepted the company's offer right away. She would make money like her dad said. She worked for a couple of freelance editing and article writing websites to have some income. Her dad gave her a check, and she paid what she owed on her mortgage. She felt guilty taking the money, like she was receiving something she didn't deserve. She should feel lucky, though a sneaky voice in the back of her mind also chastised her for her obvious privilege. Think of all the people who had no one to bail them out. If she were one of them, her future would look drastically different.

She also meant what she told Hannah. She wanted to write again. She would show Trevor that she wasn't a sellout and that it was possible to have both stability and art.

She read through her old notebooks. She had started writing a novel years ago, but the momentum had quickly faltered. The manuscript was mostly disconnected pieces so far, but she liked the central idea, a thriller in which the reader assumed the main character was the narrator, but it was later revealed to be her sister. The twist changed the reader's perspective on the entire story. Or she hoped it would if she pulled it off.

She contacted her friend Sadie, with whom she had swapped short stories during a creative writing class one summer in college. Ashley and Sadie had drifted apart in the last few years. Trevor had never warmed to her, and to a certain extent Ashley couldn't blame him. Sadie had a big personality, and it could be a lot to have around. But the last time Ashley had talked to her, Sadie had been writing a book and therefore might have some advice to give.

Fortunately, Sadie didn't hold their recent distance against Ashley. She let Ashley catch her up on all that had happened, then did the same. She had her manuscript out with agents, a step that Ashley felt was impossibly far away for her own work. Sadie offered to have Ashley join her monthly critique group, and Ashley gratefully accepted.

A couple of Saturdays later, Ashley arrived late to the critique group meeting in the back of a local hipster coffee shop. The group had already begun to discuss the first piece, so they simply waved her in while the conversation continued. She listened until they came to her submitted chapter.

"It's interesting," a heavyset man in his sixties named Jim said. "It's similar to Sadie's novel that we workshopped with her last year. You guys must think alike."

Sadie jumped in. "I don't think so. We used to take creative writing classes together. That's it."

Ashley's mind whirred. Had she and Sadie talked about this book when Ashley had started it years ago? It was possible. Ashley said, "Well, since everyone else has read the book, I'd like to get a sample of it, if you don't mind."

Sadie shrugged. "Sure."

The discussion moved on, but the comment nagged at her along with the fact that Sadie had been quick to jump in and shut Jim down. When she got home, Ashley went through her old files again and found that she had submitted an earlier draft of her first chapter to the last creative writing class she and Sadie had taken together. She may have talked with Sadie about her plans for the book back then, but it wasn't until later that she had come up with the idea of the narrator switch. She relaxed. Even if she and Sadie had started from the same point, they were sure to end up at different places. There was nothing to worry about after all.

After some prompting from Ashley, a week later Sadie sent her the entire manuscript. Ashley skimmed the first chapter, desperate to see if Jim was right about the similarities. After a few pages, the knot in her stomach loosened. The two chapters overlapped but weren't the same. As she read the chapter through more slowly a second time, it seemed familiar, beyond its connections to Ashley's own work. She guessed Sadie had also submitted her chapter during that same class. That didn't make Sadie the bad guy. She and Ashley had read each other's work and things must have seeped in.

As she continued by skimming the subsequent chapters, Sadie called.

"Sorry I took so long to send it," Sadie said. "I have an agent interested in representing it. But she wants some changes. I tried to address them on my own, but I gave up and sent it to see what you would say."

Sadie walked Ashley through the changes the agent had suggested. The lingering one that she wasn't sure how to address dealt with a pivotal emotional scene about two thirds of the way through that came across flat rather than engaging.

Ashley read through those pages for a few minutes. Overall, the book was good, she admitted, but the agent was right that it needed something else.

"I think you need to change the point of view," Ashley said. "Get in closer to the narrator. Then we would feel her more."

It was a huge ask. Ashley believed she was barely qualified to give it. But it was oftentimes easier to recognize the flaws in someone else's work.

Sadie took a moment to absorb the comment. "That would require rewriting nearly the whole book."

Ashley shrugged, trying to sound as if rewriting books was something she did every day. "Sometimes that's what you have to do."

"What do you know." The comment was a throwaway, a teasing barb with just enough sting in it to wound.

Sadie stayed silent, probably waiting for Ashley to do something, to apologize or admit that she was wrong about needing to rewrite the book. When that didn't materialize, Sadie sighed. "I knew there was a bigger problem here, but I think I needed someone else to say it too."

"Well, I'm glad I could be your inner voice for the day." In the pause after the laughter drifted away, she dared to ask for something. "Do you think you could introduce me to your agent? Have her read some of my pages?"

Sadie pursed her lips, all sense of teasing fun dissipated. "No. I haven't even signed with her yet. Ask me again when your book is actually written. Then we'll talk." She ended the call in a huff.

Ashley leaned back in her chair and sighed. Sadie wasn't wrong to decline. Ashley's manuscript was far from ready and might not even be done after a few months in Salisbury. Presumably at the end of the summer she would have to move out of Hannah's flat and come home. She could land at her dad's place, but she would need a new career, or a willingness to return to her old one. In the meantime, she would have to put the work into her book like everyone else who dreamed of publication.

Two weeks later, the reality of her move had sunk in. She wrote more than she ever had, and the book was taking shape both in her mind and on the page. She registered for a virtual writing conference that would take place while she was in Salisbury and offered the opportunity to meet with a literary agent for feedback on the premise of her book.

She told a few of her friends—Bryn, Jasmine, and Michael—who were still in London that she was returning, and they planned a blow-out get-together in the capital and a trip to one of the big music festivals later in the summer.

The commission check came through for her last house sale, which gave her a nest egg to cover her expenses while abroad. When the day came to sign the closing paperwork on her own house, she thrilled at the finality of it and pushed down any hint of regret.

This was it, then. She was moving on. With help from her loved ones, yes, but she would use that help to launch herself into independence once again. One day, there would be no stopping her.

Chapter 4

London, England, 1377

Thomas's head felt three times too big for his body when consciousness returned the next morning. He cracked open his eyes. Even with the single window shuttered, the room was too bright for his pounding head. Once his eyes adjusted enough to allow him to think clearly, he realized how late it must be. John was not in bed beside him. Outside, a horse trotted into the courtyard, and stable hands shouted instructions as they coordinated their duties. Thomas sighed. His brother would be annoyed Thomas had delayed the start of their journey this long.

Thomas pulled on his hose and boots and went downstairs, where the innkeeper offered him a slice of buttered bread and a mug of small ale. He sat at a bench in the mostly empty room. All the other travelers had begun their journeys early, as he should have. The pain in his head receded a bit after a few sips of ale. He wanted to ask the innkeeper where John was—probably tending to the horses, Thomas guessed—but a tall man in a plain brown friar's robe walked toward him.

"You must be Thomas," the friar said. He finished wrapping a fresh loaf of bread in cloth and stored it in a bag slung across his shoulder. "I've been out procuring some refreshment for our journey. The weather is fine. I think we could make it twenty miles today, if it holds."

Thomas swallowed a few times before his voice worked. "Who are you?"

The man held out his hand. "Brother William."

Thomas shook his hand. "Thomas de la Warr."

"Your brother told me you're on your way to Salisbury to be ordained. He asked me to accompany you since I am headed there myself. No one should travel alone. There are always brigands about."

Thomas had never known his brother to be friendly with any men of the church. "How do you know my brother?"

"I met him here early this morning shortly after prime. He was on his way to Greenwich, I believe."

"Yes, he is going to France."

"That's right. It's perfect for a family to have one man for the king and one man for God. Anyway, I told him I was happy to have the company. I am traveling the country, visiting every cathedral and most churches I come across."

Outside, church bells struck the hour.

"We are at terce. Will you pray with me?" William pulled a large wooden cross out from beneath his robe and held it between them.

Behind William, the innkeeper crossed himself. Thomas closed his own eyes and folded his hands. Several minutes into the silence, the resolution he had made the night before crashed into his consciousness. He was supposed to be headed to a port to catch a ship to France, not riding to Salisbury. Had John known about Thomas's plan somehow, that he had recruited this traveling friar to accompany him? Had Thomas said something in his sleep? But that was beside the point now. William was determined to accompany him, that much was clear. He seemed a friendly enough fellow. But Thomas had to figure out a way to shake him once they set off. If only his mind would work at a quicker pace this morning, he might have a better idea of what to do.

His thoughts returned to the fact that he was supposed to be at prayer. He peeked at William out of the corner of one eye, then quickly shut it again. William was deep in prayer. Thomas could probably leave right now and his new companion wouldn't notice. But could he turn his back on God in such a literal fashion? Perhaps this obstacle in his path was a sign from God that Thomas shouldn't be so concerned with his own glory. He was meant to be part of the church. There was no higher calling. He knew that. Weighing both sides of his own argument, he decided he would travel with William today and find what other signs might be sent him.

After another quarter of an hour, William stirred beside him. Thomas felt it safe to open his eyes. A moment later, William did so as well.

William sighed like a cat satisfied by a saucer of milk. "Are you ready to depart? We are already late."

"Yes, let me get my things." He stood.

The innkeeper left his stance leaning against the doorway to the service rooms and stuck a hand toward Thomas. "Tuppence for the bread."

"Right." Thomas removed a coin from a small leather pouch at his waist and handed it over. Then he turned and leaned over William to grab the remaining half of his slice of bread. Waste not, want not. He finished the small meal as he climbed the stairs. In the room, he changed his shirt and folded the few possessions that had traveled with him into his satchel.

Back downstairs, William waited for him in the courtyard. A stable boy brought the horses around. The two men were silent as they mounted and rode single file out of the neighborhood. Once there was room for them to ride abreast, William spurred his horse to ride beside Thomas.

"Have you been to Salisbury?" William asked.

"Yes. We are from Wiltshire, about two days' ride north."

"Wonderful. You will know the way better than me then. May I ask, were you educated in Salisbury? I have heard the bishop there has a very good school for choristers."

"Partly. I was taught at home as a boy and at my uncle's home for my squire training. But later I attended the grammar school in Salisbury and continued on to the theology course."

"Yet you seem rather old not to be ordained."

Thomas gazed into the distance. "I received the dispensation to be ordained when I was twenty, almost five years ago. But I…I have not felt the calling until now."

William nodded, a serious expression on his face. "I imagine it would be difficult to leave the world for the church when you have experienced so much of it. For myself, I was raised by the friars since I was a boy. I have never wanted anything else."

"I admire your strength of purpose."

"It is easy when you are given no other choice."

Thomas shook his head. Technically he had been given no other choice, but he was not finding the transition so easy. His stomach roiled, and he stopped his horse so he could jump off and be sick by the side of the road. He wiped his mouth with his hand. This day was not starting anything like as well as he had hoped.

The remainder of the day's journey was dull. William had little to talk about besides God, and Thomas often found himself only half listening, too absorbed in his own thoughts and in keeping his stomach from revolting again to pay attention to his companion's theological ramblings. John could at least have found a simple monk for Thomas to travel with rather than a friar whose mandate was to preach to the public. Thomas wondered if John had already paid William, or if Thomas would be expected to provide him alms when they arrived. He absentmindedly dipped his hand into his satchel and tested the weight of his small coin purse. He should have plenty left to get both him and William to Salisbury. Even if Thomas absconded from their journey, he would have to leave William with something, to pay for the bread they had shared at least.

For most of the day they roughly followed the course of the Thames. The river disappeared and reappeared from view as it pleased. Even though they traveled away from the great ports of the Thames, smaller vessels plied the water, taking Thomas's imagination with them. He felt tugged back the way he had come. He still believed—or, at the very least, hoped—that this was not the direction he was meant to take.

By the time they stopped for supper and a bed for the night, Thomas had reached his wit's end. He couldn't stomach the thought of his ordination taking place once they reached Salisbury. As a half measure, he considered returning home to north Wiltshire before going to Salisbury. He could use the cover of checking on his mother in her new widowhood. He quickly dismissed the idea. His mother would sympathize with his indecision, but a man should not lean on his mother's sympathy. The point was that he was past the age when he should have decided on his path. The fact that he had put it off for so long showed him the answer: he did not want to join the church.

He was quiet at supper, claiming tiredness from the day's journey. Despite the unnecessary expense, he insisted on having the small private room at the top of the stairs, saying he wouldn't be able to sleep any other way, so William was forced to share with another traveler.

Thomas slept for several hours. When he woke, still fully clothed, the inn was silent except for a few stomps and whinnies from the stabled horses behind the building. He listened closely for a while. Hearing nothing, he got out of bed and packed his satchel. He tiptoed out of the room and down the stairs to make his escape.

In the pitch blackness, it was difficult to navigate through the tables downstairs, but he kept one hand out in front of himself to identify the next obstacle. When he thought he was roughly halfway across the room, his hand bumped into something warm and soft. He gave an inadvertent yelp.

A candleflame flickered to life in front of him.

"My goodness!" William said. "What are you doing down here without a candle?"

"What—what are you doing down here at all?"

"I always break my sleep with a prayer at matins. I find that the dark keeps me focused on the Lord. Have you come to join me?" He glanced at Thomas's satchel hanging at his side. "Ah, I understand."

Thomas was caught. "I mean no insult to you."

"No, only to God himself." William shook his head. "It's not for me to judge you. You must do as you wish. Only…"

"What?"

"I did tell your brother I would get you safely to Salisbury. If you leave now, I will never be able to tell him that you were safely delivered anywhere."

Thomas deflated slightly at this reminder of his familial duty. "You can tell him I was safe the last time you talked to me. The same as he was the last time you saw him."

"You owe me nothing, boy. Do as you please."

To be called a boy at twenty-five was insulting. "I am not a child."

"You are sneaking through the dark rather than face your life's choice head on. Is that the action of a man?"

Thomas fixed his gaze on William for a long moment as the candlelight cast ever-changing shadows across his face. He had been so close to an escape, but it was not yet to be. If Thomas wanted to choose a different path for himself, he would do as William said and face it like a man. A true knight would not sneak around his duty in such a way. Thomas set down his satchel and sat beside William in prayer. When they went back upstairs, William joined Thomas in slumber in the private room as a safeguard against further escape attempts. Thomas made no protest.

****

Thomas was sullen for most of the next morning's ride, but William's consistent good humor and lack of reproach for the previous night's encounter slowly brought Thomas around. In the brightness of a summer's day, his situation did not feel so dire.

As they topped a small hill late in the afternoon, the next village came into view about a mile distant. Its church tower rose as a beacon over the scatter of small, thatched buildings. "We have found our next destination. Another church for you to visit," Thomas said.

"And not you?"

Thomas smiled. "Yes, me as well. You can show me what each church you visit bequeaths you that keeps you on your wandering journey."

"Ah, you think the destination is the churches."

Thomas raised an eyebrow.

"I find God just as much on a deserted stretch of highway as I do in the church, my friend. You will learn this one day, too, I hope."

"I have a lot to learn."

"Any man who tells you he does not have a lot to learn is a fool."

"Yet you seem wiser than I."

"I listen to God, that is all. He is constantly showing me new things."

Thomas hesitated, taking a moment to resettle himself in his saddle as they reached the bottom of the hill and the ground leveled. "Can I ask you something?"

"Of course. I am never insulted by a question asked. It is the unasked ones that cause problems."

"How do you reconcile the imperfections of some men of the church with the positions they hold?" When William did not respond right away, Thomas added, "I speak of the wealth of so many men of the church. And, when we were in London, a couple of monks went inside a poor inn with women of the night."

William smiled knowingly. "The fact is there are good and bad men, whether they wear ecclesiastical or secular garb. Joining the church will not free you from the hold of sin, if that is what you think. You must battle against it like any man. That is between you and God, of course."

"Right."

"How could a perfect man lead a flock of imperfect souls? You must understand both the church and the world in such a role."

Thomas nodded. William was philosophical about everything. His continual, unruffled calm was reassuring, like a set of ducks gliding across a pond. "Show me the peace you find along your journeys," he said.

William inclined his head in acknowledgement.

Thomas said a silent prayer that he would find whatever William had, whatever would keep Thomas to the path that had been laid out for him. He couldn't disgrace his family by running away from his duty. A true knight would never turn from what he was called to do. Thomas would have to be his own kind of knight that fought battles through the church rather than through the sword. He fervently hoped he had the strength to do it.

Chapter 5

Ashley's whole life fit into the two suitcases stacked in the back of Hannah's car. Well, two suitcases and the ten boxes she'd left at her father's house. As Hannah drove her from Heathrow to Salisbury, Ashley decided it felt freeing rather than depressing. She was starting the new chapter of her life, just like she had wanted.

Ashley had worried the drive would be awkward, but the cousins had picked right up where they left off, laughing and catching up, the tension from that first phone call weeks ago dissipated.

The day burst with sun. As they entered Salisbury, a steady stream of people walked sedately along the wandering sidewalks and paths.

Hannah pulled over and parked along a busy street just outside the city center. "This is us then."

They both got out, Ashley extracting her suitcases from the boot. She loved using the slightly foreign words again, savored their familiar strangeness in her mouth. Hannah grabbed one of the suitcases and they each rolled one along as they walked a short distance down the sidewalk. Hannah halted in front of a blue doorway next to a charity shop.

"Here we are," she announced unnecessarily. She showed Ashley how to enter the code in the keypad to open the street door, then pulled out her keys for the two flats.

Once inside, Ashley and Hannah dragged the suitcases up the stairs. On the landing, Hannah led them toward the left. She pointed at the flat across the hall. "That's the one we use as a vacation rental."

Ashley followed Hannah into the flat on the left. The place wasn't very big, maybe 600 square feet, but it had everything she needed. She set down her purse and peeked out the back window in the living room. Over the tops of the buildings, she could just make out a stretch of the Salisbury Avon flowing alongside a narrow street.

"What do you think?"

"It's perfect," Ashley said.

"Good. The couple who were staying in the other flat should have checked out this morning, so I can show it to you also."

They went across the hall. Hannah knocked, just in case, then unlocked the door.

This flat was bigger, with a view over the road. Ashley was glad her flat had the better vantage point.

Hannah returned from checking something in the bathroom. "The estate agent is meeting us so I can introduce you."

Estate agent? Hannah hadn't warned her about this. In the two months since she quit her job, Ashley had avoided thinking about the career she had thrown away. Now that it confronted her again, she couldn't help but hope it might presage a way forward, a new path she could take to support her book-writing dream. Despite the fact that she had dropped everything to come here, the promise of stability still tugged at her.

The sound of the door opening at the bottom of the stairs drew Ashley back onto the landing.

"Hello!" a male voice called.

"Come on up!" Hannah responded from behind Ashley.

Ashley moved aside as a young man in a tie reached the landing. He shook hands with both of them.

"Terry will be the person you contact if there are any maintenance issues," Hannah said.

"And if you have any other questions, feel free to reach out." He handed over his card.

Ashley decided to take advantage of the moment. She rooted around in her purse for one of her old business cards. "I've just left this agency, but my contact information is the same." Despite herself, she hoped he would google her. There had been several local articles about her that he might find. Learning about her successes could help her get her foot in the door—for what exactly, she wasn't sure yet. She just knew that in the battle of dreams versus responsibility she was still trying to find the right balance.

Terry glanced at the card. "Sounds like the place is going to be in good hands, then."

"Ashley's going to be writing a book while she's here," Hannah offered before Ashley could respond.

Ashley cringed at the non sequitur. Fortunately, Terry didn't seem particularly interested and the conversation moved on.

After a little more chitchat, they all shook hands again, and Terry started down the stairs. Ashley examined the card he had given her. She forced herself to tamp down her excitement. She had her first professional connection in the city, and she was expert at leveraging those. There was still no clear path forward, but if things kept going smoothly, she was certain she would find the way.

Terry stopped before opening the door to the street. "Good luck on your book," he said with an oddly unnerving wink, as if he had known lots of people to arrive in Salisbury to write and never accomplish anything. Ashley forced a smile. He was probably just being cute. Flirting with her, maybe. And he wasn't bad looking…but no. The last thing she needed now was another boyfriend who would bring her down. It wouldn't hurt to have a friend in town, though. Beyond that, she shouldn't get ahead of herself.

Once Terry left, Hannah handed Ashley a spare key to the vacation flat and showed her how to clean and prepare the flat between guests. It seemed simple enough. Once this was done, Ashley assured Hannah she was fine on her own, knowing that Hannah had to get back to her family in London. They hugged and promised to keep in touch. Then Ashley was left alone in her new apartment to figure out her new life.

She laughed at herself. She shouldn't put so much pressure on her first day there. She just needed to focus on getting settled in, then move on to the next thing, then the next.

By the time she finished unpacking, she struggled to stay awake. She had taken the red eye and she had never been good at sleeping on planes. Then the reunion with Hannah and the car ride… The morning had already been intense. But she had to stay awake, or she would never adjust to the time difference. She glanced at her phone. It was almost noon. She should find a place for lunch. That would occupy her for an hour at least.

On the sidewalk, her legs automatically entered speed-walking mode. She stopped, took a deep breath, and reminded herself that she was not in DC. She had nowhere to be. In fact, she had time to kill. She started again, taking her time, noticing every odd thing she walked past—a funny sticker on a window, a long-past concert poster pasted on a wall. The only time she let herself pass someone was when a couple stopped to check their phones on a street corner. She smiled at a few passersby, and they nodded at her in return. After a few minutes, she reached the city center. She stepped into a circle of pedestrian-only space and looked for a place to eat.

She passed a few chains before she finally found a small local café that looked promising. Inside, the space was quiet and cool. The middle-aged lady at the counter maintained her patience even when Ashley, in her muddled, sleep-deprived state, messed up using the chip and pin twice despite what Ashley was sure were very clear instructions on the cashier's part.

"Sorry," she said at the end of the interaction, though she was apologizing less for the chip and pin annoyance than her very obvious American-ness, which she usually hid as much as possible when she was abroad.

That ordeal over, she sat by the window with her sandwich and tea. She pulled her laptop out of its sleeve and opened it. She didn't feel awake enough to write, but she could make a schedule for her writing so she would have structure to her days.

She reached for her phone to check the calendar but knocked her teacup just enough to cause a momentary panic. She grabbed her laptop and leaped out of her seat. Fortunately, the cup wavered but didn't topple.

"Close call," someone said.

A young man had just come through the door.

Beth Ford

"Thanks," she said automatically, though she wasn't sure what on earth she was thanking him for. "That would have been a disaster," she added. The man looked surprisingly like Trevor, his hair tightly curled with a reddish tinge, dark brown eyes, and round face. It made her heart skip a beat, but she quickly chastised herself. Trevor was off in his new life in New York, and she had refused to have anything to do with him since their breakup, even though he had texted her several times.

The man nodded with a smile, then walked up to the counter to order. Ashley sat back down, her face red from embarrassment. She hoped none of those emotions had played across her face. She wanted to cry, though she couldn't put into words why. She was simply too tired, she told herself, and the last few weeks had been overwhelming. She sucked in a deep breath and returned to creating her schedule.

"Hey, I'm Antony."

Again, the man's voice startled her. She turned to him and smiled, though she was sure she was still blushing. "Ashley," she said, extending her hand. "Nice to meet you."

Antony set two cups of coffee on the table next to Ashley's, sliding one to the seat across from him, preparing for the arrival of someone else. "What are you doing here?" he asked Ashley.

"You mean here as in—"

"In Salisbury. The accent."

"Right." She bit her lip, unsure what to share with this oddly familiar-looking stranger. "I took a few months off work. To write a book." The half-truth surprised her as it came out of her mouth. She liked this new positive spin on her situation.

"Good for you." His reply lacked the veiled condescension that some people used when saying that to her now.

Ashley decided she liked him.

Antony turned as a woman in a long dress entered the restaurant. He waved to her. "Katie, this is Ashley," he said as the newcomer approached his table. "She's writing a book."

"Awesome," Katie said. Faint crow's feet at the corners of her eyes hinted she was older than Antony, probably in her forties.

Katie settled into the seat across from Antony but leaned across the space between the tables to talk conspiratorially to Ashley. "Tell me about this book."

Her schedule forgotten, Ashley talked to her new friends for the next two hours. At the end of that time, they invited her to join them and a few other friends for pub quiz on Tuesday night.

Her new friends left after they finished their lunch, leaving Ashley free to put together her schedule, into which she happily inserted her Tuesday evening trivia appointment. Her first day back in England and she had already made one step toward belonging. She couldn't let herself get too distracted, but an occasional social outing wouldn't be uncalled for. By mid-afternoon when the café closed for the day, she felt like she had a plan and was set up for success for her time in Salisbury.

On Tuesday evening, Ashley triple-checked her appearance in the mirror before she left for pub quiz, as if that would guard against her sneaking fear that Trevor and Katie hadn't meant her to accept the invite and would be surprised when she showed up.

She needn't have worried. Katie waved Ashley over

eagerly as soon as she walked in. Antony gave her a quick hug, then offered to go get her something from the bar. She settled in between him and Katie and soon everyone was laughing like old friends. She answered a few pop-culture trivia questions, but her British history knowledge was sorely lacking. The team was well chosen for its members' complementary knowledge, and the team came in third, a victory even though it only gave the whole team ten pounds to spend at the bar.

For the next week she kept her head down and stayed focused. Cleaning and preparing the rental flat between guests wasn't too difficult and kept her from feeling completely useless. She wrote every day even though not all of what she got on paper was good.

Ashley was surprised when Sadie video-called the following Wednesday. They hadn't talked much since Ashley had given Sadie the feedback on her story.

"Guess what!" Sadie practically shouted as soon as Ashley answered. "I signed with the agent! Well, almost. We're talking tomorrow, but she's definitely interested!"

Ashley smiled, pushing away her stupid jealousy. "That's great, Sadie."

"Thanks. You had a hand in it, too."

"The revisions I suggested worked out?"

"Not exactly. You know how you said the narrator's point of view was the problem? I solved it by making it an unreliable narrator. That it was her twin sister telling the story pretending to be her. And that meant I only had to rewrite the last third of the book instead of the whole thing."

Ashley's phone slipped out of her hand and landed on the bed. Despite the awkward angle of her video, she didn't pick it back up. "That's literally the plot of my novel."

"Not exactly. The rest of my story is unchanged. It's just a similar twist."

"Not similar. The same. You stole my idea."

"You gave me the idea. I'll thank you in the acknowledgements, for sure. You can read the new version, if you want, so you can see how it's different."

"Wow, Sadie. I can't talk to you right now." Ashley hung up. Her emotions wavered like a wobbly Jenga tower. She curled on her side on the bed. The pieces crashed down, and soon she was sobbing. She thought she had escaped all the negativity when she left her old life. But now the one thing she still had to hold on to—the brilliant book she was supposed to be writing—had been snatched from her also.

Eventually the tears slowed, then stopped. She lay on the bed, staring at the ceiling, deciding what to do.

She had to get out of this suffocating flat.

She stomped downstairs and headed north out of the city. She had a vague idea that she might walk across the fields to the ruins of Old Sarum. She hoped the walk would calm her. From her last trip to the area, she remembered Old Sarum as a quiet place for contemplation and maybe even a good cry if there weren't many other tourists around. That was what she needed right now.

She walked at a fast clip, barely registering the people around her as she maneuvered automatically around them. The weather was nice, bordering on hot, but she couldn't enjoy it. Once she crossed the first field on the outskirts of the city, she veered toward a small grove of trees to walk through the shade. She seethed over Sadie as she barreled forward, not expecting to encounter anyone on her way. She kept her gaze on her feet to make sure she didn't trip as her thoughts raged elsewhere. But just as she entered the woods, she ran smack into someone. She let out a little scream. It wasn't just that he was a stranger. He was the strangest-looking man she had ever seen.

Chapter 6

Wiltshire, England, 1377

Two days further into their ride, Thomas and William had Salisbury almost within their grasp. They would arrive by the afternoon, barring some unfortunate circumstance, which Thomas couldn't help but hope would come. Thomas had removed his traveling cloak early in their ride that morning, finding he didn't need it on the warm summer's day. But now clouds moved in, so they couldn't discount rain, or by extension, the possibility that in the event of a storm they might need to seek shelter at the nearest tavern and leave the rest of their journey until tomorrow. Not that he would have any more answers to his situation tomorrow, Thomas reasoned sadly with himself. But to put off his fate one more day would be enough.

William rode beside Thomas, humming a tune to himself. The man was never out of good cheer. Thomas envied him that but still wasn't willing to commit himself to the church to get a share of it. While he had given up on the thought of an ignominious escape, he still wasn't sure he could go through with his ordination. Perhaps he would meet with the bishop and discover whether that conversation swayed him. If he did not go through with it, he would face the consequences head on, as William had challenged him to do.

The rain held off. It was close to midday when they

crested a hill and the spire of the great cathedral emerged from the landscape. William pulled his horse up short and crossed himself.

"It's incredible," Thomas said, and he meant it. He had visited Salisbury many times, and that first view of the city never ceased to amaze him. That man could build such a temple surely spoke of the glory of God. Of that much he was certain.

"It is, it is," William said, wiping his brow with a small cloth. "We still have at least an hour's ride before us. Why don't we pause for sext, followed by some breaking of bread?" He patted his satchel. He had made it his mission to find the best, freshest loaf of bread every morning of their journey, and he hadn't failed them yet. Another thing for which Thomas was grateful.

Thomas pointed off at an angle down the hill. "Why don't we pause among those trees where it won't be so hot?"

William nodded eagerly and followed Thomas to the woods.

They tied the horses up at the edge of the trees and knelt to pray. Thomas had fallen easily back into the routine of prayers every three hours—though William was the one announcing each stop for prayer as they traveled, Thomas had followed the schedule rigidly during his time at school in Salisbury and knew it well. There was comfort in the steady passage of the hours marked by the pause for quiet reflection. Not everything with the structure of the church was wrong, Thomas mused. There was benefit to it. He didn't need to be a priest to appreciate that.

Thomas stepped a little farther into the woods, wishing to be alone with his thoughts and his God without the sound of William's breath and murmured prayers beside him. He knelt in front of a flat, mossy rock. He leaned his elbows on it and clasped his hands.

He prayed fervently for God to make him happy with his lot in life. To make him accept his ordination with open arms if that was his correct path. For a sign to show him that it was what he was meant to do. That going to France was an impossible dream—a dangerous one for his soul, even if he cared not for the fate of his body. Despite his fervent hopes, no such feeling came. He was still uncertain, wavering as if balancing along a tightrope.

Behind him, William called his name, but the voice was faint, as if coming from a far distance. Thomas ignored it, wanting to hold onto his prayers for a while longer. He thought suddenly of Kathryn, even though he had managed to keep her out of his mind over the last few weeks. He wondered why she had appeared now when he had given up that path in life entirely. He knew that neither she nor any other woman would ever understand his desire to shirk his duty. Either he would be ordained and never marry, or he would cause a scandal by running off, and no respectable woman would ever marry him then. Either way, the possibility of love was lost to him.

This new train of thought upset and unsettled him. His knees suddenly ached from kneeling too long. So much for finding peace.

When he opened his eyes, he wasn't sure how much time had passed. He didn't think it was more than a quarter of an hour, but there was something different in the air than when he had knelt down. Had more time passed than he thought? He peered up through the tree branches but found the sun in the same position overhead. In the distance, there was a whooshing sound that he couldn't place.

He turned his head to search behind him. He couldn't find William, even though Thomas thought he had left him right at the edge of the woods.

Thomas stood and walked toward the edge of the tree line, only fifteen feet or so away. He stopped in his tracks. William was nowhere, and the horses were missing, too. What had happened? He couldn't imagine William would leave him here on his own. Had William been robbed or, even worse, killed, while Thomas prayed, oblivious? Or had William simply wandered off, giving Thomas the opportunity to select his own destiny? Was that why William's voice calling him had sounded so faint? Had he ridden off and left Thomas behind? But in that case, why wouldn't he have left Thomas his own horse?

Thomas calmed his thoughts. He had asked God for a sign. Here was a sign, more dramatic than he would have ever imagined. With William gone, Thomas had no one to supervise his arrival in Salisbury. He could go wherever he wanted. One of them—God or William—must mean him to take this opportunity and go to France as he had planned. His heart soared at the possibility. His unease of a moment before drifted away. What matter that no woman would ever have him? He could be a bachelor knight. Such things existed.

He shifted his satchel against his hip and checked that the contents were all there. He squared his shoulders. Without his horse, he would have to walk to Southampton, the nearest port, but the journey would be a good penance. He could be like William and find God along the way.

He strode purposefully a few feet farther so he could see down the hill toward Salisbury and begin his quest. Before he fully emerged from the woods, he crashed into a woman charging up the hill. At least, he thought it was a woman. But she was not like any woman he had ever seen.

Chapter 7

Neither of them said a word. They stood in shock, each assessing the other.

Ashley stared at the young man's strange clothes. He wore a long, blue shirt over—were those tights?—and oddly shapeless leather boots. Everything he wore appeared homemade. The leather crossbody bag he wore was the only thing he had of decent quality.

She lifted her gaze to his face. His eyes immediately captivated her. They were the most gorgeous shade of blue she had ever seen. His face wasn't bad either. His hair was thick and a bit long. Even beneath the beard she could tell he had a strong jawline and fine cheekbones. He appeared her age or a bit younger.

Snapping back to herself, she took a few steps backward to put some distance between them. "Sorry," she said nervously.

The man cocked his head at her like a curious cat trying to figure out what the game was.

"Are you all right?" she finally asked.

He said something that she couldn't interpret. It was her turn to look confused.

"Are you going to Salisbury?" she asked, since he was headed in the opposite direction she was. Then tried again, "Salisbury?"

"Sarisbury," he said firmly, correcting her. The middle sound held more of a "r" shape in his mouth instead of an "l." She couldn't tell where he was from. The words he had said to her sounded like nothing she had heard before.

But they were getting somewhere. She pointed down the hill toward the city. "Sarisbury," she said, mimicking him.

He nodded, satisfied. His gaze tracked in the direction she pointed. When his eyes lit on the city, he took a few inadvertent steps back and stumbled over a tree root. Once he was steady on his feet again, he glanced wildly along the horizon. Her eyes darted between him and the view, trying to guess what had surprised him so. Between them and the city, a stretch of highway trailed along the horizon. Nothing particularly remarkable about that. But the man turned pale and crossed himself. When that didn't improve things in his mind, he pulled a necklace out from under his tunic—she had decided that was the best word for what he was wearing. The necklace was a simple leather cord holding a wooden cross. He rubbed the cross fervently and his lips formed a prayer she couldn't interpret.

"Are you okay?" she asked again.

He glared at her before he turned and dashed back into the forest.

Ashley hesitated, then followed after him. Despite the fact that running into the woods after a potentially crazy man sounded like a setup for a horror movie, she had to make sure he was okay. She couldn't just leave him here.

He didn't go very far. A dozen or so feet farther into the woods, he knelt in front of a low, flat rock. Was he praying?

He stayed in that position for several minutes.

Ashley hung back, debating what to do. All thoughts of her feud with Sadie blew away, and she focused on this new confrontation. Did he need help? He certainly seemed lost and scared. She would almost think he was a hermit living secluded in the woods, if they weren't so close to town and the highway. She considered his clothes. Was there a medieval reenactment happening nearby, maybe at Old Sarum where she had been headed? His outfit appeared of that time period. Had she interrupted some event? But no, the small copse was silent except for them and the distant sound of cars passing along the road.

She still hadn't decided what to do when his eyes opened again. He looked around. When he saw her his face fell, but he didn't appear so scared this time. He set his jaw in determination, stood, and approached her.

He said something to her. She almost understood a few words. There was something in the middle that sounded like "thu"—was he saying "you" maybe? When she showed no recognition, he said something again. It sounded different this time. The accent on a few words reminded her of French, but she didn't speak that language except for a few important phrases she had picked up through pop culture such as *Voulez-vous couche avec moi?* That probably wouldn't be the best sentence to introduce herself with. She captured a smile before it appeared on her lips.

It would be mortifying if it turned out she just didn't understand his accent. When she'd lived in England before, she had always found it nearly impossible to understand anyone from Sunderland. Maybe he was from there. "Sunderland?" she asked. He still looked confused. So much for that theory.

He watched her as if he expected her to provide him with some clue or direction.

"Do you need to go to Salisbury?"

"Sarisbury," he said. This was still the only word they agreed on.

She sighed. If he was a psycho murderer, it was probably best to get out of the countryside and back into the city where she could get help. She inclined her head toward Salisbury. He nodded and followed her down the hill.

His agitation increased as they neared the road. He gripped the cross around his neck. His eyes darted in every direction, tracking one car for a few seconds, then jumping to another. Eventually they reached a crosswalk. A red Renault sedan stopped for them. Ashley started across, but after a few steps noticed the man wasn't following her. He stood petrified on the curb. She waved apologetically to the driver, crossed again, and gingerly took the man's hand. This brought him back to himself a bit, and he allowed her to lead him across the street. Once on the other side, he straightened his shoulders in pride at his accomplishment. Ashley couldn't help but smile. As odd as the situation was, she enjoyed witnessing such a simple act make someone so happy. She would figure out a way to help this very strange stranger, she decided. She would take her power back and show Jayna and Sadie and everyone else that Ashley was neither selfish nor someone who could be walked all over without consequence.

She contemplated her next move. Across another road, she spotted a bus stop. Maybe the bus driver would have a suggestion on where to take him. The nearest police station, maybe, so the authorities could figure out who he was. She could google police stations, but she still only had her American phone plan, so any data she accessed would be expensive.

With this goal in mind, she led him through another crossing, with less hesitation on his part this time. Fortunately, within a few minutes a bus arrived. She climbed up the first step. "Do you know where the nearest police station is?" she asked.

"Not on this route," the driver, a middle-aged man, said.

Ashley was about to remark that this was not what she had asked. But the driver spotted the man behind her.

"Is it for him?" The driver watched him with an expression of barely veiled disgust.

"Yes." Ashley glanced behind her. Out of the shadows of the woods and with a slightly calmer mind, she now saw that besides his strange appearance, the man was also rather dirty. Had she just picked up a strange homeless man by mistake? Maybe she should just buy him something to eat and leave him on his way? But there was something about him, a certain regalness underneath the mess, that drew her to him. Under other circumstances, she could tell, he was a man to be contended with.

"Coming or not?" the driver asked.

"No, sorry. Thank you." She stepped down. The bus drove off, leaving Ashley alone with her new charge.

She tried a new tactic. She pointed at herself. "Ashley," she said, then pointed at him. "You?" When this elicited no response, she repeated the pointing, saying "My name is Ashley, what is your name?"

The man grinned. "Thomas," he said.

Success! They had communicated. "Thomas," she

repeated. "Nice to meet you."

The man shrugged good naturedly, showing he didn't understand the last part of what she said but was not as concerned about it now.

They watched each other for several minutes. She was out of ideas of what to do.

The police would give her some direction. She gave in and googled the local police number, accepting the data charges. She called direct rather than going through 999 as she didn't want to elicit an emergency response and risk the situation escalating. She gave a short explanation to the officer who responded. He didn't sound particularly impressed with her story but said he would send a car to check on her.

While they waited, Ashley watched Thomas as he took in the scenery around him. He seemed calmer now. She considered what his story might be. Maybe he had amnesia. You heard stories about that, people forgetting who they were and starting a new life until someone from their past recognized them years later. Or he could just be a lost tourist. Or an unfortunate local with some mental health issues. Maybe he was known to the police, though if he was, surely the officer she spoke with would have mentioned it.

Her imaginings stopped short when the satchel he carried across his body moved from its position against his left hip. Beneath it hung a sheathed knife strapped around his waist.

Shit. Had she just stupidly put herself in danger? She normally prided herself on being savvier than that. She took a deep breath. If he had been intent on killing her, he would have taken his opportunity in the woods. He wouldn't dare do anything along this busy city street.

Right?

Just then, a police car pulled up. Two officers, a man and a woman, stepped out. Ashley spoke with them quietly off to the side.

"Have you seen him before?" she asked.

Both officers shook their heads. "Has he said anything to you?"

"His name is Thomas. But I don't think he speaks English. At least not any English I understand. He also said something that sounded like it might be French."

The man rolled his eyes. Ashley sensed he thought she was just a stupid American who couldn't understand an English accent.

"Has he threatened you at all?" The woman asked after she had taken down Ashley's contact information and handed over a card declaring herself to be Constable Marvin.

"No. But…"

The woman cocked an eyebrow.

"He has a knife. Around his waist."

The woman peered at him. "I see it," she said after a moment. She stepped a few feet away and spoke into the walkie-talkie on her shoulder.

The man approached Thomas. "How are you doing today, sir?"

Thomas smiled nervously.

"We want to take you in and get some information from you. Help you out, okay?"

Thomas peered over the officer's shoulder at Ashley as if requesting help. Ashley took a step forward. The officer turned and held out his hand. "Please don't get involved, ma'am."

She stopped.

The officer asked Thomas a question in French. Thomas responded but it was clear that neither man completely understood the other. The officer looked over his shoulder at his partner. "It's not like any French I've ever heard. Maybe he's from Quebec or Switzerland or something. I don't know." He shrugged.

The officer regarded Thomas for a long moment, which only increased Thomas's tension. He seemed ready to jump at any moment. Sensing this, the officer pounced, reaching over and grabbing Thomas's arm. Thomas shook it free. When the officer grabbed him again, Thomas's other hand went for his knife.

Constable Marvin jumped into the fray, wrestling Thomas down until they pinned him on the ground and handcuffed him. The man stood and dragged Thomas to his feet. He led Thomas to the car, opened the back door, and shoved him in. Ashley watched helplessly.

"You can go on your way now, ma'am," the officer said. "We have your information, so we'll contact you if we need a statement."

"But what are you going to do with him?"

"We'll have a medical officer examine him. He may need to be certified."

"Certified, like…committed?"

The officer sighed. "That's usually best in these types of situations, so he can get some help." He elbowed past her to access the driver's side door.

"Wait," Ashley said before he could get inside. She saw her opportunity to help about to slam shut. "Can you tell me what happens to him? Give me an update?"

"Call the station tomorrow and we'll see what we can do."

He got into the car with his partner and drove off.

Thomas glanced back at her as they drove away. Even though she had known him scarcely an hour, it broke her heart to witness him treated that way and then ripped away from her. Especially since it was her fault. She shouldn't have called the police. He had done nothing wrong. Had she just ruined this man's life?

****

Thomas tried not to panic. If he kept calm, he could find a way out of this. But it was hard to keep his breathing steady as the vehicle sped down the road with nothing to guide it. Everywhere around him, people were moving, faster than he had ever seen, but there wasn't a single horse in sight.

Think, he ordered himself. Everything had been normal when he had bent to pray at the rock. He had asked God for a sign, and when he got up, he was here. There could be no stronger sign. He struggled to identify its meaning. It was so far from the message he had desired that it must be meant to shake him from his resolution. To seek to avoid his path to the church at Salisbury was literal madness. Had he gone mad? Had he died and this was hell? Or purgatory? Wouldn't one remember one's death?

He had to get back to that rock and ask God to send him back home. He would commit his entire body and life to the church. But how could he get there when he was trapped and manacled in this impossible wagon?

He shifted his focus to the present moment. He had to deal with that first before he could figure out what he needed to do with the bigger questions of his life. The man and the woman in the front seat were talking, and a third voice emerged unseen from up there, too. He couldn't understand what they said. He caught his name, though, *Thomas*, and strained to hear anything else that made sense.

No such luck. Clearly they understood something about him, but he had no clue about them. That put him at a disadvantage. With his wrists tied, he had no way to fight them to attempt an escape. And even if he did, who knew what kind of weaponry they might have that he would never predict? His all-purpose knife, mostly used to eat as he traveled, suddenly seemed woefully inadequate.

The only thing to do was to go along with everything for as long as he could, without provoking them. With this decision made, he said silent prayers over and over for the rest of the ride. He wished his hands were free so he could hold his cross, but he did the best he could to call on God's protection without its weight in his hand. After several minutes that felt like an eternity, they stopped in front of a building. His two captors got out and opened the door to the backseat. He climbed out obligingly and smiled a little at them as he did so, making himself harmless and maybe even friendly. They handled him gently, so his docility helped the situation. Good. He had adopted the right tactic.

Inside, they brought him to a small room and set him on a cold shiny chair. The man returned a few minutes later carrying a small rectangular sheaf of something, which he set on the tabletop. He spoke again. When Thomas didn't respond, the man grabbed Thomas's arm and dragged him to his feet. He went for Thomas's waist and removed the knife, his one weapon. He then patted down the rest of Thomas's body. Thomas had to restrain himself from kicking the man away. Next, the man rifled through Thomas's satchel, taking out each item—his traveling cloak, his spare shirt, his small sewing kit. The whole time, the man talked to himself. Or maybe he was talking to someone Thomas couldn't see. In this place you couldn't tell.

Once this was complete, the man left with the knife and Thomas's other possessions. Thomas sat. When the man returned, he unlocked the manacles. This was progress. He pushed the sheaf toward Thomas along with a stylus that was cool to the touch. Thomas fingered the thin sheet. It was many times thinner than any vellum he had ever felt, but it served the same purpose because there were words printed on it he couldn't read.

No, with a bit of stretching he could decipher a few words. At the bottom, it listed Salisbury and Wiltshire. Like with the strange woman he had encountered, he had these place names in common with these people.

The man was still trying to get Thomas to understand something and was growing increasingly agitated. He gesticulated so broadly Thomas feared the man would grab him again.

"I don't understand," Thomas said, but the words meant nothing to the man.

Finally, the man took the stylus and sheet and wrote something on the page. He turned the sheet back around toward Thomas and held out the stylus. Thomas took it and examined the end of it. A writing device with the ink already inside of it. He touched the tip of it to the sheet. A small black dot appeared. Fascinating. Why had no one ever thought of that back home?

The man pointed a thick finger at what he had written. "Thomas," he said, then pointed to another space and said something else.

Thomas peered at where he pointed. The man had

indeed written "Thomas," though the script he used was a bit odd. Thomas considered the tiny words already on the page next to his name, then the words next to the other blank. He mentally traced the letters and sounded them out. It looked like "name" even though it did not sound correct when the man said it—he collapsed it into one syllable with an odd long "a" sound. But Thomas would have to guess and give it a try. He spun the stylus in his hand a few times, figuring out the best way to grip it. After a moment, in the blank space, he wrote his surname: de la Warr.

The man relaxed a bit. Thomas had guessed correctly.

But there was another blank the man wanted to move on to next. Thomas couldn't make heads or tails of the words around it. Finally, the man pointed to the bottom of the sheet where Thomas had deciphered a couple of words earlier. The man must want a place. This seemed to be an exercise in getting information about Thomas, so he made another guess. Lydiard, Wiltshire, he wrote. The name of his family estate, his birthplace and home.

But this didn't satisfy the man. He read what Thomas had written and shook his head. He launched into some sentences in which Lydiard appeared and several instances of negatives—no and not. Beyond that, Thomas couldn't interpret.

Maybe he wanted to know where Thomas had come from most recently? Thomas crossed out Lydiard and Wiltshire and wrote London.

The man frowned, considering, but he found this a more acceptable answer than the first. After a moment, the man stood and walked out of the room, taking the sheet with him. Thomas waited.

After a while, a different man entered, younger than the other one. He wore the same uniform as the others, dark clothes in a stiff fabric. Had Thomas been taken in by a monastic sect? If so, it was unlike any he had encountered. However, if they were monks, then they must worship God and therefore couldn't be too bad. Unless everything here was flipped, and they worshipped the devil instead. They certainly had many items that must be possessed to operate as they did. He gripped his cross with his left hand.

The man didn't say anything but set a cup in front of Thomas. Inside the cup was a muddy brown liquid. Thomas sniffed the contents hesitantly. He held the cup to his lips, and the man nodded encouragingly. Thomas took a tentative sip. It was both bitter and sweet at the same time. He made a face. The man spoke. Thomas was already sick of not understanding anything anyone said to him. When Thomas didn't respond, the man shrugged and left.

Thomas took another sip. It wasn't bad, this drink. It just wasn't like anything he had tasted before. Maybe it was a medicinal drink made from herbs. What they were treating him for, he couldn't guess, but he hoped their intentions were honorable.

He waited even longer this time. Long enough for the adrenaline to wear off and drowsiness to settle in his limbs. He snapped alert as soon as the door opened and the younger man entered again. The man motioned at Thomas to stand up. Thomas followed him out of the room past rows of desks. At the end of the hall, they crossed through a door into a narrow, windowless room. A row of basins ran along one wall. The other wall was made up of three smaller cubicles. Everything was composed of a shiny white material he didn't recognize. He ran a finger along the edge of one of the wash basins. The man motioned at one of the cubicles and Thomas peeked inside to see an open seat. He glanced back at the man, who gave him a strange look and motioned to the stall again.

Thomas stepped inside and shut the door. It gave him a moment alone. He considered what he was supposed to do here. It had the appearance of a public latrine, but he didn't understand how it worked with a solid floor and no hole under the seat. If it was a latrine, these people were oddly concerned about privacy that each station was so separate from the others.

He leaned over and peered into the seat. It wasn't empty. He stuck the very tip of his finger into it. Water filled it. Why? The water was clear, meaning it must not have been used before.

The man spoke from his post outside the stall. He sounded impatient, so Thomas went ahead and relieved himself. When he stepped outside, the man again gave him an exasperated look. Maybe Thomas had guessed wrong as to the purpose of this visit? The man stepped around him and went into the stall. Suddenly there was the sound of rushing water. Instinctively, Thomas jumped and turned so his back wasn't to the man. His hand went to his belt, expecting to find his knife, but then remembered they had taken it from him.

The man grabbed Thomas and dragged him back to the first room, holding Thomas's arms behind his back as they walked. When Thomas was left alone at the metal table again, he was on the verge of tears. This was not the sign he had wanted, and he was ready for this vision—or whatever it was—to be over. He had never felt so powerless. By comparison, acquiescing to his ordination seemed like a laughable problem to have. With that problem he understood the stakes. What was he to do when he didn't even understand the rules of the game he was playing?

Thomas's stomach rumbled while he waited yet again. He thought of the bread William had stashed in his pack, but quickly recalled that William was in some far-off place Thomas couldn't reach. Their quiet ride across the countryside this morning felt like it had happened decades before.

It was late afternoon before anyone came in to visit him again. A new man entered, this one not dressed in a uniform. He carried a blank bound book of those same oddly thin sheets of vellum, and another stylus. He stuck his hand out for Thomas to shake. He greeted Thomas, then pointed to himself and said, "Kiran."

Thomas repeated the name slowly. It was not like any name he had ever heard before, though the man's thick dark hair and complexion reminded him of traders from the Far East he encountered during his time in London.

Kiran proceeded to ask a series of questions. He was patient with Thomas, writing down notations as they talked even though Thomas had very little in the way of answers since he didn't understand what was being asked. What did these people think was magically going to happen here? That he would suddenly understand? Though maybe he would, eventually. Already the cadence of the words felt less strange to him. At this realization, he took hope.

However, after half an hour of this, Thomas grew

frustrated. When the next question was asked, he simply stared at the man. This was getting them nowhere. Thomas had to get back to the woods—to find a way home before it got dark. He stood and headed for the door. Kiran did nothing to stop him. Thomas turned back toward the entrance to the building, but soon footsteps approached from behind and someone grabbed his arm yet again. He shook the man off—this was yet someone else in the same blasted uniform—but that only succeeded in bringing someone else to the first man's aid. Finally, he gave up.

He wasn't free here. That much was certain.

This was soon borne out. Kiran consulted with a couple of the monks for several minutes. They scribbled on more sheets of vellum. With such a focus on writing, this monastery must be incredibly wealthy. He wondered who their patron was. Maybe he could deal with that man, and he would come to his senses, realize that Thomas should not be kept here against his will. If only he knew how to ask the question in words these people would understand.

The writing seemingly complete, Kiran walked over to Thomas. Thomas locked eyes with him, telegraphing that Thomas wasn't afraid. Clearly Kiran wasn't afraid of Thomas either, because his words were as gentle and soothing as if he were talking to a child or a misbehaving cur. Thomas bristled at this view of himself. He may not be intimidating, especially now that he had been de-armed, but he was a noble and not a man to be trifled with. If they weren't afraid of him, why had they taken his knife? Why wouldn't they let him leave this place?

He forced himself to listen to what Kiran was telling him. He caught at something familiar. Hospital—now there was another word they had in common! He relaxed. With all the confusion, they must think he was an itinerant traveler in need of rest. That explained the strange uniforms—this group of monks must provide hospitality to people passing through. Though why it required so much formality and preparation, he wasn't sure.

Kiran gently guided Thomas toward the entrance, talking in the same condescending voice the entire time. Outside, another metal wagon waited for them. This one was blue, shinier than any paint Thomas had ever seen. He couldn't resist his curiosity, and he reached over and ran a finger along the smooth surface.

When Kiran opened the door, Thomas held his ground for a moment, refusing to go in. But Kiran turned as if he were about to call one of the uniformed men over, and Thomas decided it was better to do as Kiran said. That way it was only him against one other. But the other had the advantage because he knew what was going on here—and how to use the wagon. Once Thomas was in, he wouldn't know how to get out.

He acquiesced and got in. The seats here were much more comfortable than in the wagon that had brought him in. There were cushions instead of a plain bench seat. Perhaps the de la Warr name still held some sway here after all.

Kiran started to close the door, but then he leaned over Thomas, pulling a strap around him and clicking it into place on the other side. Thomas fumbled with the place the strap had been inserted. After a moment, it clicked again, and the strap released. Kiran sighed and clicked it back into place. Thomas left it there since he knew he had the power to get out of it.

Thomas closed his eyes for most of the trip. The streets speeding by made him queasy. Soon they stopped and Kiran got out of the front seat. Thomas unclipped his strap and waited for Kiran to open the door.

The building they had stopped in front of was five stories tall, its height rivaling that of the spire of the famous cathedral but underwhelming in all other respects. It was nothing more than a white box stuck on the landscape. Clearly this place didn't waste much energy or money on architects and masons. Or they had lost those skills completely along with proper language.

Kiran led Thomas inside where there were more forms and half-understood questions. They again patted him down even though he had nothing left with him. Then a woman arrived, dressed in a strange outfit that was pink on top and bottom. Like all the women here, she wore trousers instead of a dress and left her hair uncovered. It made him uncomfortable, this strange melding of the sexes.

She led Thomas and Kiran down a series of hallways—still completely white and plain—until they reached the room she wanted. She ushered him inside. A small bed and nightstand occupied most of the space, and through a door he glimpsed a washbasin and another one of those curious seats. This was not too bad, then. He had stayed in much worse inns, and he welcomed the private room after the day he had had. He smiled and thanked Kiran and the woman who had accompanied them.

Satisfied, Kiran said goodbye. The woman left briefly and returned with a folded pile of clothes and presented them to Thomas. His extra shirt was in the satchel that had been taken from him, so he was glad to have the change of clothes.

Thomas shook his head genially when the woman talked to him. She seemed nice enough, but there was no need for her to waste her words on him.

"Naaame," he said slowly, drawing out the vowel sound as he had heard the man do earlier.

"Diana," she answered.

He grinned and repeated it. This was familiar, the name of an ancient goddess. Not all learning had been lost here, then.

After Diana left, he laid the clothes she had given him out on the bed. The shirt seemed normal enough. The trousers were of a weird, loose material, gray and very soft. He slipped them on anyway. Then he went to investigate the latrine. Now that he was on his own, he could figure out what it was without someone watching over his shoulder. After pressing all over the bowl, he finally discovered it was the silver handle that made the water go away. The noise made him jump less than he had the first time.

Then he turned to the wash basin. Using what he had learned about the handle on the latrine, he pushed and pulled on the metal bits until one of them turned. Water gushed out and disappeared down the drain.

Remarkable! Water that flowed the moment you needed it. He had heard from a scholar when he was at school that the Romans had devised things like this. Maybe these people were related to the Romans. After a moment, he stuck his hand under the stream of water but quickly pulled it away with a little yelp. It was hot. How on earth was it hot?

In the next instant, Diana appeared beside him. She turned off the water and examined his finger. It had turned red where the hot water had hit it. She turned the handle on the other side of the white basin, and the water flowed there, too. She stuck his hand under the water. This stream was cold, and soothing on his burn. He smiled sheepishly. Diana smiled back. Emboldened, he acted on his new theory and asked her in Latin what this place was. Her blank look showed him he wasn't understood in this language either. Thomas sighed. So much for the Roman idea.

As Diana left, he glimpsed her shake her head at his antics. No wonder Kiran talked to him as if he were a child. To these people, he might as well be. He should act like he knew what was going on to command their respect. Despite this resolution, he indulged in one more push of the handle on the latrine and grinned in delight as the water swirled away.

Chapter 8

By the time Ashley got home, the adrenaline from her adventure wore off, leaving her exhausted. Thomas's last pleading gaze from the back of the cop car replayed in her mind. She empathized with him, but the authorities would know better what to do with him. What if he had stabbed her when they were alone in the woods? She shivered at the thought.

She made a sandwich and watched mindless TV for an hour. Then she lay down for a nap, a rare indulgence. She woke up only when her phone dinged. It was Katie, inviting Ashley to join them at the pub in an hour. That was exactly what she needed. The distraction of alcohol and her new friends that—hopefully—wouldn't screw her over like Sadie had.

The evening was warm, so their little group met on the patio outside a pub in the city center.

"You look like death," Antony said to her when she walked up.

Obviously, Ashley's attempts to pretty herself up before she left the house had not paid dividends. She couldn't even muster a "Gee, thanks," in response.

Katie returned to the table carrying two pints. She slid one in front of Ashley, unasked. "What's up with you?" she asked, making a face.

"I've had the day from hell," Ashley said after a fortifying gulp of her beer. When she told them about what Sadie had done, they seemed ready to get their pitchforks and tar and feather her. And she had only exaggerated a little, tiny bit.

"That girl is not your friend," Katie said.

"I know. I don't know why I let myself get dragged back into her drama." It was true. If Ashley had never reached out to Sadie for help, none of this would have happened. Ashley sighed. "But that's not even the wackiest thing that happened today."

"Hold on," Antony said. "I don't know if I can handle this." He took a deep breath and made a show of calming himself. "All right," he finally said. "I'm ready."

Next, she told them about Thomas. When she finished, they were silent.

"I don't even know how to react to that," Antony said after a moment.

"That's nice of you, I guess," Katie said.

"Neither of you have seen this guy around before?"

Her companions shook their heads.

"Maybe he's lost," Antony said with a shrug. "If so, I feel sorry for him."

"Me, too," Ashley agreed.

Katie watched her carefully. After a few more sips of her beer, Katie asked, "So how attractive is this mysterious guy, then?"

Ashley immediately blushed. "What makes you ask that?"

"You seem really interested in him. I can tell you're still thinking about it."

"Well, yeah, I can't decide what to do." She relaxed and smiled. "Yes, he is very attractive."

"I knew it!"

"The plot thickens," Antony said. "You have to

check on him, then. Maybe it's meant to be."

Ashley screwed up her nose. "I doubt it."

"Don't judge," he replied. "Once he gets cleaned up, he may be a prince from some far-off land. You don't know."

"Now we all know what Antony's fantasy is," Katie said drolly.

"Anyway," Ashley said, "I have even more reasons not to want to go home now." She thought back to the estate agent Hannah had introduced her to. His card was still tucked uselessly in her wallet. "I wish I could stay here. Surely, they need estate agents in Salisbury."

Katie shook her head. "That's not your problem. Your problem is getting a work visa."

"Right." Ashley's shoulders slumped. She had momentarily forgotten about that huge hurdle. "Well, I can stay six months on my tourist visa." And then? No answers came.

"Marry mysterious guy," Antony said. "Problem solved."

"Except who knows where on earth he's actually from," Katie reminded him.

"Where else do they have people named Thomas?" Ashley asked, in a half joking way. This led into a long debate on the etymology of names and where they came from, which Ashley was happy to mostly sit back and laugh along with. Her phone dinged. It was a text from Sadie. Ashley tucked her phone away and refused to read it, even after it dinged several more times.

The unquestioning support of her new friends in her feud with Sadie emboldened her. She had a second pint, and then a third. Considering how little she had gone out in recent years back home, three drinks was a lot, especially for her small frame. Her walk home was happy, if a bit unsteady. Once inside her flat, she pulled out her phone and read what Sadie had said. Ashley's anger was still fresh, and it flared like a pile of kindling as soon as she read the messages.

Hey girl, I wanted to make sure we're all right after our last conversation. It didn't go like I thought it would, the first message said.

I'm sorry you're upset. But we helped each other. It's what writers do.

Sadie clearly still did not get it at all. Ashley noticed she had left the door to the flat open and walked across the room to close it. On the way back, she tripped and fell over her purse, which she had dropped on the floor by the sofa. She stayed on the floor, letting her emotions swell. How the hell was she supposed to respond to Sadie's non-apology? Did she want to save their friendship, or should she let this rift be permanent?

She took a few deep, calming breaths. To distract herself, she opened her email.

And hit the gold mine. At least, that's how it felt in her inebriated state.

Sadie had copied Ashley on an email to her agent. Why, Ashley had no idea. A Freudian slip because she had Ashley on her mind? Ashley certainly wasn't mentioned in the email itself. It was simply Sadie thanking the agent for their phone call and outlining the changes to the manuscript they had discussed, with the final document attached. Sadie, of course, claimed the narrator change as her own idea.

Ashley's fingers hovered over the keypad of her phone. Dare she respond? She thought about Katie's support, and the way she had encouraged Ashley to stand up for herself. Could Ashley afford not to take advantage of this opportunity?

Ashley closed her eyes and gritted her teeth until the room stopped spinning. She hated being vindictive, but all she wanted right now was to reach through the phone and smash Sadie's face in. Barring that, she would have to settle for the next best thing: ruining Sadie's dream the way Sadie had ruined Ashley's.

She started typing. She wanted it to sound somewhat professional. But she also wanted Sadie to know that she couldn't screw Ashley Winston over and get away with it.

Thanks for looping me in here, Sadie, Ashley wrote.

Ms. Reyes, she continued, referring to the literary agent, *I am so glad to hear that my idea for changing the narrator and the twist at the end was what convinced you to represent this manuscript. I think I could add a lot of value to your work with Sadie and am more than happy to share my other work with you.*

It was innocuous enough, she thought, as she signed it. Then why was her hand shaking? After a long moment, she took a deep breath and hit send.

Five minutes later, however, she felt guilty, not so much on Sadie's behalf, because she pushed that down as far as possible, but on behalf of her own career. This was going to be this agent's first impression of Ashley and her work. Was that the message she wanted out there? She didn't have a choice, she reassured herself. Sadie had backed her into a corner. Ashley had to protect herself first and foremost. She pulled off her shoes and crawled into bed without undressing.

When Ashley awoke, her head was groggy, her arm pinned in an uncomfortable position beneath her. She rolled onto her back with a groan. The events of the night before drifted to the forefront of her consciousness. Oh no, she thought. No, no, no. She groped around the bed for her phone. She had several missed calls, an angry all-caps text message, and a voicemail that she dared not listen to from Sadie.

She braced herself as she checked her email. She skimmed the agent's response first, then read it slowly twice more to absorb it. The agent had dropped Sadie, but also was not interested in hearing more about Ashley's book. She suggested Sadie and Ashley needed to figure out the situation on their own, perhaps as co-authors, and said that she did not want to work with anyone she couldn't trust—implying what Ashley did was underhanded.

She wasn't wrong.

Ashley got in the shower, her mind swirling with emotions. She called up her anger from the night before—it was her work that had been stolen, after all—but she didn't feel nearly as vindicated as she'd thought she would. Sadie had been one of her few friends left back home, and Ashley had killed that relationship now.

And what had she done to her own writing career? Upon reflection, as the hot water cleared her head, Ashley saw what a huge tactical error this might be. Would the agent tell others not to work with Ashley? Was it worth apologizing, explaining that the email was sent in drunken anger? No, that certainly wouldn't make her appear any better. And why had Sadie copied her on the damn email in the first place? Sadie was the one who had set everything in motion. And was Sadie right that they had simply helped each other along the way? Why couldn't Ashley have just been happy for Sadie?

Ashley stepped out of the shower. She couldn't wrestle her thoughts away from what she had done. She had purportedly come to Salisbury to write her book. Now Sadie—no, Ashley herself—had taken that away from her. Ashley wiped the fog off the mirror and gazed at herself, still dripping wet. She had made a mess of her whole life. Worse, was she actually a horrible person? She knew she could care for other people—how else could she explain Trevor's long hold over her—but everything that had happened lately had made her care more and more for herself only. For the first time, she thought that might not be a good thing.

The water dripping down her face turned salty. She was crying. What could she do to make amends for any of this? How could she show herself that she could be the person she had been before—open, willing to help, happy?

Her mind snapped back to the previous day's encounter with Thomas. There was a person who needed help, and she could provide it. Maybe her new purpose in Salisbury could be making sure Thomas was okay. She resolved to go check on him. He could be her salvation for this trip, and for herself.

Chapter 9

Ashley readied herself to go out relatively early the next morning. She often found that after a night of drinking she couldn't sleep much. As she walked to the door, she gazed forlornly at the writing schedule taped so hopefully to the wall above the desk in an alcove in the living room. She ripped it down. Now that her prospects were fatally damaged, she wouldn't be filling her time writing. She would spend it fulfilling her new mission instead. And the first step in that mission was finding Thomas and undoing the damage she had done yesterday.

She headed directly to the police station and explained the situation to the officer at the front desk. When she admitted she had no relation to Thomas, he was loathe to tell her anything. She dug through her purse until she found the officers' cards from the day before. "Are either of these people in?"

The officer took the cards and read them skeptically. "Let me check," he finally said. He picked up the phone but looked pointedly at Ashley until she moved away and sat in a plastic chair along one wall.

Eventually, Constable Marvin, the policewoman who had helped Ashley the day before, emerged. "Miss Winston," she said formally.

Ashley stood eagerly. "Thank you for meeting me. What happened with Thomas? Were you able to find out who he is or contact anyone who knows him?"

The officer shook her head. "We weren't. We gave him over to the hospital last night when he wouldn't settle down. You can go over there and find out what they know." She checked her watch. "But he'll be held for twenty-four hours, so he won't be released until this afternoon." She regarded Ashley. "You should also know that he has fourteen days to get us some form of identification. If you can talk to him, if he trusts you, that would be helpful."

Ashley frowned at this new wrinkle in her mission. "I don't know if he'll tell me anything." Hell, she didn't know if he *could* tell her anything.

"He has to have something. He's in this country somehow. He's from somewhere."

Not wanting the conversation to continue in this vein, especially since she had no idea what the answer to their shared dilemma was, Ashley simply nodded. She got directions to the hospital and thanked Constable Marvin profusely. When Ashley exited the station, she considered the possibilities for the day. She had hours until Thomas's release. What she needed was a reset. She would be a tourist today, she decided. Get out of her own thoughts. She slung her purse over her shoulder and headed toward the cathedral. She had visited during her previous trip years ago, of course, but hadn't made her way there yet since she had been back. The cathedral was arguably the most significant constant in the city. That was what she needed right now, constancy, since she had ripped the stability out of her own life.

She spent an hour walking around the church, reading the informational signs and admiring the ornate carvings. Afterward, she lay on the grass quadrangle abutting the cathedral. The grass was damp, and she wished she had a blanket to lay under her, but she didn't let it deter her. She lay there, letting the sun warm her like a ripening fruit.

She dozed off at some point and awoke with a start, frantically reaching out to check that her purse was still there. Fortunately, it was. A group of people picnicking nearby gave her an odd look. She smiled sheepishly at them.

Her stomach growled. She wandered toward the city center to find something to eat. But as she exited the cathedral close and continued onto the high street, a shopfront caught her eye. Flyers pasted in the windows showed off available properties in the area. She perused a few, then looked up at the store's sign and recognized the name. It was the firm that managed Hannah's flats. On a whim, she walked in, her mind turning over the possibility she had brought up with her friends the night before about establishing herself here.

Fortunately, the office was empty of visitors. Even better, Terry was the only person sitting at the desks in the open main room. In a glass-fronted office along the back wall, an older man talked on the phone and paid no heed to her entrance.

Terry walked over to her, tugging on his tie. "Everything all right with the flat?" he asked. "Ashley, isn't it?"

She smiled, a big, forced smile she normally bestowed on clients. She hadn't used it since she quit. "You got it. Everything's fine," she added quickly, then paused. "I have sort of an odd request, so feel free to tell me to bugger off if you're busy." She squirmed, embarrassed at the British phrase she had inadvertently used, hoping it didn't sound too put-on. She recovered and smiled. "You know I was a real estate agent back home. I want to get information about what requirements exist here to be an agent."

"We wouldn't be able to hire someone here temporarily…"

Ashley shook her head. "I know, I just meant—" What did she mean exactly? "I just wanted to know in general what the requirements are here. Is there a test or a course you have to take?"

"Technically, no. But there is a certification you can take. It would probably help you with transitioning from the U.S. market to the U.K. one." He returned to his desk and rifled through a drawer. "Here you go," he said, handing over a pamphlet. "This has some information on courses we typically recommend for new agents."

"Thanks," she said, taking the folded paper and sliding it into her purse. "I appreciate it." She turned to leave.

"We could have lunch sometime," he said abruptly from behind her. "I could go over some things with you."

She glanced over her shoulder. He looked awfully eager, but within this professional context, surely, he couldn't mean it as a date. "Yes, let's," she said. "You have my card."

Her mood bolstered by this good result, she peered up and down the street. Her stomach had quieted down. She checked her watch. It had just passed noon, so Thomas could be released any time now, and she wanted to make sure she was there. She turned her steps purposefully toward the bus stop.

Once at the hospital, she went through much the same process with explaining the situation as at the police station. She wasn't related to him, she told the receptionist, but if he didn't have any relatives here, surely they should let her help him. After a few phone calls, the receptionist told her that they planned to release Thomas later that day and she could check back then.

"When exactly?"

"Sometime this afternoon." Her tone indicated no additional information would be forthcoming.

Ashley checked the time. It was already after one o'clock. She didn't want to miss him and have him end up wandering the streets confused again. "I'll wait," she said. The receptionist shrugged and moved on to the next person in line. Ashley claimed a chair in one corner of the waiting room and entertained herself on her phone.

****

Thomas had indicated several times since breakfast that he wanted to leave, but each time he made it more than a few feet down the hallway he was ushered back to his room. Diana was nowhere to be found this morning, and the young man who had replaced her was not as friendly. Thomas had no choice but to lie on the bed and try not to let his thoughts dwell too deeply on what was occurring.

Lunch was served, some sort of meat between two slices of bland bread, with an unnaturally red, globulus dessert. Shortly after Thomas finished eating and the young man had taken the tray away, a knock came at the door. Thomas smiled at Kiran standing in the doorway.

The same routine followed, Kiran asking questions, Thomas answering them as best he could, Kiran writing down things in his book. Thomas cooperated, hoping that would lead him to being shown the way out of this labyrinthine building.

Kiran left. When he returned, he carried Thomas's satchel.

Thomas leapt up from his perch on the bed. Kiran talked while Thomas pawed through his satchel, making sure all of his things were accounted for. He looked up expectantly when he was satisfied. Kiran smiled and with the same gentle maneuver of hand against Thomas's back, he led Thomas through doors and down hallways until they reached the lobby. Seeing the light of day again lifted Thomas's spirits.

Kiran appeared concerned as he gave Thomas final instructions, but Thomas's mind was already a world away, heading back home. Thomas took a few steps toward the doors. His eyes lighted on someone seated against the far wall. The young woman he had encountered yesterday. Ashley, she had said her name was. He was relieved to see another familiar face. He pointed to her, and Kiran also seemed relieved when she walked over to them.

Ashley and Kiran exchanged a few sentences. Then Kiran said his goodbyes and walked back into the depths of the building.

****

Ashley had expected there would be some sort of announcement, that the receptionist would tell her Thomas was coming out. Instead, she nearly missed him as he crossed the lobby a couple of hours later. These people really were just letting him out to manage by his own devices.

She jumped up and waved. Thomas did a doubletake. When he recognized her, he grinned.

She crossed the lobby to him. The doctor standing behind him seemed glad she knew him, and he left

92

Thomas in her care. Once the doctor had walked away, she hesitated in front of Thomas, unsure what to say. "Hello," she finally decided on.

"Hallo," he said, the word accented. They understood each other so far.

"Good? Okay?" she asked.

This he more or less understood also. He nodded. He still had his satchel stuffed full of his possessions, but the hospital had provided him with sweatpants and a T-shirt to wear. He wore the clothes awkwardly, occasionally tugging at the waist of his pants and shrugging his shoulders as if he didn't like the feel of the fabric. The toes of his leather boots looked out of place sticking out from beneath the sweatpants.

"Hungry?" she asked. When this received no reaction, she rubbed her stomach and mimed eating.

He nodded.

Not a stimulating conversation, but they were getting somewhere. She led him outside to the bus stop. This would be a challenge, as she had failed at getting him on the bus the day before. Fortunately, he seemed more pliable now. She hoped they hadn't been too rough with him at the station or the hospital to make him that way. When the bus pulled up a few minutes later, he crossed himself but followed Ashley up the steps. She put her fare on her bus pass and pulled out a few pound coins to cover Thomas's ticket. Ashley picked a seat for them in the middle of the bus, where no other passengers were nearby. She had Thomas sit by the window so he would have to get past her to do anything, though she couldn't quite define what she was worried he might do.

She bit her lip. Was he mentally ill? She shook her head. He seemed fine.

He reached into his satchel and pulled out his cross necklace. He put it around his neck and gripped the cross the entire ride. Ashley watched him closely. He had on a brave face, but she could tell by the way his eyes darted around the landscape passing by that he was terrified. Another bus passed them going the opposite direction, and he jumped at the whoosh. Ashley put a hand on his shoulder and smiled softly. He glanced at her but kept his expression neutral. She removed her hand. She had no idea what he was thinking or going through. Had he arrived here as a refugee, made an illegal crossing of the Channel, perhaps? If so, what horrors had he escaped from? She wanted desperately to ask, but knew it was best not to push him.

They disembarked at the city center. She paused, considering their options. Maybe he would like a pub. Someplace quiet and calm, a little dark and old-fashioned. While she was contemplating this, Thomas rushed past her. Clearly, he had plans of his own.

Ashley dashed after him. After a moment, she guessed he had spied the spire of an old stone church peeking over the rooftops in the next street. Indeed, after a brief scramble of confusion at the pedestrian crossing, that was where he headed. Ashley entered the building a moment after him.

The church was silent and empty. Thomas walked purposefully down the aisle. He hesitated slightly, investigating the setup, before kneeling at the altar. A moment later, a cleric entered, wearing his collar, an older man with close-cropped gray hair. "Can I help you folks?" he asked. Ashley marveled at his voice. It was the perfect pitch—quiet and gentle but just loud enough to reach them through the cavernous space. She guessed this had been his church for a long time.

Thomas jumped up and approached the vicar. Thomas crossed himself again, knelt, and held his hands up in supplication. The vicar's eye widened in surprise for an instant, but he reined in his surprise and made the sign of the cross over Thomas's head.

Thomas launched into the longest speech Ashley had heard him make so far. This time, the older man couldn't hide his surprise. He looked over Thomas's head at Ashley. "What is he saying?"

Ashley stepped closer. "I don't know," she said apologetically.

This obviously did not relieve the vicar's confusion. Ashley beckoned him closer.

As the vicar stepped around him, Thomas leapt up. He crossed himself again. "In nomine Patris et Filii et Spiritus Sancti," he said emphatically.

The vicar watched him quizzically, but Thomas smiled, aware that he had been understood. Ashley had never gone to church much, but she recognized the phrase from period dramas on TV. "I think maybe he wants to do confession?"

The vicar frowned and turned to face her. "I don't normally do that."

Ashley quickly explained the situation, making Thomas sound as sane as she could.

The vicar regarded Thomas carefully, who was still watching them eagerly. "There were times I could almost understand him. Maybe he's speaking Dutch?"

Ashley shrugged. "They probably tried that at the station. He also speaks French, but one of the officers spoke with him and he said it's not like any French he ever heard."

The vicar nodded slowly. "Well, confession isn't disallowed by the Church of England, so since he seems to be in distress, I'll do it."

"Thank you," Ashley said. She meant it. She needed something to go right for her new friend—or whatever he was to her. He almost felt like a traumatized pet she had just picked up from the shelter and was protecting.

The vicar guided Thomas to a pew at the front. Ashley stayed back, giving them privacy.

****

Thomas smiled when the priest approached him again. This was his opportunity to divulge his sins and his doubts, to be forgiven so he could go home. That was what he hoped, anyway. There were aspects of this church that were slightly different from what he was used to. The priest's garb, for one. He might be a lay brother instead of a priest, but Thomas would take what he could get at this point.

The priest motioned to the frontmost bench. Thomas glanced around, then sat. He didn't see a confessional booth anywhere, so perhaps people did their confession in the open here. That could be what the rows of benches were for—because surely the congregation would stand during the service still? Either way, he sensed more than ever the power of the church. Even in this bizarre world he had entered, the faith held on in mostly recognizable form.

Thomas launched into his story: his destiny as a priest himself, which he had almost run away from in favor of going to war, and his appearance in this strange place. He didn't worry about the words he used because surely God could still understand him or make the priest understand him.

When he finished, the priest patted Thomas's hand gently before conferring a blessing on him. Thomas crossed himself. He had the power now to rectify his situation. He would have to take action to get himself back home, and surely God would show him what that action should be.

****

The vicar listened intently to Thomas. Ashley admired his ability to appear so engrossed and caring even though she knew he couldn't understand a word Thomas said. After several minutes, the vicar gave Thomas another blessing and stood. When the vicar returned to Ashley, Thomas closed his eyes in prayer.

"Thank you," Ashley said again.

"Have you noticed his ring?" the vicar asked.

Ashley shook her head. She had been so struck by everything else he was wearing that she hadn't really noticed it. She leaned her head so she could see Thomas's hands. There was indeed a gold ring with a round face on his left pinkie.

"I ask because I was struck by the seal on it. It's the coat of arms of the Tregoze family."

A clue! "Who are they?"

"They *were* a family that used to own land north of here. They had connections to William the Conqueror, I think." He smiled softly. "I'm a bit of a local history buff, you see."

"So they were medieval?" she asked. She was suddenly struck by how many things pointed to that era. His indecipherable speech, his fear of cars, his obsession with praying. The clothes he had worn yesterday—the long tunic, the tights, and the oddly shapeless boots—could be medieval, too.

"Yes, the family lived at Lydiard Park. But they died out by the fifteenth century, I think."

"Is there anything at Lydiard Park now?" She vaguely recognized the name, probably from a tourist guidebook.

"The eighteenth-century mansion is there, but I think anything medieval was lost long ago."

"Right." She paused. "Do you know if there's a Catholic church nearby?"

The vicar kindly gave her directions to the nearest one. It could wait, for now, but it would be good to know where to take Thomas next time.

Next time? How long was she going to keep this up?

She pushed the question out of her thoughts. She would help Thomas for as long as he needed her.

After thanking the vicar again, she walked up to Thomas. When he opened his eyes, she inclined her head to the door. "Let's go," she said. He followed her peacefully. She smiled. He seemed buoyed by his confession. If it made him feel better, that was all that mattered.

Back out on the street, Ashley searched for a pub for them to eat at. Lunchtime was long past now, and dinner was approaching. Her stomach rumbled. She hadn't even had anything to drink since she left her flat that morning.

Her thoughts snapped back to the present moment. Thomas was gone. She glanced frantically around. Finally, she spotted him at the top of the street, walking quickly like he knew where he was going. Ashley hesitated a moment—should she just let him go? But, no, she had a responsibility to him. She remembered the doctor's relief as he left Thomas with her, glad that he would have someone to look out for him. She raced after

Thomas, desperately hoping she wasn't making a mistake.

Chapter 10

Ashley hurried after Thomas. He kept speed-walking even once they were outside of town. He didn't seem to be running away from her, necessarily, but he didn't stop to talk to her and explain himself either. Then again, why would he bother? It's not like they could really communicate.

Eventually she recognized they were heading across the same field they had crossed together going the opposite direction the day before. The copse lay ahead up the hill to their left, and Thomas made a beeline for it, disappearing between the trees before Ashley could catch up to him. She hesitated at the edge of the woods, then took a deep breath and stepped inside. She walked tentatively across the dead leaves packed beneath her feet. She couldn't hear his footsteps. After a moment, she found him kneeling at the same moss-covered rock he had retreated to after their initial encounter.

What was so special to him about this goddamn rock?

She waited silently a few paces behind while he prayed. It was something she would be doing a lot of, it seemed. She had never seen someone pray so much. After a few minutes, he cocked one eye open, hands still clasped in prayer. When he saw her, he closed his eyes again and prayed even more fervently. Eventually, she stepped forward and touched his shoulder gently.

Whatever he was doing, it obviously wasn't making him feel any better or helping the situation.

Thomas's shoulder slumped under her fingertips. He stood, but when he turned to her, his eyes flashed with defiance. He marched to the edge of the woods. Ashley hurried after him.

The city lay on the plain below them, but Thomas didn't veer in that direction. He headed away from the city instead. Ashley guessed his destination was the one she had had in mind before she ran into him originally: Old Sarum.

This would be interesting.

Thomas's pace didn't slow for the next mile. Ashley fell behind. She desperately wished she had some water or a granola bar or something. She felt a bit faint in the sun. Thomas, on the other hand, wasn't fazed by any of it. That, or sheer determination powered him.

Old Sarum eventually slid into view. Thomas stopped in his tracks for a moment, but then he pushed forward just as Ashley reached him. There was only one other pair of tourists wandering among the ruins, and they ignored Ashley and Thomas as they crested the hill.

Thomas crossed the ruins reverently. The space had that effect on people. Ashley had felt it too when she visited. The village abandoned so many centuries ago in favor of the new town of Salisbury was now just barely visible above ground but still commanded its incredible view across the landscape. The day was clear, the fields rolling for miles in every direction.

Thomas paused beside the stone foundations of the once great cathedral that the one still standing in Salisbury had replaced. Ashley stepped beside him and touched his elbow. He didn't acknowledge her. Ashley considered what his fascination with the spot meant. He clearly knew Salisbury, and Salisbury only existed once Old Sarum had been abandoned. But the buildings on the hill would have still been visible for a long time after. Their collapse into ruins and the reclamation of the building stone would have happened over centuries.

Ashley shook her head. What was she even proposing here? Thomas was just a lost tourist. She needed to raise her blood sugar before she went completely nuts.

She touched Thomas's elbow again. This time he turned to her. His eyes were rimmed in red, but no tears fell from them. His eyes held a sadness like he had given up. He watched Ashley, waiting like a lost puppy to be told where they were going next. Ashley gently led him back down the hill. They walked slowly back to Salisbury.

They had nearly reached the city center when dizziness overwhelmed Ashley. She stumbled. Thomas caught her and led her to a low wall lining the sidewalk. Ashley sat and rubbed her forehead. She felt clammy. Her vision was gray and fuzzy.

Thomas knelt beside her. His face held so much concern she couldn't help but smile a little. She stood, but wooziness overtook her again.

Thomas shook his head and guided her back to the seat. A businessman walked past. He glanced at Ashley, but his expression held contempt rather than concern, as if he suspected she might be a drunk or something else nefarious.

She mimed holding a bottle up to her mouth. "Water," she said.

"Water," Thomas repeated slowly like he might

comprehend.

Steadying herself against him, she reached into her purse and pulled out a five-pound note. She looked around. At the far corner, just visible, hung a sign for a small convenience store. She handed him the money and pointed to the store.

"Water," he repeated. Then he got up and walked in the direction she had indicated.

Ashley watched him disappear into the store. That much had been accomplished, though she hoped the scene that transpired inside wouldn't cause any problems.

A couple of minutes later, Thomas reemerged. He was holding a bottle of water. Success!

When he reached her, he held out the bottle in one hand and her change in the other. She dumped the coins in her purse, not bothering to put them away, and drank the water thankfully. When she had finished half of it, she offered it to Thomas. He shook his head and pointed to her. She finished the rest of it quickly. He mimed eating just as she had done for him hours ago when they met at the hospital. She nodded and slowly stood.

Thomas took her arm and she let him support her as they walked slowly down the street. He was sturdy—and rather muscled, Ashley thought as they walked, feeling his arm flex and his leg and chest move confidently beside her, unbothered by taking on her extra weight. He glanced down at her and smiled several times as they walked. She still couldn't get over how blue his eyes were. It was difficult to keep her eyes off him and search for a place to eat instead.

She stopped at the first pub they passed, hoping a traditional setting would appeal to him. Inside was dim, with a low, wood ceiling and thick beams stationed on either side of the gleaming bar. Thomas relaxed a bit. The pub was clearly the right choice.

Thomas led her to a booth along one wall. She slid in. He sat across from her.

The sole worker approached the table. The pub traffic was slow, with only two other tables filled. "Is she okay?" he asked Thomas.

"I'm fine," Ashley said. "Just need something to eat."

The barman handed over menus. "Anything to drink?"

"Two waters and two lagers, please."

"Carlsberg fine?"

"Do you have anything English?" That would probably appeal more to Thomas's tastes, though she couldn't clearly articulate why she thought that.

The barman nodded and returned to his station behind the bar.

Ashley watched Thomas. He stared intently at the menu. Could he understand the words after all?

"What are you going to get?" she asked.

He looked up, startled out of his concentration. He shrugged and waved the menu around a bit, indicating he couldn't make heads or tails of it.

Guess not. Ashley studied the menu. What would be a good, old-fashioned meal? The offerings didn't disappoint. She wavered between fish and chips and bangers and mash, finally deciding on the latter.

"Two orders of bangers and mash," she said when the barman returned with their drinks.

"Does he speak?"

"He doesn't speak English," Ashley supplied.

The barman regarded them strangely. Then he rubbed a hand across his bald head and turned back to the bar. The bar was only six feet or so from the table, so she guessed he had heard her speak to Thomas in English, which undermined her own statement. But she didn't have the time or energy to explain to everyone they met. Hell, she didn't even know what the explanation was.

"Anglisch," Thomas said, grabbing her attention again. The first vowel sounded a bit off, the last syllable a bit thicker than when she said it.

"English," she repeated. Another word they had in common.

"Anglisch. English," Thomas said, working something out in his head.

Ashley held up her ale, hoping the sign of clinking glasses was universal. "Cheers."

Thomas held up his glass in response. Ashley smiled, took a sip, and cut into her sausage.

Thomas followed suit, but he used his knife both to cut the food and bring it to his mouth. She watched this maneuver with interest. He managed it much more deftly than she would have. After a few minutes, she held up her utensils, and exaggerated the movements to show him how to use the fork and the knife together. He attempted it but didn't succeed in getting the bite to his mouth. Ashley smiled, but he ignored her and reverted to eating with his knife.

They finished their meals mostly in silence. Thomas finished his ale and Ashley ordered him another, but he didn't touch his water glass.

When their plates were empty, Thomas reached into his bag and pulled out a handful of something and offered it to Ashley. She hesitated but opened her hand to accept whatever it was.

A small pile of coins landed in her palm. They were a dark silver color, with slightly irregular edges. She picked one up to examine it. The engravings were an incredibly old style. The image of what she assumed was a king on one side looked almost cartoonish. But the coins themselves shone brand new, not worn and dirty like something that, based on the design, should probably be hundreds of years old. She peered at the writing that circled the king's head. With the odd font, she couldn't make out what it said.

She turned the face of the coin to Thomas and pointed at the image of the man. "Who is this?" she asked. "Your king?"

"Edward."

Edward! Again, the vowels were a bit strange, but she understood. Now they were getting somewhere. How many Edwards had there been? Lots, probably. She held up one finger, then two, then three. Thomas stopped her at three. "Edward," he said, followed by a few words she couldn't understand, then he held up three fingers again. He pointed at the floor and said something else. "Richard." He held up two fingers.

She pondered what this could mean. Why point at the floor? She had refrained from flashing technology at Thomas too much, given his reaction to cars, but now she pulled out her phone. If this wasn't a situation that called for emergency use of Wikipedia, then nothing was.

She looked up Edward III, then Richard II. Richard had succeeded Edward, so Thomas pairing them together made sense. Maybe he meant the king was now Richard? That the coins were old? It must take time to pull all the currency in a kingdom to switch them over to a new king. She returned to the Wikipedia entry. That would make it 1377.

She shook her head. Would make *what* 1377? She still wasn't sure.

She handed the coins back to Thomas. "I'll pay," she said. But she couldn't get the thought of them out of her head. She pulled a page out of a notebook in her purse and wrote that day's date and the next day's date on it plus the year, then marked a space for Thomas to write the same for himself.

She turned the page around and handed the pen to Thomas. She pointed at the blanks for him to fill in.

He ran his finger along the words and numbers she had written. After a moment's thought, he wrote below the blanks she had left for him.

Edward L Richard I MCCCLXXVII

Ashley took the page back and stared at it. She understood that the long series of letters was meant to be a number, though her knowledge of Roman numerals was not strong enough to decode what he had written exactly. She knew that M meant one thousand—largely because of the chocolate candy commercials back at the turn of the millennium. And at the very end, VII should mean seven, unless something about what came before changed it. Richard I was confusing, since he had just indicated Richard II.

She turned her attention back to the number. She had a one to start and a seven to end. A check back at her phone confirmed that Edward III had reigned for fifty years and L meant fifty. Her guess must be right. It was the year of the transition from Edward's reign to Richard's. Thirteen hundred and seventy-seven.

Thomas thought he was from the past.

Or, at the very least, he wanted her to think that.

Ashley paid and hurried them out of the pub. She googled the nearest reasonably priced hotel and headed in that direction. She needed some time to process what had just happened. She had known that Thomas likely had mental health issues, but there was something about what they had just shared that both frightened and excited her. She needed to think, to figure out the next step to help him.

At the hotel, she put down a credit card for his room and led him to the third floor, taking the stairs instead of the elevator since there was no point in stressing him unnecessarily with a new mode of transport.

At the door to the room, she demonstrated how the keycard worked a few times before pushing the door open and walking inside. He followed her inside but froze after a few steps. She turned back to face him, and he in turn spun around and walked back into the hallway.

She followed him out. "What's wrong?"

"No," he said, his face bright red.

"No what?"

He gestured vaguely toward the room, then to her. "That. You."

"Me?" She had no clue what he was getting at.

Thomas dug his cross out from under his shirt and pointed at it. "No," he repeated.

Ashley thought through what had just happened. Everything had been fine until they walked into the room. He had stopped a few steps in...when he had first been able to see the bed. Was being alone in a bedroom with a woman too much for him? Or, even worse, did he think she was propositioning him? Her face burned as much as his had. "No," she struggled to explain. "You sleep here. I'm going to leave." To demonstrate, she mimed sleeping and moved her hand as if around a clock. He didn't appear reassured. She handed over the key and gestured toward the door.

He stepped cautiously forward, took the key, and opened the door.

"I'll come back in the morning," she said. "Stay here. Don't leave." She paused. "It's not like that," she added, though she doubted he knew what she meant.

He stepped inside and shut the door quickly, eager to get rid of her. But with all the confusion, she couldn't really blame him. If she was honest, she was a bit relieved to have him off her hands for the time being as well.

She stood in the hall with her hands on her hips until a man emerged from another room and it felt odd not to move on. As she rode the elevator down to the lobby, she reflected on the day. It had probably been the strangest of her life. She wasn't sure if she had done the right thing going to pick him up at the hospital, especially now that she understood he thought of her only as a woman attempting to get in his pants. She needed to think through what her next steps should be and how much of her time, energy, and money she should invest in this bizarre situation. She headed home, determined to forget him for the rest of the evening.

****

After Ashley left, Thomas sat on the edge of the bed. This inn had a less personal touch. There was no Diana to bring him clothes or a tray of food. Why hadn't Ashley taken him back there?

He shook his head. He couldn't fathom Ashley's

intentions. She had seemed nice enough, but the fact that she came into his room… Perhaps the monks here were no more honest than the monks back home, and they had sent Ashley to him, hoping to please him. Why they would want to please him when they had first kept him prisoner, he couldn't figure out.

It was hard enough to decipher the role of women here. They all wore trousers, and not a single one covered her hair. Even a whore back home wouldn't dare dress in that way. His head ached sorting it all out.

He flopped onto his back. Another day had passed, and he was no closer to getting home. Worse, his one hope at getting home, praying at the stone, had proven ineffective. And his glimpse of the old village on the hill showed him that something here had changed. The old cathedral was nothing more than a foundation trench now, as if it had been weathering away for a millennium rather than a century. His head swam at the insanity of the thought. Why was God still punishing him with this madness?

He got up quickly, knelt, and prayed. He promised he would go straight to his ordination if he were sent home. He repeated this promise over and over.

When he opened his eyes, however, the magical transition had not been reversed. He was still in the dark square room. Had someone cursed him? William, perhaps, or John? William must travel the country for a reason. Maybe he cursed those he found wanting in the faith. Or had John gotten someone to curse Thomas so Thomas couldn't follow his brother to France? He squeezed his eyes tightly shut. It was too much for one person to fathom.

There was only one thing he could do. Wait and see

what answers he was given, from God or some other, more sinister, source.

Chapter 11

When Ashley woke up in the morning, she couldn't bring herself to face Thomas quite yet. She needed to figure out what she was doing with him—and how to avoid any more misunderstandings like last night's.

She called the hotel to check on Thomas. The clerk clearly thought it was an odd request, especially when she said she didn't actually want to speak to him, but the fact that there was nothing to report was a good sign. He clearly hadn't gone wandering the halls with a knife or had a freakout over the TV or anything, because that would have been noticed. The hotel didn't offer room service, but she called a café nearby that delivered and had them bring the food up to his room. When she didn't hear anything back within an hour, she also took that as a good sign, that the delivery had been uneventful.

After she had dealt with these most pressing items, she allowed herself a moment of feeling pleased for herself and the charity she had shown Thomas. But still, in the quiet that followed, her mind slipped back to her book first, then Sadie, then Ashley's own mortifying faux pas. Ashley still wasn't sure if she was angrier at Sadie or herself.

Despite everything, her book called to her. The only chance she had for absolution with it was to prove her story worthy. She opened her working document but couldn't focus. After half an hour of scrolling through the document and only writing a sentence here or there, she gave up. Everything was confused and clouded in her head. She didn't know what she was doing in her career, her writing, or her personal life. She missed the days back home when she had been so sure about all of those things.

A television marathon filled the rest of the day. She felt guilty about leaving Thomas alone, but decided it was too late to go to him now. She would visit him in the morning. What had happened in the hotel room was an honest mistake, considering how different his worldview was from hers. She would have to accept that little misunderstandings would occur, but that he didn't do anything intentionally to insult her.

Just as she made this decision, her phone rang from a UK number she didn't know. She picked up. Her heart fell when it wasn't Thomas even though she hadn't known, an instant before, that she'd been hoping it was him. Her stomach tightened when the police officer spoke.

"We don't have any contact info for him," the officer was explaining. "Do you know where he's staying?"

Constable Marvin's familiar voice comforted Ashley somewhat. At least Thomas's case wasn't being pushed up the bureaucratic chain. Ashley gave her the name of the hotel she had checked him in to.

"What will you do with him?" Ashley asked before the officer could hang up.

"Nothing, right now. He has limited time to get us his identification. We need to keep track of where he is until then. In his intake paperwork, he claimed to be from London. We're making inquiries."

London? Ashley wondered. He hadn't mentioned London to her at all.

"Any other questions?"

"No, just...I feel like I'm getting involved in something that isn't really my business."

"Frankly, ma'am, you involved yourself when you volunteered to pick him up when he was released from the hospital. You took him into your custody."

Was that what she had done? Unofficially, maybe. That was what came from worrying about anyone but herself, she mused, then quickly reminded herself of her pledge to help Thomas. Unlike Trevor, Thomas needed her help but didn't ask for or expect it. She was not making the same mistake.

Constable Marvin took the pause as an opportunity to end the conversation. "Thank you for your help. Let us know if you're able to find anything out," she said, then hung up.

****

Thomas lay in bed for a while after he woke up that morning. He was incredibly homesick. How he yearned to be teased by his brother again, or be comforted by his mother, even though he was a grown man. He would settle for something as simple as riding astride his horse again and knowing the steed could take him somewhere Thomas would understand.

Eventually he got up and dressed. He pulled open the rough green curtains, but the window still didn't let in much light. At the hospital, Diana had done something on the wall to create the unnatural light these people used. He went around the room and flipped every switch he could find. Each one turned on a different light source. It was like magic, which is what made it so terrifying.

Only the devil traded in magic. Was it possible for an entire city to sell its soul to the devil collectively?

He paused. What if it wasn't just Salisbury that was like this? What was London like in this strange world he had entered? Or the rest of England? Was John experiencing the same thing in France right now?

He doubted it. Thomas was the only one experiencing this strange disconnect. In his travels around the city, he hadn't recognized anyone either personally or culturally. Wherever John and everyone else Thomas knew were, right now, it was far from here.

But it wouldn't hurt to be sure. He should check. Lydiard was too far away to visit without his horse or knowledge of how to make those strange wagons move. But he could go to the cathedral and its school, see if anyone he knew was there. It was a start at doing something.

He cleaned himself up before going out. He was proud at how adept he had gotten at using their wash basins and latrines. He didn't have much with him, but he used his knife to trim his beard, as not many men had them here and he wanted to blend in as much as possible.

He walked out of the room, taking the small card Ashley had used to open the door. He studied the numbers by the door, and his surroundings, so he would remember how to get back to this room. Everyone here used the newfangled Arabic numerals. He didn't use them much back home, but he had been introduced to them at school, so he could recognize and recall them. He took the stairs down to the lobby and was pleasantly surprised to find food laid out along a counter. It was earlier than he would normally eat, but he should have some anyway since he had no way of procuring food here on his own. He watched the other guests take food and sit down. No one appeared to be paying or asking permission, so he was probably safe to do the same. He followed suit and sat at one of the small tables with a slice of buttered bread and an apple.

As he ate, he watched in fascination as a woman on the other side of the room pulled a thick skin off a yellow fruit and ate it. He had never seen such a thing. After a moment, the woman caught his eye and said something angrily to him. He shook his head and looked away. If only he could explain he was staring at the fruit, not at her. Chastened but feeling brave, he went and got one for himself. He struggled for a moment with removing the skin but was able to get it eventually. He bit into it. The texture was oddly soft, but the flavor was not terrible. He wondered what this thing was called. The woman finished her meal and glared at him as she walked back toward the rooms. He lowered his eyes meekly, not wanting to offend further.

He watched closely as several people got glasses of brightly colored liquid from a tall container. When he felt confident enough and there was no one else around the containers, he got a glass and attempted it himself. He managed to pour himself a glass of ruby red liquid. He had chosen that one because its color was less odd—the other one was bright orange. He had thought it might be wine, but when he tasted it, it was sweet and tart and nothing like wine. He didn't love it, but he finished it anyway because it seemed a shame to waste it.

Thus fortified, he projected confidence as he stepped through the magic door that opened on its own.

Fortunately, the inn was near the city center, and once he stood on the street, the cathedral spire provided a point to navigate toward. Much of the city was unfamiliar to him, as it seemed to have grown to ten times its normal size, but as he neared the cathedral close, he recognized some of the buildings. He let himself hope that this area might lead him back home. He navigated to Exeter Street, which ran along the cathedral grounds. As he neared the junction, he glimpsed the familiar landmark of St. Ann's gate. Perhaps the school was still there!

He spun slowly around three times on the corner by the gate, gazing around him in case this strange city was just slightly off, but, to his disappointment, the grammar school building he had attended as a boy was not there. To console himself, he touched a hand to the weathered stonework of the portico. He sensed nothing, however, no special magic that told him this one known edifice would send him home.

He sighed and headed back toward the cathedral. Soon he heard children's chatter. He sped up until he reached the next place he knew. The chorister's school was still here! Thomas hadn't attended the chorister's school, as he had stayed with an uncle to train as a squire when he was young, but he was pleased it continued to serve its purpose here. He watched as children moved into the building. There were girls among the group, which was odd, but each strange thing here already shocked him less and less. He watched the adults scattered amongst the children. None of them were familiar, and they all wore this world's strange, non-ecclesiastical clothes. He certainly didn't recognize the bishop or any other clergymen among them.

A man walked up to Thomas, frowning deeply. He asked something. Thomas smiled, hoping to engender the man's goodwill. But the man's frown deepened further, and he continued talking angrily. He pointed toward the street. Then he pulled a rectangular black device out of his pocket. Not wanting to find out what that thing did, Thomas turned and hurried away.

Once he was out of view of the school, Thomas paused in the cathedral close. He would have to be more careful about watching what people did here, as his gaze seemed to anger them quickly. Worse, his adventure hadn't produced any results of value. While he had found some places he recognized, he was clearly the only person in this particular predicament. Everyone else understood the rules of this world. He was no closer to figuring out how to get home. He turned and observed the cathedral. He considered going in, but his heart was weary. He had prayed. He had confessed his sins. He was still here. Was this purgatory? And if so, how long was he destined to stay here? If that was the case, he could only hope his family knew he was gone and was fervently praying for his soul to move on quickly.

A faint drizzle started. Thomas glanced up as the cool droplets fell. This place was too physical to be purgatory, too real. It was nothing like he was told the heavenly realms would be. There must be some other explanation that he was unable to grasp.

Defeated, he went back to his room at the inn and stayed there for the rest of the day, the monotony broken only by someone bringing a meal to him. By the end of the day, with no newfound clarity, he knew he couldn't figure this out on his own. He hoped Ashley would return and that he hadn't been too rude to her the night before. Despite her questionable profession, she was the only person willing to help him navigate this strange world.

He would have to take all the help he could get from whomever was willing to offer it.

****

The next morning, Ashley arrived at Thomas's hotel room carrying a breakfast sandwich and a coffee for him as a peace offering. He appeared pleased to see her and let her in the room without the theatrics of her previous visit. Once inside, she talked without worrying whether he understood every word. The more he heard the foreign language, the more he would pick up. Now that it had been a few days, Thomas already understood more of what was going on around him. He seemed calmer and less prone to immediately react. He was attentive as she talked and handed over the items. Already the two of them were establishing a repertoire of communication that was coming more easily. Gestures filled in the gaps between words, and Ashley was growing used to explaining the same thing three different ways to make sure he understood.

Fortunately, though, with breakfast there wasn't much to explain. He ate the sandwich with gusto. He examined the travel coffee cup for a moment before taking a careful sip. Ashley laughed as his mouth screwed up in disgust. Clearly, they didn't have coffee wherever he came from. She took the cup from him. "Let's get you some juice on the way out." She wiped the lip of the cup and took a sip. Given how exhausting her previous day with Thomas had been, a second cup of coffee at the start of this one probably wouldn't hurt.

Today she would take him to the Catholic church the vicar had given her directions to. Through everything so far, Thomas's faith seemed to be the place he took refuge. She wanted to give him that sense of safety.

Thomas followed her amiably through the streets of Salisbury. He slowly drank the orange juice she had bought him. Based on the sour face he made with each sip, he must not like it either but had determined not to scorn the second item she had given him. When they reached the church, she took the juice bottle and threw both it and her coffee cup in a trash can. He gave the bottle up quickly, probably relieved that he wouldn't have to finish its contents.

They walked in silence into the church. A few votive candles burned at a small table before the altar, the only sign that anyone had been there recently. Ashley hung back while Thomas prayed. The church paled in comparison to the city's cathedral, but it was still striking, and far older than anything in the States. Near the entrance she noted a sign detailing the times for confession. They were in luck. The next time block started in an hour.

When Thomas finished praying, he walked over to her. She pointed at the sign, which didn't mean much to him. "Confession at eleven o'clock," she said. She made the motion of one turn of the clock.

He gave her a quizzical look and repeated the motion.

"A clock," she said. Did they not have clocks where—or when—he was from? Since they had time to kill, she found an app that had an analog clock and showed him. "Clock," she repeated.

He shrugged.

"How do you tell time?" she asked. "The hour?" She tapped the top of the clock on her screen, even though now she doubted that meant anything to him. She just didn't know any other universal signs for time.

After a moment's thought, he pointed up in the direction of the church's steeple.

She considered this. "The bells? The bells ring the hour?"

He nodded.

"Right." She made a mental note to look up when clocks were invented.

Thomas motioned to the back pew, and Ashley sat beside him. He asked her a question she couldn't fathom. Then he said, more slowly, "No pray." He clasped his palms together in prayer.

"No, I don't go to church."

He gave her a skeptical look similar to the one he had given her the other night in the hotel, and she guessed that once again he wasn't sure she was the type of person he should associate with.

There was so much more she wanted to ask him, but it was too difficult to communicate such complex ideas. Her last conversation with the police tugged at her thoughts. She should try to get more information about him, but she didn't want to push Thomas too far. Constable Marvin would just have to wait for a response to her demands. Answers would come in time. Hopefully.

They waited in silence until the hour struck. By that time, a few other people had gathered. The priest appeared, and Thomas understood. He stood behind the last woman in line.

Ashley stayed seated while Thomas waited his turn. She wondered what the priest would make of him. But the confession went smoothly, because Thomas emerged from the booth and returned to her with a smile on his face.

"What's that?" she asked, pointing to what he was holding.

He held out a pocket Bible and a rosary.

"He gave you those? That's nice of him." She marveled at how much goodwill Thomas managed to inspire in people who had just met him, even though he could barely communicate with them. Why was she unable to do that even with people who knew her well?

They stepped outside. Thomas ran his fingers along the beads of the rosary. He opened the Bible to a page and frowned. He held the open page out so she could read it. "Latin," he said.

"No…it's not Latin, it's English."

"English," he repeated in that slightly odd pronunciation he had used before. He pointed at her. "You English."

"Yes." She took the book from him and opened it to the first page, a passage she assumed he must be familiar with. "In the beginning, when God created the heavens and the earth—and the earth was without form or shape, with darkness over the abyss and a mighty wind sweeping over the waters—Then God said: Let there be light, and there was light." She closed the Bible and handed it back to him.

He appeared confused. He said something that sounded different from his usual speech. As she listened to the oddities, she put it together with his previous question and his previous attempt to communicate with the vicar and figured he must be speaking Latin.

"That's Genesis 1:1 in Latin?"

He frowned and nodded, still peering mistrustingly at the Bible in his hand.

Someone came up behind them, another parishioner

exiting the church. "Sorry," Ashley said as she maneuvered herself and Thomas out of the way. When the woman had gone, Ashley said, "Why don't we go for a walk?" She extended her hand in demonstration. He slipped the Bible into the satchel he always carried with him and nodded.

She led him through the city center until they reached the river. She slowed, and he fell in beside her. He watched everything with interest, even pausing to stomp his foot a few times on the tarmac path to test its consistency. She fell into people-watching with him, enjoying the opportunity to view everything with new eyes, from a bright purple summer dress that delighted him to the music of a busker that they stopped and listened to for fifteen minutes. Feeling guilty as they walked away, she dropped a few pound coins in the man's open guitar case.

As they passed an azalea bush hanging over the path, Thomas snapped off one of the pink flowers and presented it to Ashley with a bow and a flourish. She laughed and stuck the flower behind her ear. Some things were universal.

As they restarted the walk, she resisted the urge to grab his hand. If she ignored all the obviously odd things about their relationship—including the fact that they could barely communicate—the sunny walk felt very much like one with a new boyfriend. She grinned at him, and he grinned back.

After a while, when they reached the fringes of town, they collapsed onto a bench and continued their people watching from a stationary position. After a while, with her stomach growling, Ashley led them back into town where they purchased a couple of pasties. Not knowing what else to do, she walked them back to their spot by the river, and there they ate their handheld meals in pleasant silence. It really was the perfect day, she thought. Occasionally one or the other of them would point someone out and say something the other only half-understood, other than knowing that it was meant to be humorous and deserved a light laugh. In this way, they got increasingly used to the other's cadence of speech, and Ashley caught the underlying meaning of what he said to her—whether it was a funny comment, a question, or an expression of frustration. He was young, clearly, probably a bit younger than she was, but he seemed more like a man than any other boy she had met at that age.

She pulled out her notebook and turned to a fresh sheet of paper. She carefully wrote out XXVIII, her age. That was a Roman numeral simple enough for her to compose. After a bit of explanation and repetition of "years" and "age," Thomas wrote beside it XXV. She had been correct. He was only twenty-five, but very mature. Maybe all the religion did that to you.

Now that she had opened the door to another round of questioning, Thomas appeared eager to know more. He asked his question, then followed it up by pointing to a family walking by, particularly at the children with them, then pointed at her and at her ring finger.

"No," she said quickly. "I'm not married. No children."

He nodded, seemingly satisfied with this answer. When she asked the same question of him, he shook his head firmly. Her stomach fluttered at this confirmation.

Daylight faded as she walked him back to his hotel. This time, she said goodbye on the street, not wanting a repeat of her previous nighttime visit to his room. When she turned back briefly at the corner, he was still standing in the entrance to the building, watching after her. She gave a little wave, which he returned, shyly, before going inside.

When she got to her flat, she tried concentrating on her writing, then checking her email and social media, but she couldn't tear her thoughts away from Thomas. She thought back to the clue the vicar had given her the other day. She had to find out more about what was going on before she got even more sucked into the situation than she already was—although recalling the flutter in her stomach as they sat by the river that afternoon made her suspect she was already in too deep to turn back now.

She googled the family the vicar had mentioned in relation to Thomas's ring and got sucked into an ancestry wiki. She soon made it to an entry for Thomas de la Warr, fifth Baron de la Warr, who was about 25 in 1377. Her head swam. Everything was starting to fit together too well. She hadn't asked the police what he had given as his surname. With no identification, the information he volunteered would have been all they had to go on. She would have to ask Thomas tomorrow.

She bookmarked the page and searched for Lydiard Park in hopes of grounding herself back in reality. As the vicar had said, only the eighteenth-century manor house remained. She scoured the website, but there was no information on the medieval history of the estate. That was a dead end.

She remembered her mental note to google the invention of clocks. Pretty quickly she learned that they would not have existed as she knew them in 1377. They would have been used only to make church bells strike the hour, just as Thomas had indicated when he pointed up to the church steeple. Then she went down a rabbit hole of different ways to tell time in medieval England, including marking the number of hours since sunrise, a system she wasn't sure she fully understood because it meant a certain hour, 9:00 a.m. for instance, would not happen at the same time throughout the year. She also delved into the different times for prayer, which she had vaguely heard about at some point in her life. Nothing else she found contradicted what had happened with Thomas so far.

She rubbed her eyes. Her options at this point were either that Thomas was having a delusion that he was actually a medieval nobleman or that he actually *was* a medieval nobleman, which made no sense, obviously. Or maybe he was just a tourist who had lost his passport and Ashley was crafting a pattern that wasn't really there. That was what the human brain was programmed to do, right? Identify patterns? But if he were a tourist, why wouldn't he have gone to London where there presumably was an embassy that could help him get home? Why wouldn't he just say the name of the country he was from?

She considered the few words that she and Thomas had found in common, the experiences of the policeman, the vicar, and herself that they could almost understand some of the words he said.

It was impossible, but if he really were from 1377, he would speak Middle English. Surely there would be some overlapping words between Modern English and Middle English even though, for most intents and purposes, each language was indecipherable for speakers of the other. Ashley had taken a couple of Middle

English courses in college, but she was hardly an expert. She recalled one of her classmates reading a passage of Chaucer aloud and commenting that it was easier to pronounce the words correctly if you adopted a Scottish accent. That was because Chaucer wrote in the fourteenth century—the same century Thomas purported to be from—and that was before the Great Vowel Shift in English. That could explain why the vowels in the words she and Thomas had found in common sounded a bit off.

She would never be able to prove it one way or the other by herself. The only place to find an expert in Middle English would be in academia. The closest university was in Southampton, and she quickly discovered on their website who taught Middle English courses.

Her phone dinged, momentarily distracting her from her quest.

Bryn had texted the group chat Ashley had set up with her old London friends. *I can't wait to see you!!*

Shit. She was supposed to be going to London on Wednesday. Yet another piece of her life that had fallen by the wayside as her vision narrowed to the Mystery of Thomas and nothing else. She considered her options.

I am so sorry, she sent. *I can't make it this week after all. Soon, I promise!*

Damn, ok, Bryn replied.

I just can't leave Salisbury right now.

So I can come there?

She hesitated but pushed ahead. She couldn't cut all ties because of Thomas. That was too similar to what she had let happen with Trevor. She needed to be someone who could support more than one friendship—or romantic relationship—at a time. *Yes! If you want.*

I already took the time off work, so might as well.

Great! Let me know your arrival details.

What was she doing? More than likely, Thomas was pulling some type of scam. She couldn't identify what he could be angling to get out of it except a couple of free meals, which she had already provided him. Well, that and a free hotel room. Damn. Was she being taken for a ride?

She had to know. She would take Thomas to the university on Monday during the professor's morning office hours. Surely no college students would attend first thing Monday. The professor would likely tell her Thomas was speaking gibberish, and then the jig would be up. She would know it was a lie.

But what if it wasn't?

Chapter 12

The next day was Sunday, and Ashley planned to bring Thomas to the 10:00 mass at the Catholic church they had visited the day before. Thomas's worldview was clearly medieval, whether it was a put-on or not. In his view, church seemed to be a daily occurrence rather than something reserved for Sundays only, but it still felt fitting to take him. She sighed as she got ready. She had already been to church more with Thomas in the last week than she had been in years. Faith wasn't a refuge for her like it was for him. She preferred practicalities, things she could touch.

Which is what made this whole inexplicable situation even more discomfiting.

She checked herself in the mirror, dressed in her usual blouse and jeans. Despite everything, she wanted Thomas to notice her, to think of her as a woman he might pursue. She grabbed a sundress and a cardigan out of her closet and changed quickly, even though she was annoyed with herself as she did it. She was not here to try to impress a man.

But Thomas was not just any man.

She did a final turn in the mirror. She looked damn cute.

On the way, she stopped to buy herself a coffee, but selected a bottle of water for Thomas this time instead. At his hotel room, he smiled when he greeted her. He scanned his gaze from her face down her dress, but looked askance at her when he came to her knees. She looked down. Was there something wrong? Had she forgotten to shave?

No, everything was fine. Except her legs were bare. Were bare legs bad? In 1377, probably. She frowned as she walked into the room and shut the door behind her. So much for making a good impression. She handed him the bottle of water. He didn't appear thrilled at this offering either, though he accepted it with grace. She wondered what the heck he drank in his daily life, because she was running out of options.

They walked slowly to the church. She didn't talk much, as she couldn't help but be disappointed by his reaction to her outfit, though she told herself she was being stupid. Thomas had been nice to her, certainly, but he hadn't shown any sign he was interested in her like that. She needed to get over herself.

The day was cloudy, but still warm enough that it wasn't an unpleasant walk even in silence. When they arrived at the church, Thomas looked doubtfully at her legs again before they entered. A couple walked into the building, the woman wearing a dress a few inches shorter than Ashley's. Thomas watched her, then shook his head but walked inside. Ashley followed, pleased that at least it wasn't only her that he judged harshly.

The church was only half full, and Ashley chose a spot for them toward the back, just in case Thomas acted weird or was perturbed by something, like he had been about reading the Bible in English the day before. She pulled the hem of her dress as far over her knees as she could, then chastised herself and decided not to care.

The service started. Ashley's mother had been

raised Catholic and gone to Catholic school, an experience that had made her vehemently anti-Catholic as an adult. As the procession came down the aisle to the altar, she recalled her mother mocking the priest sprinkling holy water over the congregation. The memory brought a smile to her lips, which she fought into a frown. It would be incredibly disrespectful to everyone here to find any part of the service funny, and if she did, Thomas would probably never speak to her again, an outcome she couldn't stomach. She tried to be serious.

She had been to mass once as a child, for a friend's communion, and the service replicated her vague memory of many calls to stand, then kneel. Some of the prayers and hymns she vaguely knew, but most of the time she stayed silent, simply observing. Thomas mouthed prayers, either in Latin or his own language, she couldn't tell. She stayed behind when it came time to line up for the eucharist. It would be disingenuous for her to take the bread and wine. Thomas motioned toward the front of the church, trying to convince her to join him, but she shook her head firmly, and after a moment he gave up. When he returned to the pew, relief lit his eyes.

After the blessing, they shuffled outside with the rest of the congregation. It was still a bit early for lunch, and Ashley didn't know what else to do to fill the time. There was only so much of it they could spend sitting or walking in silence. Despite her earlier eagerness to impress him, she found the constant struggle to communicate exhausting. Did she really need to babysit Thomas the whole time he was here? Surely by now he could find his way around the city and manage by himself for a few hours.

But he didn't seem ready to part from her yet. Before she could explain she was leaving, he said carefully, "I go Lydiard Tregoze. You go, too."

She watched him for a moment, trying not to show her surprise. Beyond the fact that he had just spoken his most competent sentences yet, she had researched Lydiard the day before. It was almost as if he knew which way her thoughts were tracking. That, or he really did have a connection to that place.

"Please," he said when she didn't respond right away.

She sighed and pulled out her phone to find out how to get there. The complex public transport timetables soon frustrated her. From what she understood, there was no direct train or bus to Swindon, the nearest town to Lydiard. They would have to take a taxi or a rideshare, and how much would that cost?

She shook her head. "It's too far," was the simplest explanation she could give.

He nodded. "Okay," he said, then finished with, "Ta."

She laughed. He was clearly practicing phrases he had heard while he was here. He was a quicker study than she would have been, in the same situation.

He didn't argue or appear surprised when she communicated that she was going to leave him. Instead of miming a clock this time, she pointed to the church bell and held up eight fingers. She would come for him at that time the next morning. She hesitated, then reached in her wallet and presented him with a twenty-pound note. He would need to buy himself something to eat while she was gone.

He stared at the bill in his hand. Eventually he

pointed to the image on the front of the bill.

"That's Queen Elizabeth."

"Queen..." he said slowly. She thought at first maybe he didn't understand the word. But before she could elaborate, he asked, "King?"

"There is no king. Just her."

"Queen Elizabeth," he repeated, pondering the portrait.

She could tell he wanted to ask more questions, so she waited a minute in case he was able to form them into words. When he didn't say anything else, she said, "I'll see you tomorrow, Thomas, okay?"

He nodded and wandered off in the opposite direction from the hotel. She could only hope he had a destination in mind and knew how to get back to where he was staying. But she couldn't restrict him to the hotel or watch him all day. He wasn't a child, after all. It wasn't until he had disappeared into the crowd that she remembered she had meant to ask him for his last name. Hopefully he would be ready the next morning at the appointed time. She could ask him then. If she never saw him again, then that would also tell her what she needed to know. That he had gotten what he wanted from her and was on his way back to wherever he belonged.

****

Thomas was disappointed that Ashley wouldn't take him to Lydiard, but it was probably for the best. Based on what he had seen of the Salisbury city center, the buildings he recognized were sparse and didn't hold any answers. He didn't know what he expected to find at Lydiard, other than the comfort of returning home. Though, depending on what was left of home, visiting it might be worse than not. It was a long journey, but he had hoped their magic wagons would get them there quickly. Maybe he would find another opportunity to go there.

He wandered back to the city center. He went into a few shops, marveling over things he didn't recognize and comforted by things he did. He bought himself a simple lunch of a small meat pie. He was relieved when the storekeeper handed him several bills and coins as change. He didn't completely understand the monetary system here yet. Though pounds were used, a year's wages were needed to buy a decent meal. He tucked the money into his satchel. He would save it in case he needed it later.

"Ta," he said to the shopkeeper. The man nodded curtly. He didn't laugh like Ashley had earlier when Thomas tested the word out on her. This encounter showed Thomas he did understand the use of the word, but Ashley was, once again, odd.

However, as he walked slowly back to the inn, he couldn't stop thinking about her and the way that, even amid the strange disconnects between them, her kindness translated. He had sworn off all women after giving up Kathryn, but maybe...

Maybe what? There was no life for him here. He had to focus on getting home. He had to assume that Ashley would only ever be a blip in his life. That he would escape this terrifying place and never see her again.

The idea of leaving her behind made his stomach churn more than he would have liked. He picked up the pace. He couldn't let himself get more sucked into this world than he already was.

Chapter 13

Ashley speed-walked to the hotel the next morning. Despite her resolution to let Thomas go if that was what he wanted, overnight she had worked herself up worrying about him and what she would do if he were gone. She held her breath when she knocked on the door of Thomas's room and exhaled only when she heard movement inside. He had made it back the day before. And today she would take him to the university, and she would know the truth.

He opened the door, dressed and with his satchel, ready to go. He followed her amiably outside, not questioning where they were going. She led him to the train station, a little nervous about what answers the professor would give her about Thomas. She wasn't sure what she wanted the answer to be. Either way someone was going to end up sounding unhinged—either her for believing Thomas's fabricated story or Thomas for putting it on. Or—she still couldn't quite put the third option into words since it was the most impossible of all.

Boarding the train went smoothly. Ashley figured that, to Thomas, there was not much distinction between a bus, a train, and a car, so the movement of the long carriage didn't elicit any new mania. Once they had left the station, remembering the question she had forgotten to ask the day before, she pulled out her little notebook and flipped it open to a blank page.

Ashley Winston, she wrote. *Thomas* _____

He pulled the notebook toward him when she had barely finished. He must understand where she was going with this.

de la Warr

Holy shit. The exact name she had found online. She had said nothing about it to him, meaning he had independently pulled this name out of thin air. Her mind reeled. This was all true. It must be. Thomas waited for her to say something, keeping his gaze fixed on her, but she hurriedly closed the notebook and shoved it back into her purse. She could find no words to express the sudden disorder of her thoughts. Thomas peered at her strangely but didn't press her for more information. She tried to calm herself, reasoning that he, too, could have researched online and taken on the identity of the medieval Thomas de la Warr. Nothing was proved quite yet. But, still, her heart beat quickly at the possibilities.

Half an hour later, they alighted at Southampton city center. Once outside the station, they found themselves along a busy downtown street swarming with people. Thomas froze on the sidewalk, his eyes wide as he took in the buses and cars speeding by. His gaze followed a cyclist until the bicycle disappeared around the corner. A passerby bumped rudely into him, impatient with his lack of movement. Thomas jumped. His hand went instinctively to his belt, and Ashley held her breath, remembering the knife he had kept there the first day they met. But the moment quickly passed. The man melted into the crowd, and Thomas relaxed, though the frown on his face only deepened.

Having to jump back into protector-and-provider mode, Ashley brushed her confusion about Thomas's situation aside and took control. Ashley held Thomas's elbow and led him gently out of the crowd. As they got among the university buildings, they left the traffic behind, though plenty of pedestrians and bicycles still swished by. Ashley consulted the campus map she had saved to her phone and led Thomas along a sidewalk that cut diagonally across a green. In front of the English department building, she stopped and explained to Thomas what was going to happen.

"I'm taking you to someone who can talk to you. Hopefully."

His expression remained unchanged.

"Someone who can understand you." She pointed at him for emphasis.

A flicker of recognition darted across his face. Then he just shrugged. Ashley sighed and walked inside.

When they got to the professor's office, they waited in the hall while he finished with a student, a young woman with pink hair. Thomas stared at her unabashedly, even as she walked past them and turned down the hall. When the student was out of sight, Ashley stepped into the office, Thomas close behind her.

Ashley had barely slept the night before. Her mind hadn't been able to stop going over what she could possibly say to this professor that wouldn't make her sound like she was hallucinating.

Now, faced with the actual situation, she froze. She gulped and forced herself forward. "Professor Melder," she said, sticking out her hand. "I'm Ashley Winston. You don't know me, but I'm hoping you'll be able to help me—us." She took a deep breath and launched into her story.

When she paused for breath a couple of minutes

later, Professor Melder leaned back in his chair, watching her with a skeptical expression. He still didn't invite her to sit.

"I know how it sounds," she tried one last time. "But if you could just talk to him, I would really appreciate it."

He sighed and waved her to a chair in front of his desk. Thomas sat beside her.

"I don't speak Middle English," Melder said. "No one does, really. We read it. We can glean information on pronunciation from texts, but no one knows what it really sounded like conversationally."

Ashley was tempted to say, "Here's your chance," but didn't want to push the impossible storyline too much. At least he was willing to talk about his field.

"Have you seen him read or write any Middle English?" the professor asked.

"Not exactly." She rummaged in her purse and showed him the first notebook page she and Thomas had scribbled on when figuring out the year. "He wrote this."

Melder picked up the page and read it without comment.

"I don't know why he used Roman numerals," Ashley prompted.

"In the medieval period, pretty much everyone except for mathematicians was still using Roman numerals."

Ashley's heart skipped a beat. The pattern held.

Melder watched Thomas for a moment. Thomas didn't squirm under his scrutiny. Again, Ashley was struck with the feeling that Thomas was somebody important back home, in his own world. Melder spun around in his chair and selected a book from the bookshelf behind him. He said something to Thomas that Ashley didn't understand.

Thomas's eyes lit up. He leaned forward and replied. His speech was quick, eager, and Ashley struggled to catch any of what he said.

Melder turned slowly back around. He stared at Thomas, one hand still holding the red-bound book aloft. Ashley desperately wanted to know what they had said but didn't want to interrupt the moment.

Melder set the book down and opened it, though he glanced at Thomas every few seconds as he flipped through the pages. Finding what he wanted, he spun the book around to face Thomas. "It's a facsimile of the original manuscript," Melder explained. "He may recognize the script better than a printed page."

Thomas pulled the book eagerly toward him. Ashley thought she caught the name "Chaucer" in what he said.

"That's right," Melder said. He listened carefully to what Thomas said next.

"What did he say?" Ashley asked when Melder did not respond.

"I think he said he knows him—Chaucer."

Ashley tapped the notebook page with Thomas's writing. "Thirteen seventy-seven. That's within Chaucer's lifetime, right?"

"Yes, he would have been at the royal court, but…" Melder trailed off.

Thomas finished reading the page and grinned at his companions.

"It's definitely Middle English, right?"

"It certainly seems like it." He didn't take his eyes off Thomas. "Maybe he's a scholar who…?"

Ashley filled in the rest of his sentence. A scholar

who had a mental breakdown? Got too obsessed with his subject? She shrugged. It was possible. But Thomas was awfully young to have completed a doctorate and then have time to lose his mind over it.

Sensing the conversation flagging, she said, "He also has these coins." She motioned to Thomas to get them out of his satchel, holding up one of her own coins as an example. He pulled one out and laid it in Melder's palm.

Melder picked it up and examined it. "It certainly looks medieval. But there are all sorts of replicas."

"Right. But does it fit in the time period?"

He set the coin firmly on the desk. "I'm not a historian."

Ashley's face fell.

"But I can call one of my colleagues to ask if he can examine it," Melder conceded.

"Would you? I'd be so grateful." She put on her best smile and had to stop herself overdoing it with a flutter of her eyelashes.

Melder spun in his chair so his back was to them and spoke quietly into his phone for a few minutes. After he hung up, he turned back around. "He'll be down shortly."

The trio waited in awkward silence. Thomas occupied himself by flipping through the pages of the book. He rubbed his hands along the surface of the paper several times, as if not quite clear what it was, especially with the edges of the original vellum pages appearing in the scanned-in copy.

Eventually, an older man, heavyset, appeared in the doorway. He was bearded, with thin white hair that fluttered away from his face. "What's going on in here?" he said at almost a shout.

"Hi, Don," Melder said, then to Ashley, "This is Professor Litchfield."

Ashley shook his hand and introduced herself and Thomas.

Melder handed over the coin. Litchfield pulled out a small magnifier and examined both sides of the coin. When he finished, he said, "How many of these do you have?"

After a bit of prompting, Thomas pulled out his drawstring purse and emptied the contents on the table.

Litchfield sifted through them, occasionally picking one up to take a closer look. After several minutes, he leaned his fingertips on the desktop and peered at Thomas and Ashley. "Where did you get these?"

"I don't know. He just had them."

"Just had them? Hmph." He pawed through the coins again. "You know I can't value them for you."

"That's not the question. I just want to know when they're from and if they look correct."

"They're definitely from the end of the reign of Edward III. They're remarkably well preserved."

"Not replicas?" Melder asked.

Litchfield shook his head slowly. "It's hard to say. They appear extremely accurate. The metal and everything is right. And you hardly ever find replicas of cut coins. Most people just assume they were broken accidentally. You see this one," he said, picking up a coin with a straight cut down the middle, "it's been cut to make change."

Ashley glanced up at him, one eyebrow raised in a question.

"You've heard of a ha'penny, right? Well, back then, when a penny was actually worth something, people would literally cut a coin in half to make it worth half a penny. If this coin were broken from being in the ground over the centuries, the edge wouldn't be straight like this." He ran one meaty finger tenderly along the cut.

"Professor Melder?" a new voice said from the doorway.

Everyone swiveled their heads around to the student who had interrupted.

Melder sighed. "Sorry to cut this short, but I do have to advise my students during my office hours."

"Of course." Ashley stood and helped Thomas gather the coins back into his purse. "Thank you so much for your time."

Professor Litchfield followed Thomas and Ashley into the hallway.

"Could you also take a look at this ring?" She pointed to the ring on his pinky. "Someone told me it's the seal of the Tregoze family."

Litchfield lifted Thomas's hand to peer at the ring. Thomas darted his eyes at Ashley, who just gave him an encouraging smile. After a moment, the professor dropped Thomas's hand.

"It's the Tregoze coat of arms, but it would be easy enough to have something like this made. I've never seen a seal ring from that family like this. Not that I'm an expert on the family."

"Right. Well, thank you so much for your time." She slipped one of her old business cards out of her purse and held it out. "In case you come across any other information that might help us…"

"Ta," Litchfield said, then after an instant's hesitation pulled her a few feet away from Thomas. "Listen, Melder told me a bit about your story over the phone. Let me caution you against getting too involved in this. There are plenty of scam artists in the antiquities trade, and his intentions could be even worse than that."

Ashley gulped. "I've had the same thoughts myself. I'll be careful. Thank you," she said again, then rejoined Thomas and led him down the hall. She glanced back before they came to the stairs. Litchfield still watched them, hands in his pockets, his large form nearly filling the hallway. Ashley gave him a little nod before opening the fire door and disappearing from his view.

Back outside, Ashley checked the campus map again. She wouldn't be able to access the university library, but the bookstore might have something useful. She led Thomas in that direction. For the first time, he seemed genuinely chatty. Professor Melder had helped more than she had hoped. She showed Thomas the map and explained where they were going. As they walked, Thomas motioned toward the sea. Ashley managed to gather something about someone named John going to France. She smiled to encourage him to keep talking. She was finally glimpsing Thomas's story.

At the bookstore, she located a thick edition of Chaucer that had a glossary in the back that might be useful. She purchased a copy for each of them as a sort of study guide, and they went outside to peruse it. They found a spot on a low stone wall in the shade alongside the walkways. Each page of the text was translated into modern English on the facing page. Thomas traced the printed characters with his finger and compared the Middle English stanzas to their counterparts. Ashley did the same. She had read *The Canterbury Tales* in school, so the vocabulary wasn't entirely unfamiliar to her and came back to her slowly. The solidity of an actual translation of Thomas's speech made it all seem more plausible. Could it be true that Thomas had known Chaucer, one of the most famous writers in English history?

After a few minutes of study, Thomas seemed ready to talk again. Through a mishmash of their two languages and a bit of help from the glossary, she learned that John was his brother, and that Thomas was a priest. He didn't look like a priest, but he was definitely interested in church, so that sort of checked out.

"No," he said when she repeated back her understanding. After further clarification, Ashley determined he had to get home so that he could *become* a priest.

"Get back where?" she asked. This felt like the last moment before she could never turn back. She had to check one last time that there wasn't a simple *where* answer that she could give the police and settle this whole thing.

"I don't know," Thomas said with a heavy sigh. It was a sentence he had memorized early on because it came into use so often.

But to Ashley it held much more import this time. She knew now in her heart that neither the police nor anyone else would ever find the answer to where Thomas was from because they were asking the wrong question.

The correct question was *when*.

She couldn't explain how it had happened, but she knew it was true. Thomas was from 1377.

She snapped her attention back to the present moment. Thomas motioned at the scene around them. Next came something about God and the devil that Ashley couldn't quite understand, then more about

John's trip to France, accompanied by a few longing looks in the direction of the sea.

"You want to go to France to fight?" she asked. "War? Battle?" She knew the Hundred Years' War had been going on during Thomas's lifetime—strange as it still was to think that way—but also knew they couldn't have called it that at the time. She had no idea what name Thomas would know it by, so she left the specifics alone.

He nodded.

"Then go."

He shook his head. "No. I am for the church."

"Can't you decide for yourself?"

He stood and gazed into the distance, making it clear that he was done with the conversation. She sensed that he understood what she was asking and didn't want to discuss it.

Not wanting to push him too far, she started toward the train station. Once they were seated, she connected to the train's WiFi and checked her email. Thomas was asking her something, but she wasn't paying attention. "Fuck," she said as she read the first message in her inbox. "Fuck!"

Thomas stared at her wide-eyed. Clearly this word he understood. After a moment, he asked simply, "What?"

She rubbed her forehead. How could she explain? With all that had been going on, she had completely forgotten about the writing conference today that she had registered for so hopefully when she was still back home. She had paid the extra $50 to secure a time to meet with an agent to get feedback on her query letter, and she had missed her appointment scheduled for that morning. Even though she had sworn to give up on her book, she was disappointed at the missed opportunity to redeem herself after her terrible behavior with the last literary agent she encountered. She should have canceled the session in advance and gotten a refund, let someone else who actually deserved it take her spot, but she had forgotten about it, and now she looked like a flake. She had to make this meeting happen.

She responded to the email from the conference organizer, claiming a family emergency had taken her time that morning. Within five minutes, she had a response offering to have her join the virtual meeting room where the pitches were taking place, to see if they could squeeze her in.

She looked over at Thomas. Her anger flashed toward him, but she quickly smothered it. This was her fault, not his. He hadn't asked to be dragged to Southampton today. And that meeting had definitely been worth it anyway.

She managed to convey some of the main information: that she had missed an important meeting. Explaining about writing a book took a bit longer.

"Like Chaucer," he finally said.

"Yes, I guess so. Though I doubt anyone will be reading my work in seven hundred years. Or ever, for that matter."

There was something about the nonjudgmental inquisitiveness of his gaze that made her want to open up to him. Hell, she needed to open up to somebody or she might explode.

She told him a bit about what she had done to Sadie. Now that she told the story to someone else, it was hard to see how she was not the villain.

Thomas frowned hard when she was done. "You

told her 'sorry'?"

"No, I didn't. I don't think she wants to talk to me."

Thomas didn't say anything, but his face suddenly didn't look so nonjudgmental. She leaned her head against the window and said nothing else for the remaining twenty minutes of the trip.

She brought Thomas back to her flat with her since she was in a rush to get logged in. He hesitated in the doorway but came in nonetheless. He seemed uncomfortable invading her personal space, standing around the edges of the rooms she moved through, not sitting or relaxing. But after a few minutes his curiosity took over. He touched everything—the stove, the microwave, the washing machine, opening them and leaning to peer inside.

"Thomas," she said, wanting to keep him in her sights while she worked. He walked over obediently, leaving the washing machine door hanging open behind him.

She waved him to the couch while she logged into her computer and clicked the link to the virtual meeting room. Thomas bounced gently in his seat on the cordial-colored sofa and ran a hand along the arm. Fabric and color always fascinated him.

"Ashley," a voice called from the computer screen. Ashley whipped her head back around to speak with the host, then muted herself while she waited. She used the remaining time to open the query letter she had drafted before everything with her book had gone south, and read over it a few times.

Eventually, a slot opened, and she grabbed a few minutes with the agent she had originally selected. The agent was a young woman, the room behind her small but stylish, just as Ashley would have expected a New York agent's home to be.

Ashley read her query letter from the screen, though she added inflection to her forced-cheery voice. She was less nervous than she would have thought, so maybe there was a silver lining to completely forgetting about the appointment.

When she finished reading, the agent asked, "Who's this, then?"

"What?" Ashley brought the window back up. She saw in her own video feed that Thomas was now standing three feet behind her, leaning forward to peer into the screen. "Sorry," Ashley said, quickly muting herself. "Thomas, she can see you." She pointed to the smaller square that showed him standing over her. "Go sit down."

"Sorry, sorry," he said and returned to the couch.

"I'm sorry about that. This is still kind of new to him."

"Right." The agent's face showed she didn't understand at all. "Well, your book sounds intriguing. I didn't hear you mention any comps, though."

"I know. Those are tough."

"Don't put so much pressure on it. Search keywords on book sale websites."

The one-minute warning came up.

"Do you have any publication credits?"

Ashley shook her head.

"That's okay. Plenty of agents take debut authors. Good luck."

With that, the meeting ended. It felt anticlimactic. Ashley shut her laptop.

"Where is she?" Thomas asked. When Ashley

turned around, he was standing over her again. Somehow the soles of his boots were silent even stepping across the hardwood floor. He pointed at the computer.

"In New York." Realizing that would mean nothing to him, she continued, "In America. Where I'm from."

"Oh."

He appeared perplexed, and Ashley feared he would bring the cross out and pray again. But that had been happening less frequently, and this time the necklace remained beneath his shirt. She imagined he had so little context to understand what he had just experienced that he didn't even know whether to be scared of it.

"It's just an image of her. A picture. She's not here."

His nose wrinkled in even deeper confusion.

"It's okay," she reassured him.

He didn't look convinced and continued flicking his gaze around the room as if making sure no one lurked in a corner. Eventually he acquiesced.

"You not from Salisbury?" he asked after a moment.

"No, I'm visiting for a while. To write." She considered describing America but figured there was no point in explaining the existence of a whole hemisphere he wouldn't be aware of. She regarded him, taking in the cheap clothes the hospital had given him. The open washing machine door reminded her that, at the very least, they must need a wash by now. His original clothes, still stuffed in his ever-present satchel, would, too. Hoping to distract him, she proposed a new adventure. "Let's go shopping and get you some clothes."

Standing in the men's section of a department store flipping through shirts a little while later, Ashley felt a twinge of heartache. She remembered all the times she had shopped for Trevor, picking outfits that everyone always complimented. Now here she was, shopping for a person she barely knew. But he was a blank slate, fashion-wise. She could buy him whatever she wanted, and he would probably accept it.

She picked out two striped button-downs, a plain black T-shirt, and a pair of faded jeans, and directed him to the fitting room. She waited just outside. After a few minutes, he said quietly, "Help."

Curious about what could require a call for help in this situation, she approached his fitting room door. "Are you okay?"

She heard shuffling before he pulled open the door and held out the jeans. Half hidden behind the proffered pants, she could see he had donned one of the button-downs but left it open. His bared chest was muscular and had just enough chest hair to be titillating.

Oh my god, stop it, she told herself. Don't look at him like that. She tore her gaze away.

Thomas pointed at the zipper. "Help," he said again. Another useful word that he had picked up over the course of his ordeal.

Right. He didn't know how to use a zipper. Somehow, she wasn't surprised. She took the pants and demonstrated pulling the zipper up and down a few times.

He nodded, satisfied, and shut himself back in the room. He emerged fully dressed. Wearing clothes that actually fit him made him even more attractive. The shirt hugged his lean body perfectly.

"Good," she said, forcing herself not to stare. "Get changed again and we'll shop for shoes."

In the shoe department, the attendant sized

Thomas's foot, then Ashley picked out a few pairs. When he tried the first one on, he picked up the right shoe and pulled it onto his left foot. Ashley stopped him and pointed out how the inner curve of each shoe matched the inner curve of each foot. Now his shapeless boots made more sense. Were they made interchangeable for right and left feet? The attendant watched them oddly, but Ashley had already become inured to other people's stares and paid him no attention.

Once they had selected a pair, they checked out. Ashley paid again, but what did it matter? She was being a good Samaritan, that was all.

By the time they emerged back onto the street, Ashley was exhausted. The day had been intense with its myriad revelations. Her stomach growled, but she couldn't face spending another hour sitting down to eat. Instead, she directed them to the nearest grocery store and picked out a couple of pre-made sandwiches, chips, and sodas. She brought Thomas back to his hotel room and started to leave, promising to return in the morning.

"No. Help," he said again, this time to her back.

This might get annoying, she thought wryly. When she turned, he pointed to the sandwich he held in his hand. She tugged the plastic seal off, then went to the small desk where the chips and soda sat and opened those for him too, just in case.

"Good night," she said. She was briefly relieved when he shut the door behind her. At times, leading Thomas around felt like overseeing a small child. At others, though, it was more like being privy to a great mystery that she was only beginning to understand but still must explain to everyone else, a mental feat that wore her out. But after that brief moment of relief, as she walked home, she found she couldn't stop thinking about him. The day had been a success overall. She and Thomas were communicating better, and her thoughts drew her back to the predicament he had explained to her that morning. She would help him understand that he didn't have to set out on a career he didn't want. Yes, she believed, as he seemed to, that there had to be a balance between duty and dreams, between what you were supposed to do and what you wanted to do, but she had changed her life, and he could change his. She wanted him to be happy, and if she could be the one to make that happen, everything she had been through this eventful spring and summer would be worth it.

****

Thomas's thoughts swarmed as he bit into the anemic meal Ashley had given him. Why did these people seal up their food so tightly? Didn't they want it to be fresh?

He pulled off his new shoes and tugged at the coarse clothing. The trousers were uncomfortable and completely impractical. He could tell that if they ever got wet, they would take forever to dry, which made them useless for travel. He walked to the bathroom and regarded himself in the mirror. He looked like one of these strange people now. He wasn't sure he liked it.

He returned to his perch on the end of the bed. The day had been full of confusing highs and lows. A shiver went up his spine as he thought about the woman Ashley had talked to in her flat that afternoon. Besides this place having disembodied voices, they also had disembodied people. There must be some sort of effect on a person's soul for that to happen. Had everyone here sold their soul to the Devil? The question had occurred to him before, but he still had no clear answer.

On the other hand, Ashley had brought him to meet the man who understood Thomas better than anyone else he had encountered so far—Melder, he thought the man's name was. That meant Thomas's own language and culture hadn't been completely lost. There was still something for him to grab at. And Melder had possessed that strange book of Geoffrey Chaucer's writings. Thomas had heard Chaucer recite poetry at court but had never seen it written down. Chaucer was known mainly as a diplomat. During their time in London, John had made a point of ingratiating himself with Chaucer, one of John of Gaunt's closest friends and supporters. John thought Chaucer's friendship would serve him well during the campaign in France.

Melder knew of real people from Thomas's world. It must follow that he would know of others. Might he know of Thomas's brother or mother? What were their fates in this mysterious place? Melder had shelves upon shelves of books in his office. Such a collection must have cost a fortune. He must be an important scribe or keeper of knowledge. Thomas had to get back there to find out what else he knew. Maybe he held the key to getting Thomas home.

Chapter 14

Ashley woke in the morning when her phone rang. It was after nine o'clock. Damn. Thomas would be wondering where she was. Groggily, she picked up.

"Is this Miss Winston?" She didn't recognize the man's voice. After she had confirmed who she was, he continued. "My name is Max Smith. I'm a curator at the local museum system. I spoke with a colleague of mine, Professor Litchfield, this morning, and he indicated you had shown him some coins."

"Yes…"

"You're aware that any group of coins classed as a horde must be reported under the Treasure Act?"

"No. I'm just here on vacation. Anyway, I'm not the one who found them."

"Yes, he did say that the situation was a bit…unique. But I would like to see the coins. Could you bring them by today?"

Ashley sighed but agreed and took down his information. She didn't want to do anything that risked bringing Thomas more to the attention of the authorities than he already was, so she would go along, get along. Then she quickly showered and dressed. Yet another adventure with Thomas appeared inevitable today.

When she walked into the hotel lobby, Thomas was seated at a table, a plate of toast crumbs pushed off to one side while he read a newspaper with intense concentration.

"Well, look at you," she said as she approached him.

He put his hand to his chest. "Look at me?" he asked, glancing around, confused.

"It's a saying…never mind. I just meant, I'm proud to see you out of your room and reading, too."

Thomas smiled. "Yes. Breakfast food. Good morning."

"Yes, good morning. We need to take another trip today." She explained about the coins as briefly as she could. Thomas frowned and clutched protectively at his satchel. "I'll try to keep him from taking them," she reassured him. Not that the coins were useful to him here, but she understood that he didn't want to feel completely dependent on her. She had given him twenty pounds here and there for food, but that wasn't enough to support himself.

Fortunately, Max Smith's office was in the Salisbury Museum, right in the city center, so they didn't have far to go. The day was drizzly, so Thomas pulled out a hooded cloak and put it on as they walked out of the hotel. Ashley wore a light jacket, but it was far from waterproof. Seeing her glance at his cloak, he held it out in offering, but she shook her head.

At their destination, they were shown to a part of the building away from the public collections and into a small office stuffed with books. With the rain outside, the one window let in only dim light. The lamp on the desk did little to offset the gloom.

After brief introductions, Thomas presented his coins and spread them across the desk. Max examined several of them carefully just as Litchfield had done the day before. "They're in remarkably good condition," he said. "Did you clean them?"

Thomas scoffed and shook his head.

Max sifted through them one last time. "Well, there's not quite enough here to qualify as a horde. Did you find them all in the same place?"

"Did you get all the coins at the same time?" Ashley asked Thomas, hoping to prompt him to a negative response.

"No," he said.

Ashley forced down the corners of her mouth to keep from smiling at this success.

Thomas seemed to sense she was pleased anyway, his own smile toying around his lips. "Different times, different places," Thomas added.

"Well, they certainly are an interesting collection. Would you mind us taking one for the museum?"

Thomas looked at Ashley. She saw in his eyes that he was exasperated at Max's fast speech.

"Sure," Ashley said, answering for him. She picked one coin up at random and handed it to Max. "If you learn anything interesting about it, please let us know."

"Will do."

Thomas collected his remaining coins, and the trio shook hands before Thomas and Ashley left.

In the lobby, Thomas asked, "You pay him?"

"No, not really. It's not payment here anymore. It's just historical. He thinks it's interesting."

"I pay you."

"No, that's not necessary."

"What then?"

"I don't know." She peered out the glass doors. The rain had stopped. Thomas had a point. He was getting expensive, and her savings wouldn't last forever. She watched him stand there, unflustered, waiting for her answer. Since that first day at the bus stop, he had done nothing to indicate violence. He had been in her flat once, so if he had wanted to murder her, he could have done it already. She made a decision. "Why don't we check you out of the hotel and you can stay at my flat instead? That will be like paying me since I won't have to pay for the hotel anymore." Her cheeks flushed the instant she said it. Would he think she was propositioning him again?

But Thomas immediately agreed. Either he hadn't fully understood what she said, or he was finally accepting her using the standards of this time. Either way, she was leading them into new and potentially dangerous territory as far as her heart was concerned. Her breath already quickened when he stood too close to her. What on earth had she just gotten herself into?

They were walking to the hotel when Ashley heard her name called. Across the small square, Katie waved. She hurried over and wrapped Ashley in a hug.

"Who's this?" she asked, gesturing at Thomas.

Ashley introduced them.

"This is that guy you were telling us about?" She grinned at Thomas. "He's just like you described him." She turned toward Ashley and winked. "I was just about to meet Antony for lunch. Join us."

Ashley smiled a little at Katie's invitation-cum-command. "You guys have lots of time to have lunch during the work week."

"We get together once a week during our lunch hours. We've coordinated the times perfectly."

"Well, we have something to do right now, but maybe we can join after."

Katie turned her mouth into an exaggerated pout. "Can't it wait? We only have an hour."

"I want to check him out of the hotel. We're already past checkout time, but I'm hoping they'll still let us do it without charging me for an extra night."

Katie raised an eyebrow. "You're paying for his hotel room?"

"Yes." Ashley was sick of explaining the situation. "Where will you be?" She got the information, then hurried Thomas toward the hotel.

Once there, a bit of cajoling convinced the clerk to let him check out late. Thomas rushed upstairs to gather the few belongings he didn't have with him. The receipt the clerk presented Ashley for the few nights' lodging was a hard pill to swallow, but Ashley reminded herself Thomas had no one else.

They headed to the café where Katie had said she would be. She and Antony were sitting drinking coffee when Ashley and Thomas arrived.

"Good, you made it," Katie said, though her tone showed she had harbored no doubt that Ashley would follow her instructions. "We waited to order food until you got here."

Katie led introductions, then Ashley helped Thomas determine what to order. The more he learned to do for himself, the better. The café menu was just one page. Ashley leaned towards him and pointed a few things out, saying the words as she did so—chicken and turkey she thought he might know, but French fries were harder to explain since potatoes would be foreign to him. He pointed at the word "sandwich," and she mimed peeling back the plastic on the sandwich container she had had to open for him the other day. After a second, he nodded vigorously to show he understood.

The conversation ended, Ashley stayed close to him, their elbows casually touching. Thomas furrowed his brow as he studied the menu. The waitress's arrival startled him out of his concentration. Thomas pointed at an item on the menu, perhaps randomly. Ashley couldn't be sure. Chicken salad. "I'll have the same thing," Ashley said, in a strange show of solidarity that she couldn't fully explain.

The waitress walked away, and Ashley returned her attention to her friends. They were staring at Ashley and Thomas as if they had just witnessed two unlikely animals interacting at a zoo.

"I see you guys have learned to communicate," Antony finally said.

Ashley blushed. She hadn't thought too much about their weird amalgamation of speech and gestures, but now that she did, she realized how strange it must appear to others. "It's how we've figured out to talk to each other."

Katie glanced at Thomas. "So, does he understand us?"

"Yes," Thomas said with a mischievous grin.

"I don't think he understands everything yet, but he's getting much better."

"Where are you from, Thomas?" Katie asked.

"Wiltshire."

Katie sat back in her chair. "I don't think that's true," she said as if scolding a recalcitrant child.

Ashley sighed. "Let's not start an interrogation, okay? How are things with you guys?"

"I asked one simple question."

"Yes, but I don't think there's a simple answer."

Ashley had only known Katie and Antony a few weeks, but she assumed telling them that the person sitting at the table with them was a time traveler would be a nonstarter. If anyone had told her that a week ago, she would have called the insane asylum personally. But the more time she spent with Thomas, the less any other explanation seemed plausible.

Fortunately, Katie allowed the conversation to take a new track. They had a relatively normal lunchtime conversation, with Thomas even occasionally joining in. Whenever he spoke, everyone stopped to listen carefully and encourage him along. Thomas said as much as he could in modern English; he was picking up an impressive amount. And Ashley had listened to him enough that she was often able to interpret a strange phrase or accent in the context of what else he was saying. She had also spent more time than she was willing to admit with her new copy of Chaucer in hopes of picking up even more. The others got the hang of the cadence of his speech as they talked with him, too. Ashley appreciated their attention to him. It took some of the burden off her, albeit only for a little while.

Eventually, the subject of her writing came up. When Katie asked how it was going, Ashley simply sighed and said it was fine.

"That is a response that says it is definitely not fine."

Ashley gave in and expanded on her reply. "I think I'm just not meant to write this book," she concluded.

"That's bullshit," Katie said as Antony nodded agreement. "Is this about what that friend of yours did? So what if she's using the same plot twist? Do you seriously think you were the first person to come up with it?"

"There is nothing new under the sun," Antony quoted with a serious expression and tone made less effective by the large bite of food in his cheek.

Ashley squirmed in her seat. "No…" Her mind flashed back to the drunken night after trivia when she had emailed the agent. She had done it at these people's behest, because of her friends' support of her against Sadie. Ashley mentally slapped herself. No. She couldn't keep foisting blame onto others. It was her choice to do what she did. But even still she didn't tell the others about what she had said to Sadie's literary agent. She burned at the shame of it, especially now with Katie denigrating what Sadie had done as not even really being a problem. She couldn't let her new friends believe she was that vengeful a person.

"Yours will just be different. And better, for sure," Katie said as Ashley tuned back into the conversation.

"It's literally what you came here to do, so you have to do it," Antony added.

"I've had other things to occupy my time." Ashley inclined her head in Thomas's direction.

"That's an excuse, too," Katie admonished.

"I wouldn't even know how to write a book," Antony said, "so you're already ahead of most of us. You have to follow your dream."

"I agree," Thomas jumped in. "Like you told me to go to France. It is the same."

"No one likes to get their own advice thrown back in their face," Ashley said, trying to pass it off as a joke.

"See, even your protégé agrees with us," Katie said. "Now what is this about wanting to go to France? Is that where you're from?"

"No. I'm from Wiltshire. France is for war. Here is

for being a priest."

Katie frowned and furrowed her brow. "You want to go to war with France?" She glanced at Ashley for help, but there was nothing for Ashley to clarify.

"We're not at war with France now, Thomas," Ashley said instead, hoping to move the conversation along.

"Who won?" he asked.

Ashley sucked in a breath. Clearly Thomas's assessment of his experience here had reached the same conclusion as hers. "I don't know," she said, because she honestly didn't. Her knowledge of the Hundred Years' War was basically that it was a thing that had happened. "But England and France are allies now. No one is going to war with France," she added quickly with a reassuring smile to her friends.

Thomas frowned and gazed into the distance.

Ashley glanced down at their empty plates. Now would be the perfect time to make an exit.

Ashley stood. "We've got to go, guys. Thanks so much for your company. It's good for Thomas to practice talking with someone other than me." She rushed through the goodbyes and hurried Thomas out the door and around the corner where they could gather out of sight of everyone else.

"Let's not talk about going to war with France in front of other people anymore," Ashley said.

"Why?"

"People will think you're crazy—mad," she corrected herself out of habit even though the distinction between American and British word choice hardly seemed pertinent in the face of the much larger language gap between her and Thomas.

"Maybe I am." He gestured at the bustling street around them. "God has abandoned me here."

"No, he hasn't. We'll figure out a way to get you home, okay?"

Thomas didn't bother to voice the obvious question, *How?* It hung between them but offered no answer.

After a long pause, Thomas said, "I must rededicate myself to the church. I will pray in the forest again."

Ashley followed him, but he stopped.

"You don't have to come with me. I can find my way back."

Ashley bit her lip. Even with all the progress Thomas had made, she didn't feel comfortable leaving him alone. "It's okay," she said. "I like going with you."

"You should write your book."

"You should go to France."

"It's different." Abruptly, he walked off. With his long strides, Ashley had to run to catch up with him.

They walked in silence the rest of the way. The rain had stopped, but dark gray clouds still hung across the sky. Thomas's pace didn't relent until they reached the woods where he and Ashley had originally met. Once again, he found the stone and knelt in front of it to pray. After a moment's hesitation, Ashley knelt beside him and copied his posture. He gave her a curious look out of the corner of his eye, but then closed his eyes and prayed. Ashley followed suit.

She hadn't prayed since the church services her family had attended on holidays when she was a child. She wasn't entirely sure what to do but appreciated the silent moment. It took a few minutes to clear her thoughts, but then she knew what she needed to ask for: guidance for herself and for Thomas. What should they both do, and how could she help him? She hoped for answers, but in the darkness none came. She wasn't surprised. She had never really felt connected to a higher power. And this showed her that wasn't going to change just because she ran around with a medieval near-priest who saw everything through the lens of God and the devil.

She contemplated this place. This was the third time Thomas had returned to this rock in the woods: immediately after they had first met, then after he had been released from the hospital, and again today. It must hold some significance to him in this journey. The most likely explanation was that he had been praying at this rock when he had found himself in her world. He must think—or at least hope—that it also had the power to send him back.

The question was, did it?

But even with her eyes closed she could feel the solidity of him beside her never waver. She only opened her eyes when Thomas stirred beside her. He stood and helped her up.

"You're still here," she said.

"Yes." He sounded less disappointed than she had thought he would.

She tried not to smile as she gazed up at him. Her stomach fluttered with the realization of how crushed she would be if he disappeared from her life forever.

Without warning, the clouds released a torrential downpour. Even though the trees provided some protection, within moments, Ashley and Thomas were both drenched.

Thomas looked up at the sky and laughed, unbothered by the raindrops splashing on his face.

Ashley couldn't help but think of the unpleasant mile-long walk back to town in this weather. She pushed the thought away and instead lifted her face to the sky, too. The rain was warm and felt surprisingly nice splashing on her cheeks.

After a minute, she felt Thomas's hand on her arm. When she looked at him, he said, "A sign." He pointed up at the sky.

"A sign?" she asked. "What does it mean?"

"God is here," he said. "There is an answer. We have to find it."

Ashley was bewildered at how he managed to find that much meaning in a rainstorm. He needed a sign, she reasoned, and interpreted it so it said what he needed it to say. She couldn't blame him for searching for that little bit of hope. She would let him have it.

Thomas started off slowly down the first short slope. Already his new sneakers were sliding in the mud. He paused at the bottom of the slope and held out a hand to help her down. Following in the tracks he had made that had already torn up some of the grass, the slope was even more slippery as she traversed it.

"These shoes are bad," he said when she was beside him again.

She looked down at their already filthy shoes. Neither pair was made for outdoor walking. "Yeah, your boots would be much better. Sorry."

"Right." He nodded firmly, then continued toward town.

The rain didn't let up, and they focused on watching their footing rather than talking. They crossed a thin line of residences strung along a road and crossed another narrow field. They could have taken the longer route along the road, but the lashing rain had darkened the afternoon, and Ashley didn't blame Thomas for leading her away from the oncoming cars. She glanced up, relieved to see the river nearing, which meant the walking path would appear soon and they would be out of all this mud.

But even this short distraction was too much. The ground sloped down subtly enough that her brain hadn't registered it. Her right foot landed awkwardly in the middle of the slope and slid out from under her. In an instant she was falling sideways. Her foot, now stuck at the bottom of the slope, couldn't move any farther even as her ankle was pushed forward with the force of her fall.

A shearing pain snapped through her ankle. Thomas scrambled back up the slope to reach her. He slipped and tumbled forward, landing on his palms and knees, but his fall *up* the small hill was gentle enough. He stood again and helped her stand. Both their hands were covered in mud, their grips slippery and unsure, but eventually she managed to right herself. She leaned against Thomas's chest, unable to put any weight on her right foot. His heart pounded underneath his T-shirt.

He helped her the dozen or so yards to the river path where the trees once again offered some protection from the deluge. She pulled out her phone, leaning forward to block it from the rain, but knew it was useless. She studied the map. They were almost exactly halfway between the road they had just crossed and the next one. They would have to get to one of those spots to get a ride. It would be better to keep to the path for as long as possible, so she determined to move forward. She held out the map to show Thomas, pointing to their location and to where she wanted to go. He frowned and shook his head. Could he not read a map? She pointed down the path instead. "We need to get to a road," she explained.

"Good," he said. Without hesitation, he scooped her up and headed toward town.

"Thomas," she said once the surprise of being lifted in the air had faded. "I can walk with your help."

"This is faster."

She couldn't argue with that.

She tentatively moved her ankle to get a sense of the damage. Pain shot through her leg. Damn. It might be broken. She had sprained her ankle before, and it hadn't felt as bad as this.

Thomas didn't slow until they reached the road. He set her gently down, and she stood, leaning with one hand on his shoulder. His strength and closeness were intoxicating. Once again, she was drawn into the immense blueness of his eyes, like a morning sky hiding that day's coming secrets. They both were breathing heavily, Thomas from exertion and she from pain. Her gaze drifted down to his lips. She was overcome with the wish that he would kiss her. No matter that he would probably think that scandalous—he was practically a priest, from what he had told her, for god's sake, and he had already misinterpreted her intentions once before. Plus, she would probably be taking advantage of the fact that he felt he owed her something for all her help. No. She tore her gaze away.

To distract herself, she pulled out her phone again. How much would a rideshare driver hate her if they got into a car in the state they were in right now? Soaking the seats with rain and mud and needing to go to the hospital? Would an ambulance be worth it? Since it was the UK, it shouldn't cost anything, right? She sighed and dialed 999.

A few hours later, Ashley hobbled out of the hospital, her right foot encased in a walking boot up to the calf. The doctor had told her she was lucky the fracture was small and stable so she could avoid surgery if she was careful during the next six weeks, keeping the walking boot on and not walking more than necessary. Those restrictions would make the rest of her time in Salisbury interesting.

Thomas had handled himself well at the hospital, answering questions from paramedics, nurses, and the doctor as best he could and observing the x-ray in wide-eyed astonishment but without making any comment. His hand clutched the cross on his necklace, but he refrained from crossing himself, and the gesture appeared absentminded rather than terrified. For the first time, no one asked Ashley where Thomas was from or if he could speak. Everyone accepted him as a foreigner but nothing more exotic than that.

Thomas and Ashley had cleaned themselves up at the hospital, but their clothes were still caked with quickly drying mud. Ashley called a rideshare anyway, leaving a larger than usual tip. Thomas helped her in and out of the car. At her flat, faced with the prospect of scaling the stairs with her injury and boot, she gave in and let Thomas carry her up. Nestled against the warm strength of his chest, she decided she could get used to that mode of transportation.

At the landing at the top of the stairs, he set her down and she finished the few steps to the front door. Once inside, Thomas slung his satchel onto the floor and immediately pulled a new set of clothes out of the store bag from the day before to replace his mud-covered outfit. Ashley hobbled to her bedroom. Changing took much longer than normal. She had to take the boot off to switch her pants, which required her to hop around the room on her good leg until she was ready to put the boot back on. She considered asking Thomas for help but decided against what he might consider an indecent request from a woman.

When she returned to the living room, she dropped onto the sofa, exhausted by the day. Thomas sat beside her. "Food?" he asked.

Ashley's stomach growled. She pointed to the fridge, but when Thomas opened it, there was nothing of note in there—just a small jug of milk and a container of leftovers she should probably have thrown out a few days ago.

Thomas stuck his hand inside. "It's cold."

"That's how we keep the food from going bad."

"There is no food."

She thought she caught a smile toying at the corner of his lips. "Very funny. Let's order in," Ashley suggested, picking up her phone.

Thomas smiled. She was learning that when he plastered that big smile on, it meant he had no idea what was going on but was amenable to it.

She fumbled in her wallet for her credit card. She left the wallet open as she entered the information and submitted their order. Thomas reached down and pulled out a card. Ashley eyed him, unsure what he was doing. Was he just taking her money now?

But once again he proved himself innocent. He simply tapped the plastic against his fingernails and put it back before pulling out her other credit card and similarly inspecting it. When he got to her ID, he looked between her and the photo. He had seen many photos by now, in advertisements along the street if nothing else, but never one of her. He grinned at her.

"It's not a good photo," Ashley said in her defense.

Fortunately, the buzzer rang, and she sent Thomas downstairs to collect the pizza. When he returned and set the box on the coffee table, Ashley said, "You are in for a treat. I wish I could have pizza for the first time again." The smile after he took his first bite showed she was right.

The room was too quiet while they ate, so Ashley put on some music. She laughed as she watched the continual change in Thomas's expression—surprise at the recorded sounds first, then switching from pleased to disturbed to concerned to blissful as the songs changed. She envied him his ability to wonder at all the things she found mundane.

After they had eaten, she turned the music off and they talked like two old friends. While the glossary had to make a few appearances, Ashley was astonished by how much they understood each other now. Even if she didn't always understand everything he said, she could usually fill in the gaps between his words to make meaning.

They told each other more about their lives. She talked about her time in London, a place Thomas was also familiar with. She recalled Constable Marvin mentioning Thomas had told them he was from London. It had struck her as odd at the time, but now she was certain they had misunderstood. Who could blame them, given the circumstances? He had been on his way home from London when he ended up here, that was all.

She told Thomas about Bryn coming to visit, and he said he was happy to know she wasn't completely alone. She scoffed at the comment. How pathetic did he think she was? He had met Katie and Anthony, seen her call or text her parents back home. He knew she wasn't alone.

Seeing Ashley's frown, Thomas explained his reasoning. "It's strange to live by yourself like this," he said.

"Not in this time," she rebutted, then caught her breath at the first explicit admission of what she thought had happened to Thomas.

He didn't react. "But still. Good to have a friend."

Ashley relaxed. "I can't argue with that."

They smiled at each other. In that moment, he felt like the best friend she had. Like they had known each other much longer than one confused week. As backward as Thomas seemed here, she guessed that he was well-respected where he came from. He carried himself with the confidence of someone who knew he had a place in the world. Now, with some of the language barrier removed, he spoke with increasing ease and, she was pleased to discover, was rather lighthearted.

This especially became apparent when he asked her about her cell phone.

"What is that thing you are always looking at?"

Where should she even start answering a question like that?

But he didn't wait for her to construct a response. "You ask its permission for everything. If you know something, if you don't know something, if you need to go somewhere, if you need to buy something. It tells you what to do."

"Not exactly." But she smiled. Without really

171

understanding the technology, he had already grasped and encapsulated the world's problem with its smartphone obsession.

He became more serious. "What does it tell you about the war with France? It must know who won."

"I thought we agreed we weren't going to talk about that anymore."

"Not going to war with France. Past war with France." He grinned.

"Now you want to be Mr. Exact." She shook her head. "I don't think I can tell you that." She took a deep breath. "That's a standard time travel conundrum. Will knowledge of the future change the future?"

He sat up straighter. "You know others?'

"No, no. That's not what I meant. Not real time travelers. But we have a lot of stories about time travelers. People have thought about it a lot."

He appeared skeptical. "People have too much time now. Because they let those things do everything for them." He motioned to her phone.

Ashley shrugged. "You're not wrong. But it's complicated. There can't be just one winner in a war that lasts a hundred years."

"One hundred years?"

"Yeah. More or less. It's called the Hundred Years' War. I can't tell you more than that."

"I learn to use this master you have."

She held it up and waved it teasingly. "Only my face can open it."

"Your face…?" His words drifted off, and he gave up on understanding anything further.

After a short silence, the conversation returned to his predicament.

"I don't know if this test of me is from God or the Devil," he said, "but there must be a way to get home so I can make things right."

"Maybe some old manuscripts talk about it or about that place in the woods. Maybe they have an answer."

Thomas frowned. "Are you talking about witchcraft?"

"Well, witchcraft isn't real, so…" Though time travel wasn't supposed to be real either, so what could she believe anymore?

Thomas crossed himself. Ashley sighed. Maybe he wasn't making as much progress as she liked to think. Though who said her measuring stick of what constituted normal belief was any more valid than his?

"We can go back to the university. They probably have some medieval manuscripts. Maybe we can talk Melder into letting us view them." After a quick check of the university website on her phone, she said, "Since it's the summer term, he doesn't have office hours again until Monday, but we can go then."

"I also want to ask him about my family."

"Why would he know about your family?"

"He has a book about Chaucer, why not de la Warr?"

"Well, you don't need a book for that." Ashley cringed as soon as the words left her mouth. She hadn't meant to let it slip that she had searched for information on him.

Thomas straightened. "You have some knowledge?" He glanced at Ashley's phone. His eyes lit up. "Your master has the knowledge!" He picked up the phone and held it out to Ashley. "You look. You tell me."

"I really, really shouldn't."

"What bad will it do? They are all dead." When

Ashley didn't budge, he held his hands together in supplication. "Please."

Ashley sighed. Was she really going to do this? Instead of taking her phone, she reached for her laptop so it would be easier to show him the webpage. "I have something bookmarked on here. From before."

"You already looked? You already know?"

Thomas sounded a bit frantic. Ashley shushed him. "It's nothing big. I was just curious about you, is all."

Thomas nodded but kept an intense stare fixed on her laptop. Ashley opened a browser window and dragged her finger down the bookmarks list until she found the wiki page she had saved from before, the one that had given her Thomas's last name and a short history of his life as a priest.

Except when she clicked the link, the page came up as 404 Page Not Found.

That was strange. Where did it go? She refreshed it just in case.

Nothing.

Maybe something with the wiki URL changed? She followed the search path she had taken before, starting with Lydiard Tregoze and working through to de la Warr. But nothing she found spoke about Thomas and his family.

"It's not here," she said. "I swear there was a page before. It's how I knew your last name. It said you were a priest in Lincoln."

"Yes," he said eagerly. "That was the post I was promised."

She regarded Thomas. Something had changed, and in that moment they both knew what it was. Thomas was here. And the past, it seemed, was still racing to catch up.

Chapter 15

Ashley was still contemplating the implications of the missing webpage—were they changing the past, and Thomas's future, as they sat here?—when Thomas startled her out of her thoughts. "Do you want to go to bed?" he asked.

She sucked in a breath. Was he suggesting…

He glanced out the window. "It's dark," he added, cutting off her thoughts.

She deflated. When would she learn Thomas didn't see her like that? "Right."

"Don't you go to bed when it gets dark?"

"We have lights." She pointed at the overhead fixture in demonstration.

"Yes, but don't you need to sleep?"

"Of course, but… Do you just go to sleep when it gets dark and get up when it's light?"

"Yes," he said in a tone that suggested she might be a complete moron. "But there is time between first sleep and second sleep to do things."

She stared at him for a moment, but it had been a long day and the pain in her ankle was returning. She didn't have the energy to figure out what first sleep and second sleep was. "Well, we can do that, I guess. Let me make you up a bed on the sofa."

She found an extra blanket in a closet and grabbed one of the pillows from her bed. She laid them out on the sofa. Thomas seemed satisfied. She turned off the living room light and shut herself into her bedroom. She used the time to check her email and send a photo of her ankle to her parents with reassurance that all was well. She also booked train tickets for herself and Thomas for Monday morning, the next time Melder held office hours. Melder would probably hate seeing them in his doorway again, but she had to do whatever she could to find an answer for Thomas. She hoped they wouldn't encounter Litchfield while they were there. She had no time for him now that he had turned them in to the museum curator for no good reason.

She eventually fell asleep but was awoken a few hours later by the sound of clattering dishes. She glanced at the clock. It was just past midnight. She rubbed her eyes and got out of bed, following the noise to the kitchen. Thomas stood at the sink with his back to her, washing the dishes she had left in the sink from the last few days. With so much going on, she hadn't been bothering to clean up. And clearly Thomas had noticed.

"What are you doing?" she asked.

He twisted around to observe her as he set a mug in the drying rack. "I thought you didn't do first sleep and second sleep."

"Well, I don't think I do. But I heard you up."

"Sorry," he said with a sheepish shrug.

"No, it's fine. Thanks for washing up."

He returned to his task. "I also prayed at matins. Now I think we were meant to find each other. Together, we find the answer."

She hesitated. "I think so, too," she said quietly. There was something pre-ordained in the way they had bumped into each other in that field and hadn't been able to shake each other since. After a moment, she asked, "You'll go back to sleep soon?"

"Yes." He set down the last dish and dried his hands. "I don't think it's healthy for you, to just sleep once during the night. Not enough sleep."

"It's what everyone does."

He shook his head with a smile. "Not everyone. Do you think animals have just one period of sleep per day?"

"We're not animals."

"Not so different." He walked over to her, wrapped one arm gently around her so his hand rested on the back of her neck. He kissed her on the forehead. "Good night," he said.

She thrilled at his touch. It felt so long already since she'd had a sense of intimacy with anyone. The peck on her forehead didn't feel sexual, but it was nice all the same. "Good night," she finally said, and left him to his own ways.

Back in her room, it took her a while to turn off her thoughts enough to fall asleep again. Soon they might find the answer that would get Thomas home. The idea saddened her more than she wanted to admit. It was nice having him here, sharing her space and challenging her just enough to look at things in a new way. Plus, if nothing else, it would be much harder for her to get up and down the stairs without him here. She smiled lightly at the thought. Getting Thomas home would be the best thing for him. She would just have to improve at navigating with the walking boot. And at connecting with someone in her life besides a random man she had met in the woods. Her smile intensified into a grin. The absurdity was part of what made it so marvelous. She was taking her own path, like she had always wanted. It just appeared completely different than she had imagined, populated by people she never would have thought to rely on in her past life. She was making progress, she told herself. Soon, she would be whole again. Thanks to Thomas.

Bryn texted Ashley first thing in the morning, stating she was on her way and would arrive in Salisbury that afternoon. Ashley was awake but still curled up in bed, groggy from her odd midnight interlude. So far, first sleep and second sleep weren't helping her much.

She snapped her attention back to the matter at hand. Ashley was starting to lose track of the days of the week and hadn't fully realized it was Wednesday, the day Bryn was supposed to arrive from London. Ashley was excited to see her friend after five years, but her mind immediately went to Thomas. When she'd told Bryn she could stay with her, Thomas had still been at the hotel. Now her couch was taken and there was nowhere else for Bryn to sleep. She sighed and stretched. She could ask Thomas to stay at a hotel again while Bryn was here. She felt bad, but she doubted he would mind. He had been amenable to most everything she had suggested so far— except "magic," that is. She smiled at the thought of Thomas's fervent belief in those things. It was endearing in a world that no longer allowed much room for magic at all.

She got out of bed and dressed while trying to sort herself out. Why hadn't she just left Thomas at the hotel to begin with? She had known Bryn was coming, but the thought had slipped her mind yesterday. Thomas occupied all her mental space lately. She would have to claim some of it back. Otherwise, her time with Bryn wouldn't amount to much.

Before she could decide what to do with Thomas, the local estate agent, Terry, called. Yet another reminder that she needed to focus on the present reality of her life here.

"If you're still interested in learning about being an estate agent, I'm happy to talk over lunch," Terry said. "Are you free today?"

Ashley peeked into the living room where Thomas waited patiently for her on the sofa, already dressed and ready to go. She needed to sort out what to do with him before Bryn arrived, which didn't leave time for lunch. "Not today. Would this weekend work?"

"Sure, how about Saturday?"

They agreed on a meeting place, then hung up, and she went into the living room. "I'm not sold on this first sleep and second sleep thing," she teased Thomas as she plopped down beside him.

"You sleep late," he said with a grin. "Not my fault." Then he asked, "Who you talk to? Your friend is coming?"

How had he remembered Bryn's visit and she hadn't? "No. I mean, yes, she's coming, but that wasn't her I was talking to." She explained about Terry and that Thomas would be on his own for a couple of hours on Saturday.

"I go," he said.

The demand surprised her. She made a face. "No. I don't think—I mean, it's not that kind of lunch."

"Man you don't know," he said defiantly.

She smiled slightly. The protectiveness was sweet, even though it would be easy enough to point out that she barely knew him either. "I can take care of myself. Besides, it's in public. Other people will be around."

He frowned but let the subject drop.

Spurred by Thomas's midnight dishwashing, she spent the morning taking care of chores that had fallen by the wayside over the days she'd spent with Thomas: cleaning the flat, doing laundry, grocery shopping. She wanted everything spic and span when Bryn arrived, to give some credence to the claim that Ashley had her life together. Thomas helped where he could. Rather than fearing new things, he now showed interest in what machines did and how life worked here. He watched the washing machine spin in fascination for a good ten minutes before she was able to distract him with another task.

With his help, she managed to finish an hour before Bryn's train was due to arrive. In the lull, she knew she had to deal with Thomas's housing situation. She considered buying an air mattress, but then thought Bryn might not want to share the flat with a strange man. And who could blame her if she didn't? If the situation were reversed, she would ask Bryn what the hell she was doing, too.

"Thomas," she said slowly, "do you mind if you stay at the hotel again while Bryn is here? I told her she could have the couch."

He shrugged. "Your choice."

That was easy. "Great."

She checked the time. "Let's get you moved back in there and then we can meet Bryn at the train station."

His satchel was always packed, so he didn't need to get ready. He never needed anything other than what was in that bag, either. It must be nice, to be able to travel that light. She frowned, though, as she considered what he probably didn't have in there. She resolved to stop on the way to the hotel and buy him a toothbrush. Surely that wouldn't be too much for him to handle.

As they walked into the hall, he asked, "Is Bryn a normal name for a girl?"

Ashley laughed. "No, it's not that common."

He nodded seriously, as if she had imparted some deep knowledge.

"What do you think of Ashley?" she asked.

He screwed up his mouth and shook his head. "This is a family name, not a woman's name."

"Really? Well, you'll be glad to hear that Thomas is still a good old, boring English name today."

"Not everything has changed."

She smiled and squeezed his hand, then opened the door to the street.

And almost ran into a police officer standing in front of the door. She jumped backward and bumped into Thomas.

"Sorry to startle you," the officer said. "I must have buzzed up just as you were leaving." The officer was young, his voice eager. "You're Miss Winston, I presume?"

"What happened to Constable Marvin?" Ashley asked.

The officer furrowed his brow. "I was just asked to come check on you. I don't know anything else."

Ashley let out a breath. Maybe Constable Marvin was busy and had a lackey come check on them—because Thomas's situation wasn't that important to the police, she reassured herself.

The officer glanced behind her at Thomas. "I came to check on Mr. de la Warr's whereabouts. The hotel called us to say he had checked out."

Ashley's eyes widened as her hopes were dashed. The police were clearly checking up on Thomas more than she thought.

"He's staying with you now, is he?" the officer prompted.

She straightened. "For now. But he'll be back at the hotel tonight."

"Right. Any luck with the ID?"

Ashley shook her head.

The officer frowned and scribbled something in his notebook. "Ma'am, you need to understand that this is a serious matter that could be turned over to immigration at any time. We need that ID. We need to know that he is lawfully in the country."

"I am English," Thomas said stiffly from behind her.

The officer startled. "I was told he didn't speak any English."

Ashley quickly decided to use his surprise to her advantage. "Like he said, he's English. This is all just a misunderstanding."

"Then it shouldn't be a problem getting us a copy of his ID."

"He's just waiting for a copy to arrive. From…London," she said, using the police's mistaken understanding as the foundation for her lie to increase its credibility. "There's been a little mix-up, that's all."

The officer darted his gaze between Thomas and Ashley as if trying to peer through them and suss out their secrets. "Right," he finally said. "Just make sure you keep us informed."

"Will do."

The officer walked away, though he glanced back at them once more before he rounded the corner.

Ashley and Thomas started down the street in silence. Ashley was surprised at her own lie about the ID. What was she going to do when it became clear that it wasn't true?

"Who are these monks?" Thomas asked, breaking into her thoughts.

"Monks?" Communication had become easier between her and Thomas lately, but this demonstrated that even when they could understand each other's words, the ideas behind them could be flummoxing. This time, she didn't even have a guess as to what he could be referring to.

When she didn't reply, Thomas continued. "These monks are everywhere. You took me to them when I first got here, and now they come to your house. Who are they?"

They walked down an entire block while she parsed through this line of reasoning. Who could he possibly think were monks around here?

"They took me to hospital. Like monks have. They are on all the streets."

Ashley could hear the frustration building in his voice. Was she being dense? They're on all the streets, she repeated to herself. They're on... "Oh! You mean the police." She laughed. To Thomas, anyone in a uniform must be a monk, she supposed.

"Po-lice," Thomas repeated, indicating he didn't recognize the word.

"Sheriff." Hadn't they had those in the Middle Ages? Robin Hood and the Sheriff of Nottingham?

"Ah, yes, 'sheriff'! I understand. They represent the king."

"Technically, yes."

Beth Ford

"Yes?"

"Yes," she repeated, dispensing with "technically" as an unnecessary word he didn't understand. She was suddenly exhausted by these mental gymnastics, and she didn't explain further. How could she make someone from the fourteenth century understand representative democracy, constitutional monarchy, or even the fact that there was a queen instead of a king? Good thing he hadn't landed in twenty-first century America. Then he would really be thrown for a loop. She smiled slightly at the thought.

"Why so many?" Thomas asked.

"So many police—I mean, sheriffs?"

Thomas nodded.

"I don't know. I guess because there are so many people."

Thomas nodded sagely, accepting this answer. "Yes, there are many more people here than in my home. Many, many people."

They reached a chemist's, and Ashley darted inside to buy a toothbrush and toothpaste for Thomas. Then they went back to the same hotel and checked him into another room. Upstairs, Ashley explained the concept of the toothbrush to Thomas and hovered over him as he doled out a bit of toothpaste onto the brush. He regarded her skeptically as he raised it to his mouth. He passed the brush across his teeth a few times before saying, "Ow," and removing the brush.

"Not so hard," she advised. "Gently." She took his hand and moved the brush lightly across his front teeth a few times. The moment was tender rather than awkward. She let go. But again, he stopped after a few strokes.

"Spit it out," Ashley said, handing him a cup from

184

the sink and filling it with water.

When his mouth was clear, he reached into the back of his mouth and tapped a molar. "This tooth is bad," he said.

She shouldn't be surprised, she supposed. Brushing couldn't undo the damage that had already been done by twenty-five years of no dental care. Would a dentist here see him without an ID? And they would do what? Either fill the cavity or extract the tooth. She couldn't send him back to the past with a cap on his tooth that no one could explain or with stitches that needed to be removed. The best she could do was try to mitigate the damage that occurred while he was in her care. And how much longer would that be?

She cleared her throat. "Well, try again tonight," she said and led them back outside.

They soon stepped into the train station, dodging the stream of people exiting the train and heading out. A few people wore face masks, a lingering fact of life after covid.

"Why do they cover their faces?" Thomas asked.

"To protect themselves from germs. The things that cause people to get sick."

"You have found out the magic of sickness? That's why so many people."

"Yes, sort of. Seriously, Thomas, if you ever make it back home, just tell people to wash their hands."

Thomas looked like he was about to ask another question, but just then Ashley's name was called behind them. Ashley turned and spotted Bryn farther down the platform. She squealed, "Oh my god!" and ran toward Bryn. They hugged, and Bryn spun her around.

"It is so good to see you, girl!" Bryn said. She had

long blonde dreadlocks and a nose ring that hadn't been there the last time Ashley had seen her.

"What's this?" she asked, tapping the metal ring.

"Something to make me not feel so old. You know I turned thirty last year."

"You're not old."

"Easy for you to say." She peered over Ashley's shoulder at Thomas. "Who's this?"

Ashley introduced them. "He's kind of the reason I couldn't come to London this week."

Bryn raised her eyebrows. "I see."

"I mean, not like that."

"Uh-huh." She tilted her head and regarded Thomas. "He's not bad-looking." She paused, expecting a response from Thomas. "He's not a big talker, huh?"

"Not really." She grabbed Bryn's hand and dragged her toward the exit, running roughshod over the moment. She hadn't figured out how to explain the situation, so for now she'd just avoid the subject. "Let's go get a drink."

An hour later, they were all laughing like old friends. They had picked a pub with a full bar, more upscale and modern than the one Ashley had first brought Thomas to. With her obviously injured ankle, she was able to abscond with a stool from another group, and Thomas and Bryn stood on either side of her. Bryn bought them all shots of tequila, which made Thomas turn green after he drank it, and their giddiness largely sprang from the alcohol coursing through their veins. It was easy to pass off Thomas's awkward speech as a simple foreign accent made worse by a few drinks. With her own beverages imbibed, Bryn didn't ask too many questions.

After a couple of hours, Ashley ordered a plate of chips to get some food in their systems. She hadn't seen Thomas drunk or tipsy, and often that was the best way to tell who someone truly was. She hoped alcohol would reveal a pleasant version of him, but no need to push it.

She needn't have worried. He kept his good humor, even as his cheeks turned red above the edges of his beard. He even indulged Bryn in a dance—Ashley had to turn her down because of her injured ankle—though he didn't do much more than hold his arm above her and let her twirl around him. Probably not the way they danced in the fourteenth century, Ashley smiled to herself.

Pausing at the end of a song, Bryn pointed a finger in Ashley's face. "Why are you smiling like that?"

"No reason." She took a sip of her beer.

"I know the reason. I know exactly." She cast her eyes playfully from Ashley to Thomas and back again. "Oh my god, I love this song!" she shouted as the intro to the next song came over the speakers.

The barback gave her an exasperated look. Bryn apologized more to her beer as she drank it than to the bartender.

"I think we may be a bit boisterous for a Wednesday night," Ashley said.

"All right. Finish that and let's get the fuck out of here."

They stopped for more chips—this time smothered with cheese—on the way back to the flat. They were halfway home when Ashley stopped short.

"Shit," she said. "I forgot to drop Thomas off at the hotel."

"Do not make that man stay in a hotel."

"No, I can go back," Thomas said.

"It'll be better. That way we can do whatever we want tomorrow."

"If that's what you want," Bryn said.

Ashley explained to Thomas that she wanted to spend time with her friend alone, which he acquiesced to easily, like he did most things. She already knew she would miss having Thomas around tomorrow.

Ashley tripped over the toe of her walking boot as she went to hug him goodbye, so her face smashed awkwardly into his chest.

"Are you okay to get home?" he asked.

"I got it from here, sir," Bryn said, wrapping an arm around Ashley's shoulders. They said their goodnights and went their separate ways until Friday. Ashley glanced back. Thomas was watching her with concern and a touch, she liked to think, of something else. Affection, maybe? Or regret? When he caught her eyes, he gave a little wave, then turned back toward the city center.

Chapter 16

Thomas woke with a purpose in the morning. His head hurt from the strange drinks he had imbibed the night before, but he wasn't going to let that delay his quest. Ashley would be occupied with her friend today, the odd young woman with the even odder name, so this was Thomas's chance. He had been stuck in this bizarre world far too long already, and he feared he was enjoying it. He needed to get home to Lydiard to remember what he was missing and to discover if there was a solution there. Since Ashley had refused to take him, he would have to take himself.

He got ready and gathered all the money he had saved up that Ashley had given him for food. It seemed like a great deal of money. Surely it would be enough to get him to Lydiard, or close enough that he could walk the rest of the way.

With Ashley, he had traveled in public wagons—the bus and the train. But he still wasn't sure how to figure out which one to get on for his destination. He went down to the lobby and walked up to the front desk, which was staffed by a young blonde. She smiled as he approached.

"I need to go to Lydiard," he said.

"Lydiard Park?"

"Yes," he said as a guess.

"There's not a direct bus or train there,

unfortunately."

This was too much information for him to process. "How?"

"I can call you a taxi? It will be more expensive."

He peered at her, trying to grasp her meaning. Finally, he said, "How much?"

"Let me call and ask. You need a return?"

"Return here, yes."

She picked up the phone beside her. She talked to someone, and Thomas was glad not to have to follow the conversation. She covered the handset with her hand and said to Thomas, "They can do eighty pounds return."

Thomas frowned and pulled the bills out of his satchel. He spread them on the counter.

"How much?"

She gave him a weird look but sifted through the bills. "This is only seventy."

"Not eighty." He reached in his satchel again and fished out the coins.

She also sorted through these. "Still only seventy-four, I'm afraid." She pursed her lips, then said something into the phone. "Okay," she said, returning her attention to Thomas. "They will do it for seventy-four."

"Okay! Where do I go?"

"They'll come here."

"They come here. I wait?"

"Yes, you can wait over there." She motioned to the couches on the other side of the lobby.

Thomas slid the money off the counter and deposited it back into his satchel. Then he sat on one of the couches facing the doors so he wouldn't miss his wagon. He was very pleased at the success of his plan.

He was suddenly aware of how much more of an adventure he was having than John right now. He grinned at the thought.

Only a few minutes passed before a bald man walked into the lobby. He had a brief exchange with the woman at the counter before she pointed at Thomas. The man approached him.

Thomas leapt up. "You go to Lydiard?"

The man nodded. He waved Thomas toward the door and to a black wagon parked on the street. He opened the back door for Thomas. Thomas got in and clicked his strap in right away. He was getting good at navigating this place.

The man slid into the driver's seat and pushed a few buttons on his console before pulling off into traffic. After a moment, he asked Thomas, "Where are you from?"

Since no one here wanted to believe he was from Wiltshire, he decided to make something up. He went with the most exotic place he had ever heard about, some place this man was sure to have never been. "Palestine," he said with more conviction than he felt.

"Really?" the driver asked as he made a right-hand turn. "Must be difficult being from there. Sounds dangerous from what we hear in the news."

That hadn't changed from what he knew. He had chosen wisely. "Danger, yes. Many battles."

"Not battles, mate. You mean bombings, I think. Between Palestine and Israel."

He knew this name, too. "Israel, yes. The Holy Land."

"How do you like England? You just arrived, I take it?"

"England is strange to me," he said slowly.

The man chuckled and shook his head, enjoying a joke at Thomas's expense. He gave up on the conversation, allowing Thomas to watch the scenery pass by. Thomas was getting more used to the motion of these fast wagons, so it didn't make him nauseous anymore. This allowed him to keep his eyes open and investigate the landscape out the window. Just like within Salisbury, along the way there were landmarks he recognized amid a slew of unfamiliarity.

After a while they passed a sign for Swindon. He perked up. The village by Lydiard! They were close. After a few minutes, however, it became clear that Swindon was not the quaint village he remembered. It was swollen and full of movement and mechanical noise. How many people must live here now!

Shortly after that, they pulled into a small, paved area for wagons. "Here we are," the driver said.

Thomas peered out the window but couldn't make out anything familiar.

"We're here, mate."

Thomas pulled himself together and collected his satchel. "I pay you now?"

"Give me forty now, but I'll come back for you. How long do you need?"

Thomas didn't respond because he was focused on determining which bills would add up to forty. When he had decided on an answer, he handed two bills over.

The driver accepted them. "Ta. What time should I be back?"

Thomas studied the digits on the clock in front of him. He had been practicing with this device in his hotel room and with Ashley, but he didn't have one of his own with him to tell how much time passed as he explored Lydiard.

"One hour, two hours?" the driver asked.

Thomas thought it was ten o'clock. "Two hours," he decided. He hoped there was a church bell nearby that would toll the hours and alert him when it was noon.

"Okay. I'll be here at noon. Come right back here, okay? I don't want you to get lost."

Thomas smiled. He could tell the man was worried about him. "I'm okay. Not lost."

The driver made a face that showed he didn't believe him. Thomas climbed out of the car, gripping his satchel, and prepared to find out what home was like in this reality.

Small groups of people were also exiting their wagons and walking up a path that extended from the parking lot. He followed them since they seemed to know where they were going. Soon they came to a building, which they entered. Inside was a counter with a couple of people selling something. Thomas considered the sign above them. There were prices listed. Why would people have to pay to enter his home? What sort of hospitality did this new family have?

He considered his options. He had used up all his money getting here and back. The lobby was busy, so he bypassed the counter and hoped no one noticed, pausing only to take a pamphlet off a small table. He would analyze it later and discover what sense he could make of the words.

Again, he followed the others, trying to appear inconspicuous as they walked out the back of the building. After they passed through a tree-lined walk, the vista opened a bit. Once again, he experienced the familiar and the strange all bound up in one. The landscape itself was not that different, but where his fine stone manor house should be instead stood a rectangular monolith, all symmetry and straight angles. Behind the house, however, he spied St. Mary's church, right where it should be. Again, the trappings of the church were what had managed to survive here. There was probably a lesson to be learned in that, he mused.

The pamphlet in his hand displayed an image of the current house. How the image was so lifelike, he couldn't say, but it would be another thing he would have to accept here. It at least demonstrated that the arts hadn't died out completely in this strange place.

Most people headed toward the house, but that held no interest to him. He continued instead around to the church. The familiar square tower reassured him. He reached the front and turned the handle, but the door didn't budge. What kind of people locked a church? He gave the door a forceful push with one hand in his frustration. When he turned to walk away, a family of four was watching him carefully. The mother set a hand on the little girl's shoulder, as if afraid they might need to turn and run from Thomas at any moment.

He smiled to set them at ease and started to walk around them. The father, however, stopped and asked him a question. He held out the rectangular device everyone here carried around, like the one Thomas had teasingly told Ashley was her master. When Thomas didn't respond, the man pointed at the church. His family moved into position in a line in front of the door.

Thomas took the proffered device into his hand. He couldn't tear his gaze away. The device appeared to be showing what Thomas was seeing right at that moment.

As he took the device, it showed the ground, then one corner of his finger. He lifted the device up and suddenly the man standing in front of him was displayed in miniature. He startled and almost dropped the object.

The man huffed in frustration. He said something and moved Thomas gently into position, then moved Thomas's hand holding the device up so that the church and the family were shown in the view. The man pointed at the circle at the bottom of the image, then went to join his family. The four of them stood expectantly in a row, arms draped over each other's shoulders.

The circle must mean something, Thomas reasoned. He hit it with his finger. The image flashed with a little click. Thomas hit it again. And again. By that time the man had returned and was taking the device away.

"Thank you," the man said.

His wife approached, though the children hung back. "Where are you from?" she asked Thomas.

His previous answer had served him well with the driver, so he repeated, "Palestine."

The wife gave her husband a knowing look as if Thomas had just proved something to her.

"Goodbye," Thomas said as they walked away. He observed the church, expecting it to look different, thinking the device must have taken something from it, but it was unchanged. He frowned. As much as he hated magic, he couldn't suppress the desire to try the device again and figure out how it worked. How could he get one for himself? After a moment, he decided to ask Ashley. Surely, if this random man had let Thomas use his device, Ashley would let Thomas, someone she knew, use hers.

To be on the safe side in case he had inadvertently

participated in some magic, he crossed himself and said a little prayer directed at the church even though he couldn't get inside.

He turned and walked down another path that led away from the church and house. There was no sign of the berm and bank walling off the deer park. Instead, out in the open parkland, people played and laughed. The noise invading what should have been a silent area reserved only for the hunt disgusted him. He turned and headed back to the parking lot and waited for the driver to take him back to Salisbury. There was no home for Thomas anywhere in Wiltshire. That much was clear to him now.

****

While Thomas waited for his taxi, Ashley and Bryn were just waking up, nursing their hangovers from the night before. As soon as they were halfway mobile, around noon, Ashley's thoughts turned to Thomas and what he had been doing all morning. He didn't seem like the kind of person who would lie in bed all day, and in that respect it was probably good he wasn't at her flat that morning seeing them laze around like this. She wanted to go get him even though she had said she wouldn't, but she stopped herself, decided Bryn would find that suspicious, though even Ashley herself wasn't sure what she was hiding. She didn't mention him while they ate the takeout they ordered for lunch, though she was obviously distracted.

"Ash," Bryn said forcefully.

Ashley startled, nearly dropping her forkful of sesame noodles. "What?"

"I asked you what your book was about."

"Right. Sorry. Still not feeling great."

Bryn's wry "mm-hm" showed she didn't really believe that excuse, but she made no comment about it. Ashley tried her best to explain her book. Even though she had poured her soul into it and broken a friendship over it, still it seemed totally indescribable as soon as anyone asked about it. She stumbled over the plot and finished lamely with, "That's all I've got for now."

Bryn nodded politely.

If Ashley didn't even know what her book was about, how was she going to sell it to anyone else? She sighed in frustration. Eager to change the subject, she asked, "What do you want to do today?"

"If I ever stop feeling like death, I'd like to go to Stonehenge. I've never been."

"Really? No school field trip or anything like that?"

She grimaced. "I didn't go to that kind of school. Anyway, I hope that's not too cheesy."

"No, we need to fix that. I haven't visited it since I've been back."

After another hour's recuperation, they forced themselves to leave the flat so they would have time to travel to Stonehenge and visit the monument. The bus ride made them both a bit nauseous. Ashley spent the whole ride with her forehead leaning against the cool window, and Bryn rested her head on Ashley's shoulder. The only positive was that the focus on keeping her stomach from revolting distracted Ashley from thinking about Thomas for the duration of the ride.

When they disembarked at Stonehenge, Ashley gulped the fresh air, grateful for the sturdy, unmoving ground below her. She wondered if that was how Thomas always felt riding the bus. She felt sorry for him if it was.

The other tourists pushed around her, and she returned her focus to Bryn. Her friend looked even worse than Ashley felt, but they pushed on. They walked around and took pictures, only half-listening to the narration on their audio guides.

After they had made one slow circuit of the giant circle, Bryn said, "Okay, I've seen it, let's go."

"Are you sure? We can come back tomorrow if you want."

Bryn shook her head. "Let's just catch the next bus back."

Ashley agreed. Bryn was pale and a bit sweaty despite the cloudy day, and Ashley was in no condition to argue with her. Sitting on the bus felt like an inviting proposition. As they walked back to the bus stop, however, Ashley couldn't help feeling that the visit had failed. Bryn had wanted to experience this one thing while she was here, and they had barely looked at it. They shouldn't have indulged so much the night before, letting themselves believe they were at university again, at an age when hangovers were kinder.

As they neared town, Thomas's increasing proximity felt like a gravity well dragging her toward him. Ashley gave in to her thoughts and asked, "Are you okay if we stop by Thomas's hotel?"

"As long as there's someplace I can lay down there." Bryn closed her eyes for a minute, this time leaning back in her seat rather than on Ashley. Without opening her eyes, she asked, "Where is he from anyway?" When Ashley didn't respond, she opened one eye. "Ash?"

Ashley desperately tried to come up with a normal answer. She recalled the policeman's suggestion the first day she met Thomas that Thomas spoke some variant of

French. "Quebec," she said.

The answer didn't satisfy Bryn. She refocused, shifting her whole body toward Ashley rather than move her head. "Quebec? He doesn't sound very French."

"Different sort of French. And he's from the countryside, not the city."

Bryn frowned. "Okay. Where did you meet him?"

"Just out and about."

"What's he doing here? Does he have a job?"

Ashley bit her lower lip. "I don't think so," she said eventually.

Bryn's tone changed from passive curiosity to concern. "You spend a lot of time with him."

Ashley glanced over. Bryn stared her down. "So what if I do?" The comeback was weak, and they both knew it.

Bryn took a new tack. "Don't you want to call to see if he's there?"

Right. Bryn assumed Thomas was a normal person who went out and did things without her. There wasn't a reasonable counter to Bryn's point. "He doesn't have a phone," Ashley said.

"Doesn't his hotel room have a phone?"

She had never shown Thomas how to answer the phone, something she would have to rectify soon. Fortunately, the bus pulled up to the city center stop before Bryn could interrogate her further. "We're here anyway. Let's just go."

Thomas appeared subdued when he answered the door to his hotel room, his greeting pleasant but forced. He let them inside with no fuss about women being in his room.

Ashley sensed something had happened. "What did

you do today?" she asked.

"I went to Lydiard."

She hadn't expected that. Thomas was more resourceful than she'd given him credit for. "Lydiard? How?"

Bryn interrupted. "Where's your suitcase?" She scanned the room again to locate it.

Thomas glanced at Ashley for a translation. She didn't offer one.

"Aren't you little miss interrogator today?" Ashley tried to sound playful. Fortunately, Bryn collapsed on the bed and had no more energy for questioning.

Ashley wanted to know more about Thomas's adventure but didn't want to rouse Bryn's suspicion further. Any conversation about Lydiard was bound to lead to a discussion of it being Thomas's home, which made no sense from the perspective of here and now. She pulled out her phone to check the time, a nervous tic since there was a clock on the nightstand.

"You show me," Thomas said, pointing to her phone. "The paintings. Portraits."

"The camera?" She brought it up and handed her phone to him.

He perched on the edge of the bed and swung the camera slowly around the room, occasionally taking a photo. When he swiveled to take in the bed behind him, the camera clicked.

Bryn sat bolt upright. "Don't take a picture of me in bed. Fucking creep."

Ashley swiped the phone from Thomas. "He didn't mean anything by it."

"You better delete that."

"Deleted," Ashley confirmed. Awkward silence

followed. "Anyone ready for dinner?" she finally asked.

The meal was quiet and awkward. No one felt very well, and Bryn watched Thomas out of the corner of her eye while she ate. Ashley's attempts at cheering everyone up failed miserably, so she let the meal fall into silence. When they dropped Thomas off at the hotel, Ashley promised to retrieve him in the morning. Bryn grumbled disapprovingly as Ashley said it, but Ashley ignored her. It wasn't fair that she should have to choose between her friends, especially when Thomas hadn't done anything wrong besides end up in a place he never wanted to be.

He held her elbow a bit longer than necessary when they said goodbye, as if silently asking her not to go. She patted his arm and tore her gaze away. Just a few more days, and then they could return to their quest to find Thomas some answers.

Friday passed uneventfully. Bryn and Ashley picked Thomas up in the morning. With her hangover gone, Bryn was in a better mood and left off interrogating Thomas, satisfying herself with mostly ignoring him instead. They wandered around the city, touring the cathedral and museum, and popping into shops that seemed promising. Thomas shared tidbits about his previous day's adventure—the taxi ride to Lydiard, the church being locked, it not looking like he expected, though Ashley knew he really meant it didn't look like he *remembered.* She appreciated Thomas not bringing up that particular subject around Bryn, who continued to be unimpressed with him. However, as they sat down to dinner and Thomas helped Ashley into her chair, Bryn leaned over and whispered, "Okay, he is very sweet with you." Ashley smiled, grateful for this small victory.

After dinner, they met up with Katie, Antony, and Antony's date, Rajeet, at a bar. Ashley paced herself better than she had on Wednesday night. She had to meet Terry for lunch the next day, and showing up hungover would be unprofessional. The others didn't seem quite so concerned about holding back—it was now the weekend, after all—except for Thomas, who this time refused Bryn's offer of a shot, content to sip his ale.

At one point, a few drinks in, the three women gathered to one side. Ashley glanced at Thomas as Katie and Bryn pulled her aside, making sure he was okay without her, but he was laughing at something with Antony and Rajeet and didn't even notice. Maybe he didn't need her as much as she liked to think. Her heart sank.

"Any updates to the mystery?" Katie asked Ashley, interrupting her thoughts.

"What mystery?" Bryn asked.

"About Thomas, of course. And where the hell he came from. Didn't she tell you the story? He seems nice enough, but he started out very strange." She turned to Ashley for confirmation. "Right?"

"Yes," Ashley said slowly.

"You told me he was from Quebec," Bryn said.

"Oh, that's news!" Katie said. "How did you find that out?"

Ashley glanced back and forth between her two friends. Her lies had finally caught up to her. "I…didn't," she finally said. "It was just easier to tell you that, Bryn, than to explain the whole thing in a way that didn't make me seem crazy."

"You lied to me."

"About something that didn't matter!"

"Of course it matters. If my friend has been hanging around with someone questionable, that affects me. And now I've been forced to be around him, too."

Thomas stepped over and touched Ashley's shoulder. "All okay?"

"Get the fuck out of here," Bryn said.

Thomas startled. He gave Ashley a look. She sighed and nodded that it was okay for him to leave. When he had stepped away, Ashley said, "Why did you do that?"

"Katie, tell me the true story," Bryn said, ignoring Ashley. "Apparently she trusts you more than she trusts me."

Katie looked pained at first, but she relayed what Ashley had told her, warming up to the story as she went on, ending with a laugh at Thomas's comments about going to war with France.

At the end of the story, Bryn gaped at Ashley in disbelief, her mouth open and one hand poised at her throat. "I'm questioning your sanity now. What is going on with you? It was strange enough with you running out here and away from your life to write a book, but this is too much."

Thomas took a step toward them again. Bryn shook her head firmly and downed the last of her drink. "I can't deal with this. You need to get your shit together, girl. I'm not going to watch this mess. I'm going home in the morning. Just leave my stuff on the landing and I'll come get it before my train leaves."

"Bryn, don't go. Where will you stay?"

"There are plenty of hotels here. Maybe I can find somebody to pay for mine, too."

Ashley reached for her, but Bryn was already pushing through the crowd and gone. Ashley turned her attention back to Katie. "Thanks, Katie. For being a terrible friend."

"You needed to hear it from somebody, and it's better coming from an old friend than from me. I know we laugh about it, but we're worried about you, too."

"Fuck off."

Ashley slammed her pint glass onto the bar so hard the liquid splashed over the edge. She grabbed Thomas's glass from his hand and did the same. She took his hand and dragged him into the night. She had cut ties with her old friends and her new ones, the only people she knew in this country. Except for Thomas. It would be the two of them against the world from now on.

Chapter 17

Thomas stayed with her again that night, and Ashley resolved she wouldn't foist him off on the hotel or anyone else again. Nobody else understood what he meant to her or how much he needed her. And no one understood her like he did. He didn't question her choices or how she lived her life.

Okay, maybe he did. But he questioned her gently and didn't cut ties with her if she did something he didn't agree with.

Ashley put out Bryn's suitcase as requested and texted her the keypad entry code for the street door. By the time Ashley woke up and checked in the morning, the suitcase was already gone. Bryn must be safely on her way back home to London. She texted both Katie and Bryn apologies for storming off but did not apologize for Thomas. Neither responded.

Ashley and Thomas were both subdued that morning. When Ashley explained what had happened, that the argument was about him, he apologized and offered to leave.

"No, that is absolutely what we are not going to do," she said, and that was that. She had invested so much of her time and energy in Thomas, there was no turning back now. She would get him home somehow, even if it broke her heart to do so.

As lunchtime approached, Ashley attempted to

smooth out her mood so she could make a good impression on Terry. The last thing she needed was for him to question her sanity, too, especially since he was in contact with Hannah. She considered what Hannah would think of the situation with Thomas—it was her flat Ashley had brought him to, after all—but quickly pushed the thought away. She was allowed to have a…whatever Thomas was to her.

Thomas walked with her into town. His calm, steady presence reassured her. With him by her side she didn't feel quite so abandoned. He said no more about needing to go with her to meet Terry. Instead, he promised to meet her at the Poultry Cross, an easy landmark to find in the old city center he was familiar with, when the church bells rang two o'clock. She had no idea where he would go, but knew she needed to let him have some space from her and vice versa. Hell, he had found his way to Lydiard and back without her, so clearly he was more self-sufficient than she gave him credit for.

Terry was waiting for her at a table in the Indian restaurant. He was more handsome than she remembered, with blond hair swept back over his head and shaved at the sides. His white dress shirt highlighted the muscled curves of his arms perfectly. He was too young for her, Ashley told herself. He barely looked out of school. Besides, her thoughts were all about one person these days, and that person wasn't Terry.

He stood as she approached. He wavered nervously at her elbow as she pulled out the chair and sat, unsure whether she needed help with the walking boot, but not providing any useful assistance either. She waved him off. Once they were both seated, he asked, "What happened to you?"

She sighed. "I went walking outside of town when it was really muddy and slipped and fractured my ankle."

"Smart," he said.

"That's me, through and through."

As they spooned mango chutney onto pappadums, he explained he had reviewed her website and was impressed by what she had accomplished in such a competitive market. It felt nice to have her work appreciated again, especially since being so unappreciated was part of what had made her quit. She felt a twinge of nostalgia for her old life, but quickly pushed it away. There was no point in looking back. She had made the right choice.

"Have you investigated the market here?" Terry asked.

"No, I haven't had a chance, besides what I saw in your window the other day." Not that she could remember any of the listings she had glanced at—that meeting felt like eons ago.

"Let me give you an idea." He pulled a tablet out of a backpack at his feet. He brought up his company's website and they browsed through some listings. He explained the terminology that struck her as odd, such as pcm (per calendar month) for rentals, and the difference between "guide price" and "offers over" in for-sale listings, a distinction never made back home.

She reconsidered Terry, watching him as he talked. He clearly had experience. He was confident and eager, like she had been. She intuited he was not someone to underestimate. He would never fold under pressure, like she had.

Their entrees arrived, causing a momentary break in the conversation. As Ashley took her first few bites, she said, "I really appreciate you giving me the lay of the land. But as you and all my friends have rightly pointed out, I can't just decide to work here. That gets into immigration law. It was a passing fancy, is all."

"There could be ways if you really want to make it happen. Get yourself a UK boyfriend and hurry up the wedding." He laughed, but his gaze was a bit too serious for her liking. Sensing her hesitation, he asked, "Do you have one already?"

"No," she said quickly. "Well, not really." Thomas flashed through her mind, but in the next instant she thought it was ridiculous to even consider him as a possible boyfriend. She was sure he certainly wouldn't describe their relationship that way if someone asked him. Besides, with no legal papers himself, he would be no help to her in this visa situation.

She blanched. Was some part of her helping Thomas in hopes of getting to stay in the UK? No. Their relationship was more real than that, and she would never—

Terry cleared his throat, breaking her train of thought. "Don't mess around with 'not really,'" he said. "A woman like you should have a bloke who knows he wants to be with her unequivocally." He edged his fingertips closer to hers on the tabletop. She drew her hand into her lap.

"What about you?" she asked. "Got a girlfriend?"

This line of questioning perked him up. "No, but I'm ready when I find the right person." After an expectant pause during which Ashley kept her expression as neutral as possible, he shifted and changed tactics. "How long do you plan to stay in Salisbury?"

This led to a getting-to-know-you conversation that

was not unpleasant. If only she could dissuade Terry from coming on to her anymore, she might still have one friend besides Thomas in town. They segued into stories of their worst and strangest clients. She told him about Mrs. Porter, a septuagenarian who, against Ashley's advice, insisted on attending every showing and regaling every visitor with stories of her health woes and the time the entire basement flooded and she hadn't done anything to fix it. Then she was surprised that after two months she didn't have a single offer. Terry told her about a young man from a rich family who had been drunk every time they met, including at the open house. Ashley laughed at his impression of the man's slurred posh accent.

By the time that story wrapped up, their plates had been empty for a while. She glanced at her phone. It was two forty-five. "Shit," she hissed and shoved her things back in her purse. "Sorry. I was supposed to meet someone at two o'clock," she explained.

She pulled out a couple of bills to pay, but Terry waved her away. "Don't worry about it," he said. "Just promise me we can meet up again."

Ashley nodded, but she was only half listening. Her thoughts were already out the door. She could only hope that Thomas had waited for her. She said a hurried goodbye and hobbled toward the exit as fast as she could.

"I'll text you!" Terry called after her.

When she reached the market cross a few minutes later, she searched the square but didn't recognize Thomas's now-familiar profile anywhere. Defeated, she settled in to wait, occasionally standing on a different side of the cross since she didn't know what direction he would come from. After a few minutes she considered the possibility that, after all that had happened with Bryn and Katie, he had taken the opportunity to escape from her. She refused to believe it, but the thought nagged at her nonetheless. Escape meant he was a prisoner, and she knew that Thomas wanted to be with her.

The clock was striking three o'clock when he finally came hurrying across the cobblestones. His excitement was unmistakable. "Come see!" he called as soon as he was within five feet of her. Intrigued, she followed.

They walked a few blocks through the medieval part of town, past the cathedral and down the close toward the museum. As they neared, Ashley heard the muted roar of a crowd. People milled around a small table under a marquee at the courtyard entrance.

As they approached the table, Ashley glimpsed the courtyard. There were large and small marquees, lots of dressed-down tourists, and small children darting among the adults. Someone wearing a medieval costume weaved through the crowd.

"Two-pound suggested donation." Ashley tore her gaze away from the hubbub and looked at the woman who had addressed her.

Ashley fished in her purse for a five-pound note. "What is this?" she asked as she handed it over.

"Festival of archaeology. We close in an hour, but we'll be here tomorrow as well, if you want to come back. Need any change?"

"No, thanks."

They stepped through, and she let Thomas lead her where he wanted to go. Off to her right, a man's voice carried through a tinny speaker system, giving some sort of lecture. Farther off, renaissance-style music played.

Thomas led her to the left, maneuvering through the

crowd until they reach a cleared area where two boys were preparing to shoot arrows at a target under the tutelage of two men dressed in long red tunics and linen pants. The boys let their arrows loose. They both hit the target weakly, the arrows bouncing off the edge onto the ground.

Momentarily free of his charges, one of the instructors stepped toward them. "Ah, our expert archer has returned."

Thomas grinned bigger than Ashley had ever seen.

"Rick," the man said, sticking his hand out.

"Ashley. Nice to meet you."

"Thomas has been demonstrating his skill for us. Practically destroyed our targets. They're not really meant for actual archery." He ended with a wink.

"Really? I'd like to watch." She looked up at Thomas, who appealed to Rick for confirmation.

"All right. One last time." Rick went over to where a set of bows leaned against the stone wall and selected one. "This is the heaviest weight we have," he said, handing the bow to Thomas.

Thomas walked back as far as he could in the crowd. Rick cleared everyone out of the arrow's path. Thomas pulled back the string, then let the arrow loose. With a whoosh, it landed dead center. Bullseye.

She joined the other observers in cheering and clapping. Finally, Thomas appeared in his element. He bowed slightly to the audience, then handed the bow back to Rick. Rick set the bow down and returned to the line of children.

"That was amazing," Ashley said.

"No one here can use a bow," Thomas said.

"Yeah, no reason to nowadays." Did they have guns

in the fourteenth century or was that another technology he wouldn't understand?

They walked back the way they had come. Another man in medieval garb approached them, carrying a falcon on a leather-gloved wrist. "Back at the archery?" he asked Thomas.

Ashley laughed. "How many friends did you make here while I was at lunch?"

The falconer smiled. "He's knowledgeable about falcons. I think my bird likes him better than me."

A girl ran up to them, wanting to pet the bird, so Thomas and Ashley moved on. Thomas took her to another table with a line of people three deep along it. In a glass case sat a beautiful, green-glazed jug. An identical jug sat on the table. A man picked it up and showed it to his son, who pretended to drink out of it.

"What's this?" Ashley asked when they got close.

The dark-haired young woman at the table pointed at the glass case. "This is one of the museum artifacts. From a pottery kiln near here, never used, that's why it's in such pristine condition. Thirteenth to fourteenth century. This was very commonly used at the time. Feel free to touch the reproduction."

Ashley moved down the line with the crowd. She had just a second to run a finger along the handle of the jug before the momentum pushed her away. Once they were out of earshot of the museum worker, she said to Thomas, "So that jug was familiar to you? That's what you used back home?"

"Yes," he said. "Exactly like that."

The festival was winding down for the day. People shuffled toward the entrance. The speakers were silent, and a few of the tables were packing up.

Ashley squeezed Thomas's bicep. "I'm glad you found somewhere you are so appreciated."

"I'm not appreciated elsewhere?" He raised an eyebrow, but a smile toyed on his lips.

She blushed. "Of course, you are. I just meant…"

He slung an arm across her shoulder. "Let's go," he said, leading her out.

It felt nice to be able to follow for once. She leaned against his side and smiled.

The next day, Sunday, was a quiet day. Ashley still hadn't heard from either Bryn or Katie, but she resolved not to worry over it further. They would come around in time. Either way, she felt more at peace with the way her life was going than she had in a long while.

Ashley and Thomas left the flat after breakfast. Thomas attended mass while Ashley read in a café nearby. Then they visited the festival again, where they listened to every talk that was offered. Thomas said hello to his friends from the day before but understood that taking over the archery again would not be particularly welcome. That was, until the day's festivities were drawing to a close, when Rick came to find them.

"Care to give a quick demonstration to the masses?" he asked Thomas. He led them back to the area where the targets were set up. "Ladies and gentlemen," he said with a flourish to the small crowd gathered, "prepare to be amazed by this next demonstration of skill."

He pulled a bow out of a hidden corner of the stone wall and handed it to Thomas. "Brought it special for you today," he said conspiratorially. Thomas tugged at the thick string appreciatively.

Ashley backed away with everyone else as Rick cleared the field. She jostled for a space toward the front, where she could watch over the children's heads with no obstacles. Everyone clapped politely as Thomas hit his first bullseye. Checking behind him, he backed up another ten feet and loosed the arrow a second time. This time the applause was slightly more enthusiastic. As the crowd thinned in the rest of the festival, he was able to back up two more times before Rick worried about people wandering into the path of the arrows.

As Thomas was bowing after his final performance, a woman hurried over. "Rick," she called, "what are you doing? That's a real hunting bow! That's not safe."

"Run," Rick hissed.

Thomas dropped the bow, grabbed Ashley's hand, and managed a final wave to the crowd before slipping out of the courtyard. It was them against the world again, but it was a good feeling now, like they were part of something special that only the two of them understood.

Out in the close, Ashley stumbled over the toe of her walking boot. Thomas caught her and pulled her up against his chest. She gazed up, his breath against her face. His lips were so, so close.

A man squeezed past them, pushing Thomas forward into her, causing her to stumble again. Thomas deftly held her steady, but the moment was broken. They moved on, walking home side by side, their fingertips occasionally brushing with the rhythm of their steps.

Chapter 18

Terry texted Ashley first thing the next morning, saying he had enjoyed their lunch and wanted to take her out again. She sighed. The way he had worded the text along with everything else he had said meant she couldn't pretend that he just wanted to be friends. She replied that she had enjoyed talking to him and left it at that. She hoped he would get the hint from her innocuous message.

No such luck. Two minutes later he texted asking her to dinner the next night. She considered how best to let him down easily.

Given that we will continue to be working together on Hannah's flats, I think we should just stay as friends.

The three dots came up instantly. A moment later, his response.

That is a lame excuse. We can keep things professional.

She tried another tack.

How old are you?

19.

I'm about to turn 29.

Her birthday wasn't until September, but still, that was close enough. A ten-year age difference made it sound worse.

That doesn't matter, he responded.

She sighed and locked her phone screen. She

215

couldn't deal with men who refused to take no for an answer right now.

Out in the living room, Thomas puttered around. His presence was comforting after the frustrating conversation with Terry. She and Thomas were meant to visit Professor Melder again that morning to hopefully unearth more answers for Thomas. She both wanted to help him and dreaded what would happen if he found a way to leave. Ashley had damaged and maybe even ruined her relationships with Bryn and Katie over Thomas. She would be so alone here without him. Terry would be small consolation.

But she couldn't contemplate that depressing future now. She had to get them back to Southampton and pretend she was happy for Thomas to make it home. She occupied herself with the next task she needed to complete, then the next, until she forgot about what lay farther ahead.

Professor Melder did not look thrilled when they appeared in his office door a couple of hours later. In fact, his frown pulled down not only the corners of his mouth but his eyes and forehead as well.

"I have a lecture in thirty minutes," he said, not taking his gaze off them, as if they were wild animals that might jump at any time.

Ashley stepped inside but didn't sit down. "We won't take up too much of your time. We were just wondering if the university has a collection of medieval manuscripts that we could view."

"You think I'm going to let two random people who aren't even students here examine our rarest books?"

Ashley ignored his question. "We're searching specifically for any information on the forest around

Salisbury, anything written about—" she hesitated and dropped her voice, still embarrassed to admit what she suspected, "time travel."

"What?" He shook his head. "I don't think we have anything that's so specific to this region." He considered Ashley. She put on her best puppy-dog eyes. He sighed. "I'm not supposed to do this, but I can get you into the library. We have some database subscriptions that you can search. But I'm not going to let you access any physical books."

"Thank you so much!"

"Thank you," Thomas echoed behind her.

She glanced over her shoulder at him. Had he understood what had been said? If his story were true there was no way he could have. But Thomas shrugged at her and smiled that same big smile. Ashley relaxed. He must have just said thanks because Ashley had, or because he sensed Melder's acquiescence.

But Thomas wasn't quite ready to go. He pointed at the shelves behind Melder and said something in Middle English.

Melder squinted. Ashley could almost hear the gears whirring in his mind, interpreting what Thomas had said.

Thomas said something else in encouragement. Ashley caught "Lydiard Tregoze" and "de la Warr."

This time Melder shook his head. He replied in words Ashley could understand. "I told you, there's nothing that specific. You can search the databases." Melder gathered a few books and a binder from his desk. "I'll drop you off at the library on the way to my lecture."

Ashley and Thomas dutifully followed him across campus and into the library. They stood off to the side while Melder spoke with the librarian. Ashley took the opportunity to ask Thomas what he had said to Melder.

"If his books had any information on my family," he was saying when Melder returned holding two sheets of paper.

"Fill these out," Melder explained. "Then she'll show you how to access the databases." He inclined his head in the direction of the librarian behind the checkout desk. He gave a curt nod, then walked off.

"Thank you!" Ashley called after him, but he didn't acknowledge her. She sensed they had used up their last favor with him. If this search failed, she didn't know what they would do. As much as she wanted Thomas to stay, the clock was ticking before the authorities would close in on him, and that would be worse than losing him to his own world. They had to find answers.

Ashley led the online search for answers, but Thomas proved useful in deciphering the ornate medieval handwriting on the scanned manuscript pages they came across. After the first hour, they didn't have anything to show for their efforts, and her ankle was already swelling inside the walking boot. Thomas left for a few minutes and returned with a small footstool. Lord knows where he got it, but it felt good to prop her foot up. Thomas was nothing if not resourceful.

By the end of the next hour, they had found several manuscripts that referenced Wiltshire or Salisbury but nothing useful for their situation. Ashley paused and reflected. They had searched every term they could think of and browsed the manuscript categories as best they could to broaden the results. The last thing that potentially limited the results were the dates. She had started with Thomas's time, but did the answer have to be in a fourteenth-century manuscript? Maybe the secret was older than that—or hadn't been written down until later.

She would try one last thing. She searched again, but this time didn't limit the date. When she read the words half an hour later, she almost couldn't believe it. They appeared in a sixteenth-century manuscript, which meant it mercifully was printed text and the language was much less unfamiliar to her. She read it twice, just to be sure, before she ran her finger along the screen to point it out to Thomas.

There is sayde to be much magik and manye secretes on Salisbury plain. A person can fynde their greatest heart's desire in that playce. A prayer sayde at one of the stanes will allmost certanley be answered. Without knowing the power of these stanes, a person may unwitingley receive an answer they did not know they were asking. This person shoulde return to the same stane with a clere purpose in his heart and mak the prayer again. But ev'ry time the magik is called on, there may be other consekwences, therfor it should be used only when absolutly necesary.

Both Ashley and Thomas sat in stunned silence for a long moment. It seemed so simple, and yet it was an answer. Even though it wasn't explicit in what the magic was, it was proof that whatever had happened to Thomas was not a figment of their imagination but something that had happened to others before him. Thomas crossed himself. She remembered his previous reticence about the use of magic and guessed that was what disturbed him.

Ashley photographed the screen with her phone so they would have the text with them to ponder over later. She clicked back and skimmed the search results she hadn't read yet but determined they weren't useful.

She gathered up their things, but Thomas laid a hand on her arm to stop her.

"You look for my family now," he said, pointing at the screen.

They were back to this again. "I don't think that's a good idea."

"You look." His voice was more forceful now, his grip on her arm a bit tighter. She flashed back to that moment at the bus stop the first day they met when his hand had gone for his knife. She shook her head to clear it. Thomas had proved that he wasn't dangerous. Still, they were here for answers. She couldn't refuse him when there would be no other opportunity to look. She sighed and sat back down. Satisfied, he released her.

They found a few references to Lydiard Tregoze, mostly dull inventory lists for tax purposes, and one reference to a property case Thomas's father had won at the assizes in 1361. Ashley was relieved to not have to risk destroying whatever time travel continuum they were in while still being disappointed for Thomas. She knew he had hoped for answers of a more personal nature.

Then she came to the last page of results. The final reference highlighted the one thing she had been sure they would not find: Thomas's name. She clicked on the thumbnail to view the whole page.

Ashley's eyes slowly scanned the page, interpreting each word as she went along. Thomas, with less mental gymnastics to do, reached the end of the passage much more quickly.

"John is dead," he said.

"What?" She struggled to finish reading the passage.

Frustrated with her slowness, Thomas ran his finger along the screen, translating the words for her as best he could.

It sparked a memory of the lost wiki page Ashley had found and been unable to find again when Thomas had asked for information. The story here was roughly the same. Thomas de la Warr, now fifth Baron de la Warr, had refused his summons to Parliament to tend to his parish instead and was now ordered to come, by the king, on pain of death. Presumably, he went.

Ashley's mind whirred. John was dead. Why had Thomas said that? A piece slid into place. "John is your older brother."

"Yes. No sons."

Ashley nodded. Thomas would only have the title if John had died and left no heirs. Ashley scrolled back up to check the year in the document information. Fourteen-oh-three. Almost thirty years after the point Thomas had left and ended up here. That must mean he returned. A knot formed in her stomach.

The screen flashed, then went dark. Ashley fumbled for the power button. When the screen came back up, all that appeared was the blue screen of death.

"Oh, no," Ashley said. She moved the mouse, hit control+alt+delete, anything she could think of to bring the computer back up. The blue screen stayed, staring at her menacingly.

A heavy sigh came from behind her. Ashley spun around. The librarian stood there with her arms crossed.

"I don't know what happened," Ashley said. "I didn't do anything."

"I'll have to get IT in." When Ashley didn't budge, she continued, "I think that's you done for now then, eh?"

"Right, thank you." Ashley rushed to grab her purse and hobbled outside as quickly as the walking boot would allow. The last thing she needed was to pay for breaking a university computer. She hoped Melder wouldn't hear about this.

Out front, Thomas asked, "What happened?"

"The computer broke."

Thomas frowned deeply. "What does this mean?"

"It doesn't work anymore."

Thomas pursed his lips, then laughed a little. "No, what does it mean that the comp-u-ter broke?" he asked, sounding out the unfamiliar word slowly.

Ashley smiled. Thomas was beyond needing her to explain words to him in different ways. She had forgotten how much progress he had made. "Well, the website didn't work when we accessed it the other day, and while we were reading this document about you, the computer crashed. Something doesn't want us to learn about you. That, or…" she paused to consider the right words, "you being here is changing these documents. Something about your story has changed. The records are different now."

"I don't exist now."

It was Ashley's turn to frown. "Not necessarily. It's like you're in some sort of limbo—"

"Purgatory," Thomas interrupted. "I knew this was it!"

"No, not literal purgatory. I just meant, it's undecided where you end up. Somehow the end of your story hasn't been written yet."

Wind suddenly whipped through her hair even though the day had been calm so far. The gust carried with it a smattering of rain droplets. Ashley glanced up at the sky and thought about the last rainstorm they had been in together, and how Thomas had read it as a sign. What was this new storm telling them? She sighed. "We'd better head back."

They trekked back toward the train station. She was getting used to the way she needed to walk in the boot and could walk faster now. But she didn't push herself. She didn't want to get back to Salisbury any quicker. That would only bring her sooner to the moment she would have to say goodbye to Thomas, and she wasn't ready for that farewell.

Then there was the whole conundrum of what exactly was happening. The failure of the computer couldn't be coincidence. She was focused on disentangling those thoughts when a shadow fell across her path.

"Miss Winston, isn't it?"

She glanced up. When she saw who it was, she immediately plastered on a fake smile. "Professor Litchfield."

"Just the two people I wanted to see. I heard from Professor Melder you were sneaking around again today." He followed the statement with a wink, but it made him appear creepy rather than friendly.

"Been talking to your curator friend?" Ashley asked, letting a touch of ice invade her voice.

"I have, in fact. He loves the coin you left him. Says it appears perfect and legitimate. We would love to know where exactly you found it." Understanding Ashley wasn't going to offer any information, he peered hopefully over her shoulder at Thomas, who just shrugged. "Hmph. Well, if you find anything else, make sure you log its exact coordinates. Drop a pin in a map or something. That would be incredibly helpful."

"Will do." Ashley started to step around him.

"I know Melder wasn't interested in your story, but I know someone who might be."

In spite of herself, Ashley stopped walking.

"I talked to a friend of mine who teaches at a university in London in the linguistics department. He was intrigued, to say the least. I don't suppose I could entreat you to meet with us, just virtually? In exchange for the free use of university facilities?" He inclined his head meaningfully in the direction of the library.

Ashley sighed. The last thing she needed was for him to discover the computer fiasco and charge her to replace it. "Sure, I guess. When?"

"Our class load is pretty light on Wednesdays. How about ten o'clock?"

They agreed and shared their contact information. Ashley couldn't help but glance back at Litchfield as he walked away. When she had first met Litchfield, she had been desperate for someone to give her answers about Thomas. Now, she felt protective of Thomas and didn't want to share him with anyone else. She could only hope Litchfield's intentions were good. But it may not even be an issue, she told herself. Thomas might be gone before Wednesday. There was no reason to wait, now that they knew the answer. It might be better for him if he were gone before then, though it would devastate her. She gritted her teeth and forced herself to walk forward as if she were not in turmoil inside.

Thirty minutes later, Ashley and Thomas were comfortably seated on the next train back to Salisbury. She was calmer now and ready to figure out a solution.

She couldn't leave Thomas here with no future. The only way to get him out of this strange limbo he had entered was to get him home.

"We should go back to the woods tomorrow," she ventured. "That will give you time tonight to get your purpose clear in your mind."

"I don't like magic."

"Well, it already happened to you without your consent, so what's the harm in doing it again?"

Thomas looked at her sharply.

Giving up on this thread, she asked, "What will you do when you get back? Go to France or to Salisbury?"

He rubbed his beard. "I don't know."

"You know what I think."

"Yes. But you don't follow your own advice."

"What are you talking about?"

"Your book. Sadie. Not writing."

They had circled around this topic before. She knew she had been using her adventure with Thomas as an excuse to avoid dealing with her own situation. After Sadie's initial flurry of calls and texts after the incident, she had fallen silent. Ashley didn't know how she could possibly fix the mess she had made. But soon Thomas would be gone, and she could figure out how to deal with it then.

Thomas didn't let the topic go. When they returned to her flat, while she was still hobbling across the living room to the bathroom, he said, "You need to talk to her. Do something that makes you feel like you can move forward."

Ashley stopped halfway across the room. "I don't want to talk to her."

"Too bad." When she glanced back at him over her

shoulder, he was grinning.

"What would I say to her?"

He shrugged. "Apologize."

Ashley scowled. Thomas had a knack for getting right to the heart of a situation, especially if it was a heart she didn't want to face. "Let me use the bathroom first."

When she returned to the living room, Thomas was seated on the couch holding her laptop out to her. "Talking to Sadie," he said.

Ashley laughed. He had figured out what that device was for, and he wasn't holding his cross out or praying over it or anything.

"What?" he asked as she sat next to him.

She took the laptop. "I'm just proud of you, is all. How much you've learned and how much more comfortable you are with technology now."

"Tech…"

She waved vaguely at her laptop and her phone resting on the coffee table. "This stuff."

"Right."

"Anyway, I'm proud of you." She started up her laptop. "I'm going to write her a letter," she said. "Calling her out of the blue would be too much. For both of us."

"Fast letter," Thomas said.

"Yes, fast letter." They sat in silence while she typed an email, deleting sentences over and over until finally they resembled something like contrition. When she finished, she read it to Thomas without looking up. She needed his approval like she had never needed anyone's before. The only way she would get through this was to avoid seeing his reaction until the end.

"Dear Sadie," she read. "I am so sorry for how I took

advantage of our friendship. I have no excuse for what I did other than to say I was scared for my future and took it out on you. I know this doesn't magically make things better. I really do wish you all the best. I know your dream is just as important to you as mine is to me and that we worked together, nothing more." The last sentence struck her as what she needed to admit. After the breakup with Trevor that followed the years of taking care of him, Ashley had jumped headfirst into focusing on her own dreams. But she understood now that her dreams weren't the only ones that mattered. Sadie had had her own needs, and so had Jayna. Trevor, for all that he had done to her, had his, too. A fiery mixture of guilt and regret roiled in her gut. A single tear welled up in her eye. Another followed it, and both trailed slowly down her cheeks.

Thomas listened without comment. When she finished and he still said nothing, she braved a glance up. She was surprised to find his face only a few inches from hers. He wiped the tears away with more tenderness than anyone had ever shown her. She could feel his breath on her cheek. His blue eyes drew her in again. She couldn't look away. He leaned in another inch. She took in a deep breath, drawing strength into her. He was leaving tomorrow. What was the harm? She closed the final two inches between them.

His mouth was warm but rough. His fingers, too, were rough when he brought them up to cup her chin, but his touch was gentle. The kiss lingered. When they separated, they didn't say anything for a long time. Everything that needed to be said had passed between them in that kiss. The moment seemed too delicate, like words might damage it. She gazed into his eyes again.

"Okay?" he asked finally.

"Yes, very okay," she answered.

A shiver ran up her spine. How on earth was she going to let him go now?

Chapter 19

In the morning, Thomas kissed Ashley in greeting when she joined him in the living room, but it was restrained, without the passion from the previous night. Still, it showed it was not a fluke. He really did care for her the way she cared for him. She asked, "Are you ready to go to the woods today?" and held her breath as she waited for his response. She knew they were down to his last few days before the authorities came for him, but she would still have to try hard not to cry if he said yes.

To her great relief, Thomas shook his head, his thick hair bouncing against his cheekbones. "I'm afraid to use that magic," he said.

"It's probably the only way."

"Not yet," he said.

She accepted the answer, hoping the "not yet" also had something to do with her. There was no long-term solution, no way she could see for them to be together, but a couple more days together would have to be enough.

"What did Sadie say?" Thomas asked eagerly.

"She hasn't replied. I doubt she will."

Thomas frowned.

Ashley set a hand gently on his arm. "Thanks for helping me. But I burned that bridge and now I have to live with it." There were a lot of things she would have to live with. At least she had tried to reconcile with

Sadie, and because of that her own conscience felt slightly assuaged. "What about you?" she asked him. "Your purpose has to be clear, according to the book. Will you pick duty or dreams?"

For a moment, she thought Thomas wasn't going to respond. Finally, he said, "If John dies, my duty will change. And my old duty will conflict with it."

Ashley knew he was thinking about the document they had read the day before. "But things could change now. The future could be different."

He looked at her fiercely. "Yes, it could."

He pulled her to him. His grip was warm and exciting, his body pressed along the length of hers. Again, it seemed like he would never speak. She wished she could know the calculations going on behind those blue eyes.

"My future could be different," he said. "I can't go back to the same way I was before I came here. Before I met you."

"Sounds like dreams it is, then."

"Dreams of a certain kind."

She didn't know what to say to that, but fortunately she didn't have to come up with any words. He kissed her long and hard again. But when he pulled away, his face held a hint of sadness. She feared he was already saying goodbye.

Ashley pretended as she moved through her day that everything was all right, that they weren't waiting for some terrible thing to collapse the world she and Thomas were building for themselves. Terry texted her, and this time she outright said she wasn't interested. He asked her if it had to do with the guy she had mentioned sort of dating. Why would men only accept a no if another man was involved? She shook her head but went with it. She told a white lie and said that they were definitely dating now. Which she was sure they would be if Thomas had any concept of modern dating. She hoped that would shut Terry up for good.

She had barely put the phone down when Constable Marvin called. She gritted her teeth and answered it.

"I'm following up about Mr. Thomas de la Warr. Is he still with you?"

They must know he was, since they were tracking his every move. "Yes," she said.

"Have you succeeded in getting any identification for him?"

"I don't have any more information for you."

"Is that a no?"

"Yes, it's a no."

"How has he been? No further incidents?"

"He's been fine. I'm sorry I called the police that first day, honestly."

Constable Marvin sighed so forcefully Ashley was surprised she couldn't feel the air coming through the phone line. "Well, we still need to get him home. Do you know where we should be searching for documents? A certain embassy, perhaps?"

"I would help you if I could, but I don't have any information." What was she going to tell the police? That they should search in the medieval archives for the county to find proof of Thomas's existence? There must be some records based on what she and Thomas had found so far online, though who knew what would happen to those records if someone accessed them now—a spontaneous fire, perhaps? She shook her head. Any mention of this would get her committed along with him. "I really don't know anything," she said.

"You see, I find that increasingly difficult to believe. I know my colleague spoke with you last week about what would happen if we don't get any ID from him. The clock is running out. We need paperwork from him within the next forty-eight hours or we will have to bring him in again."

"Yes, but that doesn't change the fact—"

"How are you in this country, Miss Winston?"

"Excuse me?"

"Are you here on a work visa? Or just a tourist visa?"

"A tourist visa."

"Right. I'd like to have your information on file as well. Can you come down to the station today so we can make a copy of your passport?"

"Is that really necessary?"

Instead of answering, Constable Marvin pushed ahead. "And what is your relationship to the property you're currently living at?"

"My cousin owns it. I'm helping her out. Why are you asking?"

"Miss Winston, I really am being reasonable here. I like you, I really do. But based on the scant information we have now, it seems that you are assisting a potential refugee from who knows where evade the law. We need to get some answers."

Ashley gulped. This is what she got for helping somebody. "I'll come in later today with my passport."

"Good. I'll see you then."

When Ashley hung up the phone, she leaned forward, covered her face with her hands, and let out a little frustrated shriek. But when she saw Thomas's concerned gaze, any resentment she might have held toward him faded away.

"I have to go to the police station. I'll deal with this as best I can. But…you can't stay here for much longer. You're going to have to give them something. What, I don't know."

"How much longer?"

Ashley shook her head. "Technically, you still have two more days to get an ID to them, but they're pushing so hard, I don't know that they'll wait that long."

Thomas nodded slowly. "I can go instead of you."

"No, don't do that. We'll figure something out." She stood and grabbed her purse. "It's just…you may have to try the magic whether you like it or not."

He crossed himself, his face a serious mask. She couldn't tell if he wanted to return home or not.

"I'll be back soon," she said. "Don't go anywhere without me." She would have to keep him in her sight now as much as possible, just in case.

As Ashley made her way to the police station, her mind raced through the worst-case scenarios. Maybe Constable Marvin's call was a ruse and they would arrest her when she got there. How would she explain that to her parents? After all the help they had given her to rescue her life, for her only to end up in jail. Jesus. Would Hannah help her find a lawyer if that happened? Or maybe the police wouldn't arrest her, but what if they wanted to keep her for a formal interview? How the heck would she explain any of this satisfactorily? They would commit her and deport Thomas to god-knows-where just so he wouldn't be their problem anymore.

Outside the front entrance, she paused and took a few deep breaths. She gazed at the little group of smokers gathered farther down along the side of the building. She envied them their soothing break, their easy camaraderie with each other, even if she wouldn't envy them their cancer later. A middle-aged man glanced up from his phone as he took a drag and caught her eye. She turned away quickly.

Realistically, none of those things she had imagined were likely to happen. Constable Marvin had threatened her obliquely on the phone, but surely, if specific threats like criminal charges or forced confessions existed, she would have called on them. Ashley just needed to go in there and get out and not raise any suspicion. The key was to look like she knew what she was doing. Confidence helped in any situation. She steeled herself and walked inside.

The officer at the front desk didn't know where Constable Marvin was or that Ashley was supposed to come by and have them make a copy of her passport. He dutifully scanned the document anyway and then sent Ashley on her way. Ashley couldn't believe her good luck. She shouldn't have worried so much. For now, she and Thomas were safe. She would have to make sure it stayed that way.

When she returned to the flat, Thomas was on the landing along with the couple currently staying across the hall. They were all gathered around the open door to the vacation flat, peering at the door handle.

"What's going on?" Ashley asked.

All three faced her. Thomas swung the door shut and nodded proudly.

The young man—she couldn't remember his name, people were always coming and staying for a couple of days—said, "We were having trouble getting the door to lock. The handle was a bit loose. But your boyfriend fixed it."

Ashley gawped at Thomas, who grinned proudly and brandished a screwdriver. Ashley had had to change a bulb in a wall sconce the other day and had left the toolbox out in her flat. Apparently, screwdrivers hadn't changed much in seven hundred years. She started to protest the characterization of their relationship, but Thomas seemed oblivious. "Boyfriend" was probably not a category that existed in 1377, so she let it go.

"Great. I'm glad," she said. "Let me know if you need anything else."

The couple went back into the flat, and Ashley and Thomas returned to theirs. She watched Thomas, who was clearly happy to feel useful. Part of her wanted to admonish him for answering the door while she was gone—what if it had been the police?—but she couldn't bring herself to. He was clearly picking up a lot more of the life and language of the modern world. She almost felt sad, like he may not need her so much anymore. But that was the goal, right? You helped someone until they didn't need it anymore. Then you could walk away. Which was exactly what she was having trouble doing right now. She could keep Thomas to herself for another couple of days, then he would have to go. They had both better prepare themselves for it—Thomas for partaking of magic, and Ashley for losing him.

The next day was Wednesday, and, with nothing further from Constable Marvin, in the morning, Ashley and Thomas joined the video call with the professors as promised. Professor Litchfield's London friend, Professor Singer, was remarkably like him. Singer was a bit thinner, and his white hair a bit thicker, but Ashley was sure that from a distance she would mistake them for each other.

After Litchfield ran through introductions, Singer shared his screen, displaying a passage from a Middle English text. He asked Thomas to read and took notes as he listened. Thomas's reading was fluid. Ashley smiled at the change compared to the halting speech she usually heard from him when he was communicating in the modern tongue.

When Thomas finished, Singer looked up and asked, "Have you studied Middle English? Taught it, even?"

Thomas screwed up one corner of his mouth. Ashley could see him contemplating how to answer this question. Her first instinct was to jump in to save him, but she restrained herself. This was his show today. For better or worse, her decisions had gotten them here, but she had to let him take the lead more. He was clearly ready.

Finally, he said, "I studied it, yes. The way you study your language."

"You're a professor?"

"No. I have studied it all my life."

"Your parents were professors?"

"You don't understand."

"Clearly not." Singer rearranged the papers on his desk before peering into his computer screen again. "Why don't you read this for me?"

Thomas sighed but did as he was asked. This time, he was less fluid and even stumbled once or twice.

"That sounds familiar," Ashley said once he had finished.

Litchfield guffawed. "It should. It's bloody Shakespeare."

Thomas raised an inquiring eyebrow at Ashley, but she gave a quick shake of her head. Now was not the time to explain Shakespeare to him.

Singer tapped a pencil against his lips. "You were raised speaking this language." He said it more as a statement than a question.

"Not this," Thomas said.

"Right." Singer switched back to the previous passage. "This one."

Thomas nodded.

"And you were raised in Wiltshire, you say?" Singer muted his line and leaned his head back, clearly shouting at someone unseen behind the door. When this display ended, he unmuted. "Sorry about that. Is there a specific group you lived with that taught you to speak this way? A religious group, perhaps?"

"I am meant to enter the church."

This perked Singer up as a possible explanation. "Fascinating. I would love to speak with you more. Is there any chance you can come to London? The university can cover the cost of the train ticket for you and your, uh, friend," he finished, nodding in Ashley's direction.

"What would he do there?" Ashley jumped in.

"I'd like to hear him speak in person. Make some recordings, perhaps. And some measurements of his mouth movements."

"You want to study him."

"I would like to learn more about him and this group he claims to be from. If this form of the language has survived somewhere in this country—which up until today, I would have said would be highly unlikely—then it is of immense interest to the academic community."

Ashley frowned. "We'll talk about it and get back to you."

"She always make the decisions for you?" Litchfield butted in.

Thomas gave a tight smile but didn't dignify the comment with a response.

"Thank you for your time," Ashley said, sounding cheerier than she felt. "We'll be in touch."

Once they signed out, Ashley turned to face Thomas. Their knees brushed, but neither of them moved. "I don't think you should do this. It sounds like a bad idea to me."

"Why?"

"Studying you will just draw more attention to you."

"You asked for the attention in the first place."

"I didn't know, then. I just didn't know." It was all she could find to say as an explanation.

Thomas rubbed her back reassuringly. Then, with renewed determination, he said, "I want to see London."

Ashley's eyes widened. "If you think Salisbury is different from what you're used to…"

"I want to see," he repeated. "Before I go home."

She kept her eyes locked on his. Did he understand how this might all go wrong? He didn't waver and returned her gaze unhesitatingly. "All right," she said, "I'll take you." It would have to be as soon as possible. Tomorrow was the deadline for Thomas to turn in his identification to the police, so he might not be free to go anywhere after that. On the one hand, escaping to London might be good to keep him out from under the local police's scrutiny. On the other hand, they might not like him leaving town. Probably wouldn't, in fact. But with no plan on how to put the police off any longer, the easy way out was to delay with distance. And worry about the consequences for herself later, once Thomas was safely home. They could sneak to the woods on their return from London and send Thomas back. She would simply say she didn't know what had happened to him. Her stomach churned. What were the chances it would be that simple?

There was one last possibility. What if Thomas was using the trip to London as a means of escape from her? He said he had been in London before he came here. What if he disappeared into the crowds there and left her behind forever? He must know he was in trouble and that she hadn't been able to get him out of it. Maybe she would be expendable once she got him back to the capital. She shook away the doubts, but they lingered in the depths of her mind like an itch she couldn't reach.

Ashley told Professor Singer of Thomas's decision, pressing him to let them come the next day, and Singer sent two return tickets to London on the train, leaving Thursday morning and returning Friday evening. Ashley had requested the extra day so that she and Thomas would have time to sightsee. And one last day together before he left her life for good. She briefly considered calling Bryn, but decided that, considering how they had left things, showing up in London with Thomas still at her heels wouldn't resolve the situation. Again and again, she found Thomas was the only person she had left. She could deal with rebuilding bridges once he was gone.

For the rest of that day, Ashley's breath caught in her throat every time the phone rang. But it was never Constable Marvin or the immigration authorities. There were no warnings in advance of the next day's deadline.

But still, no solution to Thomas's quandary presented itself besides hoping the manuscript's information would prove accurate.

That afternoon, after much cajoling, Ashley agreed to read Thomas a few pages from her book. Despite her initial reluctance to share, it was a welcome distraction from worrying over the outcome of the next few days. She stumbled as she read her words aloud for the first time and made notes, hearing phrasings that she needed to fix. This made for a choppy presentation, but Thomas listened carefully without comment.

When she finished, he said simply, "It's not verse."

"No, it's not." It seemed an odd comment at first, but then she recalled his connection to Chaucer and remembered the Middle English texts she had read in college. In his time all creative writing was probably verse. The modern novel hadn't even been invented yet.

"It's a good story. It sounds like you are this other person."

"Thanks," she said. She closed her laptop, eager to close the conversation as well.

"You should continue it."

"I will. Someday."

Thomas shook his head but must have been sick of remonstrating her because he said nothing else.

She appreciated his gentleness with her. She wanted to know more about him and what had made him the man he was. "Tell me about your life back home," she said.

"Life there is very different from life here. But also not." He smiled. "Here everything is noisy and fast, and you use way too much water for everything when other things would do just as well. But the main things are the same. To go to work, to go out with friends, to want to improve your life. Not so different."

"What do you miss the most?"

"Being normal." He grinned.

"Makes sense." She laughed. "Do you think your family knows that you're missing by now?"

"Probably. I should have arrived for my ordination long ago." He said more thoughtfully, "Since they probably already think I've run away, I might as well do it when I return."

Ashley forced a smile at the mention of him leaving. "Might as well."

"I will go soon," he said. "Then you won't have to care for me anymore."

"I like caring for you, though."

They locked eyes for a moment. Then he leaned in for another long, sweet kiss. When they pulled apart, he stayed close to her on the couch, the sides of their bodies pressed against each other. "I should be the one taking care of you."

"We don't go in for traditional gender roles so much anymore."

His eyes widened as he tried to translate what she had said.

"Don't worry about it," she said quickly. "It's nice that you want to take care of me."

He nodded slowly, still unsure. "I will do my best," he said.

The statement summed up what he had done ever since he arrived.

"You already have," Ashley reassured him.

Thomas glanced away, but she thought she caught him blushing. She smiled to herself. If only this perfect moment could continue forever. But it was not to be.

For dinner, Ashley ordered from a café across the street and, with careful instructions, Thomas went out and returned with their sandwiches so she didn't have to tackle the stairs in the walking boot, which she was already heartily sick of. The ankle wasn't hurting much anymore, and she debated whether to take it off sooner than the doctor had advised. In a compromise, she removed it and determined to leave it off while she was at home.

They ate mostly in silence. As he finished his meal, Thomas appeared thoughtful. "You never talk about where you're from, or why you're in Salisbury," he said. "You're not a traveler like me, are you?" He grinned cheekily.

"No, just a regular traveler."

"That's why they wanted to see your travel documents?"

"Yes. I'm only here temporarily."

She could see him about to ask why, so she sighed and plunged ahead.

"I lost everything back home. My job, and my house, my boyfriend, my friends. Hannah is only letting me stay in this flat for the summer as a favor to me. I have no idea what I'm going to do after this."

When she finally took a breath, Thomas looked bewildered. She laughed. She had clearly been talking too fast. "I needed a change," she said more slowly, hoping this explanation would suffice.

"Your family is back home?"

She nodded.

"Didn't they help you?"

He had clearly picked up enough of what she had said to intuit that she needed help. "Yes, they did. They bailed me out and got me here."

"What about your village? Don't they help you?"

"We don't operate like that over there. The opposite, in fact. Besides, where I live is much, much bigger than a village."

"Still, even neighbors in London know each other."

Her knee-jerk reaction was to argue, but she stopped herself, knowing it wouldn't get them anywhere. Thomas might understand more once he saw modern London for himself. "Things are different here," she said instead. "And that doesn't mean they're better. I've always done everything myself, and look where that got me."

"This place looks pretty nice." He waved a hand across the room in demonstration.

His outlook took her by surprise, but in a pleasant way. She looked around the room with new eyes. She was provided with everything she needed. "You know, you're right. But, even so, it would have been better if I hadn't been so stubborn and had asked for help earlier. Or stood up for myself more with Trevor. It took me a long time to see that, but now I do."

Thomas leaned his elbows onto his knees. "Everyone is connected," he said. "The tenant works the land, the landowner provides it, the miller mills the wheat, the baker bakes it into bread. Everyone eats."

"Everyone eats," she repeated with a smile. "That's very true. For you especially. Everything you want to do is for other people: fight for your country or save souls. I've never seen myself doing something like that." Everything he had said about his world sounded good enough, but it must be easy for him to be so philosophical. She doubted the peasants who worked his land would be so positive about the life they led. But when you didn't know anything different, how would you know to complain?

"Tomorrow is another day."

Right, tomorrow. The thought of what would happen the next day darkened her thoughts. She would take Thomas to London because he wanted to go, but she felt as if they were walking into a trap. Drawing more attention to him couldn't end well.

This led her thoughts back down the trail of what had happened that morning. During the call with the professors, Singer had struck on the idea that Thomas's knowledge was academic, that he had been a professor of Middle English somewhere. What if he was? What if he had amnesia or a mental breakdown that blurred the line between reality and his accumulated knowledge and that made him *think* he was medieval?

While Thomas cleaned up the remnants of their meals, she typed a few search terms into her phone browser. If there was a professor missing, someone must be searching for him. She found stories on other missing persons, but even after expanding her search from Wiltshire to the rest of the country, she found nothing. With the thought of how to appease the police always in the back of her mind, she also searched the Wiltshire records database for any (modern) birth certificates for a Thomas de la Warr. Maybe the police hadn't searched there because they still thought he was from London even though he insisted he was from Wiltshire. She tried any variation of the name she could think of. Again, nothing. Even though it meant their immediate problem wasn't solved, she breathed a sigh of relief. She so much wanted what she and Thomas had to be real. In the next instant, she felt immensely guilty that she still doubted his story. Hadn't she seen enough proof yet? Either way, soon enough everything would be tested. Whether he disappeared at the rock in the woods or not, she resolved to believe him. If it did work, she would be shattered. If it didn't, nothing else would matter except the fact that he was still here.

Her phone rang, dragging her out of her thoughts. It was Terry. She didn't want to answer in case he was still trying to convince her to go out with him. But there was a chance it could be about the flat, so she decided she ought to.

She didn't understand him at first through the agitation in his voice. But she picked out Katie's name. He had talked to Katie about her.

"Wait, how do you know Katie?" she asked.

He finally paused to take a breath. "Everyone knows Katie."

Ashley could believe that was true of her gregarious friend. "And what were you saying about me?"

"She told me what's been going on with you and that guy. It's dangerous."

"You don't know him. Please stay out of my personal business." She was about to hang up, before she heard his next sentence.

"The police would disagree."

She snapped the phone back to her ear. "What did you say?"

"I talked to the police, and they said he's already known to them. Did you know that?"

"Yes, I did, actually. And it's all bullshit."

She hung up, this time for real. She blocked Terry's number for good measure.

She sat there in shock for a moment, until Thomas gently asked her what was wrong. Not only were people cutting her out now, she explained, but they were actively working against them. Thank god she and Thomas were leaving for London in the morning. After that, she may have to find a way to disappear like Thomas. Or at the very least escape back home. She couldn't work with Terry, that much was clear. Salisbury would be too painful for her, anyway, without Thomas in it.

By the time she calmed down, the sky was darkening. To keep her mind off the impending events of the next day, she began the same preparations as the night before for setting Thomas up in the living room. Before she went into her bedroom, Thomas grabbed her arm and pulled her close. He kissed her, long and tenderly. When they pulled apart, Ashley felt weak. If this went any further, she wouldn't be able to let him go when they got back from London. She smiled softly at him, then turned and shut herself in her bedroom. Under the covers, she found tears streaming down her cheeks for too many reasons to put into words.

****

When Thomas was alone in the living room, he sat heavily on the sofa, made up once again as his makeshift bed. He pulled his feet out of the awkward shoes Ashley had bought for him. He appreciated the gift, but they had no give like his old leather boots did, and the tops and sides of his feet were rubbed raw.

He reached for his satchel and pulled out his clothes from back home, folding them neatly on the coffee table. He would don his tunic, hose, and boots before they left for the stone, which he hoped to do on Saturday, the day after they returned from London. If everything went well, he would be back home before midday, giving him enough time to reach Salisbury before nightfall. And then what? How would he explain his many-week absence to the bishop? Maybe word hadn't reached him that Thomas was on his way, and Thomas could simply say he had been delayed in London. Yes, that would be the thing. Then Thomas would explain that he wouldn't be going through with the ordination, which shouldn't come as a surprise to anyone, considering how long he had delayed it already. Then he could go anywhere he wished.

What he still hadn't grasped was how to explain his experience to himself. Here, in the hard reality of this magically cooled room with its hot water on demand and furniture made of materials and dyes he had never seen before, it was hard to dismiss any of it. He imagined the version of London he would visit tomorrow would be even more inexplicable. Once he got home, though, he might be able to pass it all off as a dream.

Except how would he pass off Ashley as a dream? She was as real as any woman he had ever met—more so, even. She had taken care of him when she had no obligation to. Yet there was also something in her that suggested that she needed taking care of, too. Thomas wanted to be the one to reciprocate that care.

But how? Could his two worlds continue to collide or would they be forever separated?

A thought occurred to him, a way to reconcile his desires, to make this extraordinary experience worth it. It was absurd. He shook his head in resignation and brushed the idea away.

He focused instead on getting home. The question

was how often the magic could work. Thomas had been sent here against his will, but if the magic worked when he wanted it to, did that mean that anyone could move back and forth whenever they wanted to? And would they always end up in the same place?

His breath caught in his throat. It had never before occurred to him that the stone might not send him home at all, but to another strange world altogether. The thought was too much to bear. He dropped to his knees and prayed more fervently than he ever had before.

Chapter 20

Ashley fiddled with her necklace. The train was nearing London, and she watched Thomas carefully as the landscape passed by. So far only rows of houses passed by the window, but she worried how the enormity of the capital city would affect him. He had made great strides in the time he had been here, but still. It would be a shock.

Fortunately, as they pulled into the train station, the scene roofed over, blocking the city from view. If she could keep him from freaking out on the train itself, they would be okay. Out in the city streets no one would notice. There would be more absurd things going on.

They left the platform and entered Waterloo station proper, with its huge open space and soaring ceiling. Thomas clutched the cross he wore around his neck, a move he hadn't made in a while, but he held himself together.

He craned his neck, gawking at the glass panels high above. "It's a cathedral?" he asked without glancing down.

"No, just a train station," Ashley said. She watched the people passing by, but none of them seemed the least interested in what she or Thomas was doing. She relaxed. "Come on," she said, giving his elbow a light tug. "We don't want to be late."

She wasn't surprised, however, that outside of the

train station, Thomas stopped again to take everything in. After her weeks in more demure Salisbury, even she was taken aback by the noise of the city. Everyone honked, and people pushed past them, annoyed that Thomas and Ashley were standing instead of moving.

"Let's get a taxi," she said, moving toward the road. She had debated the best way to get around while they were here and, while her knowledge of the Tube was still pretty good, she figured it would be too difficult to keep Thomas with her during the trip. And he might think they were moving through the bowels of hell or something, she thought with a smile. Besides, in a taxi he could watch the city out the window as they drove, which was ostensibly why he had wanted to come to London.

Thomas came up behind her. "This is the south side of the river," he said.

"So?" she asked as a black cab pulled up.

"It's not London."

She opened the door and waved him inside. "It's all London now."

He frowned but slid into the seat. "It's Southwark, maybe," he said.

"Where in Southwark you going, lad?" the cabbie asked.

Ashley slid in next to Thomas. "No, not Southwark," she said, and gave him the address for Professor Singer's department building. The cabbie shrugged but pulled out into traffic.

Thomas spent the ride craning his neck to observe the buildings, his right hand gripping his cross the entire time. Traffic crawled, and the ride was slow going. The cabbie made harmless chitchat as they wound their way through the streets, which only Ashley responded to.

By the time the cab dropped them at the university, they were late for their appointment, but Ashley knew that with his strong interest in Thomas, Professor Singer would wait for them. In the lobby, the secretary directed them to the sixteenth floor. Ashley cringed. There was no way around it. They would have to take the elevator.

Students walked quietly down the halls carrying tablets and books. A few waited for the elevator. Ashley waved them into the first lift but didn't enter behind them. She hoped no one else would show up before the next one came so she and Thomas could ride up alone.

The elevator returned a few minutes later. Instead of the previous three passengers, one heavyset lady walked out.

Thomas took a step back. The woman gave him a dirty look.

"What is this?" Thomas asked. He leaned forward to peer inside.

"It's nothing to worry about," Ashley reassured him. She put a hand on his shoulder. "It's just going to take us to the top of the building."

"Where did those people go?"

"Just get in, please," she hissed as she spied someone at the end of the hall headed their way. She pushed him inside and managed to hit the close door button in time.

The elevator lurched upwards. Thomas wobbled and spread his legs wide.

"We're just going up," Ashley said.

Thomas crossed himself the entire ride. By the time the doors dinged again, he appeared a little green at the unfamiliar motion. As soon as the doors slid open, she pulled him out to the hallway.

Thomas swallowed hard and glanced around them. "Where are we?"

"The same place, just sixteen floors up."

The hall ended to their right, lit by a window. Thomas stepped slowly toward it. As soon as he caught sight of the view, he stumbled back and crossed himself again. "How…" he said.

A young woman was walking toward the elevator. "Excuse me," Ashley asked her. "Is there a toilet nearby?"

"Sure, just down here to the left."

Ashley thanked her and dragged Thomas in that direction. She had to calm him down before they met Singer. They couldn't give anyone any more cause for suspicion than they already had.

She took him into the men's and locked the door behind them. Thomas raced for the first cubicle and vomited. Ashley crinkled her nose but said nothing.

A few minutes later, Thomas emerged. He splashed cold water on his face, letting it drip down his beard. Ashley handed him a wad of paper towels.

Once he was dried off, he said, "We have to do that on the way back?"

"Unless you want to walk down sixteen flights of stairs."

Thomas nodded numbly, which Ashley took to mean he would much prefer to walk down sixteen flights of stairs. Ashley lifted her right leg, indicating her walking boot. "You'll have to do the stairs without me, I'm afraid. I'll take the easy way down."

After a few deep breaths, he collected himself. "Fast stairs," he said in a half-hearted joke, "like fast letter."

"Exactly. Now are you ready to see Professor

Singer?"

He nodded. Outside the bathroom, a man made a confused face as they exited. Ashley gave him a curt nod before following the signs toward the correct office number.

Professor Singer's office door stood open. As they approached, he rattled his pen against the desk and frowned at his computer screen. Once they arrived in the doorway, he smiled.

"Ah!" he said. "I was starting to think you weren't coming."

"Sorry," she said. "It took longer to get here than we thought."

"Isn't that always the case," he said. She wasn't sure if it was a friendly commiseration or a reproach at her lack of planning.

He shook hands with both of them and waved them to a round table squeezed into a corner of the room. Already, his attention locked on Thomas. Ashley sat and crossed her legs, ready to be nonexistent for a few moments. It was a relief to not have to think about what to do or say next. Despite his recent meltdown, Thomas smiled and portrayed confidence, meeting the professor's inquisitive eyes dead on.

Singer set a small digital recorder on the tabletop. "I'll record you, if you don't mind."

Thomas's eyes darted toward Ashley's.

"It's just to record his voice so you can listen to it later, right?" she asked, as a way to give Thomas an explanation.

Singer glanced at her as if surprised to discover she was still there.

"That's fine," Thomas said.

Singer returned his focus to Thomas. He slid a few sheets of paper across the table to him. "I've prepared a few passages in Middle English for you to read. Just as you normally would." Singer leaned back in his chair and closed his eyes as he listened to Thomas read, as if he were hearing a moving piece of music.

When Thomas finished, Singer hit pause on the recorder. "It's remarkable," he said, "just how we thought Middle English should sound. Well, I was a bit surprised by the quality of the 'a' sound in a few words, but that just shows some of my colleagues were correct." He made a low grumble, then said more quietly, "Bully for them."

Brightening, he moved another sheet of paper to the top of the stack in his lap and started the recorder again. "Next, I will ask you a series of questions. I want you to respond just as you would if you were in conversation with somebody." He asked the first question in a Middle English even Ashley could tell was in tatters compared to Thomas's.

Thomas raised an eyebrow. Singer caught the motion out of the corner of his eye. "I'm sorry, remember I haven't had much reason to speak the language. Continue."

Thomas responded dryly. With each question, he seemed less and less enthused by the meeting, his answers short and succinct.

Sensing Thomas's waning interest, Singer moved on. "Now, that odd 'a' sound you made, can I take a short video of your mouth as you say it? It will help to map the exact position used to form the words." Thomas scrunched his nose up, but repeated the sentence while Singer used his smartphone to zoom in on and record his mouth movements.

Once that was done, Singer hesitated, tapped his fingers on the tabletop. "The preservation of the language in this form is unique," he said. He leaned in, probably hoping to appear conspiratorial, but Thomas scooted back at the sudden motion.

Singer plowed ahead anyway. "Where did you learn it? If there is a group speaking like this, it would be of immeasurable academic interest to study them—the way they speak, I mean." He waited expectantly for Thomas to answer. When Thomas didn't respond, Singer continued, "I understand you may want to protect them, but such a study could be of benefit to them too, drawing academic and tourist interest, which could translate into financial improvements."

"They don't want your improvements."

"Quite right, quite right. Do they follow traditional ways, like the Amish, perhaps?"

Thomas muttered something in the strange French he had used before.

Singer leaned forward again. "What was that? Can you say it again, please?"

Thomas repeated himself, more firmly this time, his gaze locked on Singer like he was bestowing a curse on him.

Singer dropped back in his chair as if he had received a physical blow. "My god, is that Old French?" he said, more to himself than to the other two. "I've never studied it myself, mind you, but my colleagues... Would you mind waiting while I pulled a few passages from Old French for you to read as well?"

"I think we've taken up enough of your time," Ashley broke in.

Singer seemed poised to argue, but then relented. "Right." He returned his focus to Thomas. "Did you learn Old French in the same place?"

"It's just French."

"Of course, of course."

"Everyone speaks it."

"Everyone speaks both English and French. Just as they would have in the post-Norman period. This just gets more and more fascinating."

Ashley stood to give Singer a hint to wrap it up.

"Right, right. I'll contact some of my colleagues. They may want to schedule time to speak with you as well."

Thomas stood, and Singer followed suit.

"You really must tell me more about this community. A formal interview could be done virtually."

Thomas moved past him.

"Nothing untoward about it," Singer said.

They reached the door. "Thank you for your time," Ashley said in her best sugary sweet realtor voice. That last open house she had used it at felt like another lifetime ago now.

"No, thank you," Singer insisted, shaking Ashley's hand, then Thomas's, for an extended period of time. "Please keep in touch."

Ashley followed Thomas into the hall. With his back turned to the door, Thomas rolled his eyes, and Ashley suppressed a giggle. They walked down the hall, Thomas braving the stairs, and Ashley waiting for the elevator.

Ashley had reserved two hotel rooms in the City, assuming Thomas would be more comfortable in the original footprint of the capital. Plus, they wouldn't have to travel too far to sightsee. It was the last time she would spend money on Thomas, so she accepted the expense. And, honestly, if continuing to pay his expenses meant Thomas stayed with her, she wouldn't mind the cost.

They had a quiet dinner near the hotel, talking over the day's events. Thomas didn't seem worried about Singer's plan to announce Thomas to his colleagues. Ashley worried, though, that something bad was bound to come of the extra attention. To distract her, Thomas regaled her with stories of what London had been like in his day: the streets thick with mud after a rain, the royal borough of Westminster, separate from the rest, the countryside flowing by along its outskirts.

"Have you really met the king?" she asked.

"Just to say we are his men," Thomas said slowly, taking time identifying each word.

"Is the palace incredible?"

Thomas shrugged. "There are many people who live and work there. There is no privacy. I think everyone here is richer than the king. He has none of this."

"But compared to everyone else…"

"Compared to everyone else, he is very rich."

There was a pause that only felt awkward after it dragged on.

"Listen, Thomas," Ashley started. "The last few weeks…"

He set a hand over hers. "I know," he said.

She nodded. There was no more to say. They were at the end. Why discuss a future that couldn't exist?

They walked the short distance back to the hotel in companionable silence. When they arrived, they again split at the elevator and the stairs. Ashley had considered booking them only one room but, remembering his reaction that first night that she had dared to step foot in his room, she had decided against it. She wanted to keep his good opinion of her. Even so, as she gazed into his blue eyes, she tried to transmit what she so desperately wanted.

He didn't receive the message, or if he did he refused to act on it. She should respect him for that, she supposed. Instead, he gave her a long, tender kiss, then went his separate way.

Ashley tossed and turned throughout the night, her mind always drawn back to the fact that Thomas would soon be out of her life forever. When she finally woke for good in the morning, away from the professors and the Salisbury police, it was easy to discount the dangers. She let herself hope that something would happen to postpone the inevitable. That some answer would appear that would keep everything from coming to a head. If only she had more time to figure something out.

The day started off with a warm, pleasant breeze. It was sunny, growing too hot by lunchtime. They walked with the other tourists along the Thames and through Westminster Abbey, where Thomas marveled at the mostly familiar structure containing tombs of so many notables that had lived and died in the time separating his world and now.

By the time they were debating where to eat lunch, Ashley had convinced herself that they could hide out in London for a few days while she figured something out. She could find someone who could forge documents. That must exist within this massive city. She wasn't sure how she would do it—her connections to the criminal underworld were currently nonexistent—but she couldn't stand the thought of Thomas leaving tomorrow. She worked up the courage to ask Thomas to stay just a bit longer. "Do you think—" she began but was cut off by her phone ringing.

It was Hannah, and it quickly became apparent that it was not a social call.

"What on earth is going on over there, Ash?" Hannah asked as soon as Ashley had answered. She didn't wait for Ashley's response. "A review came through for the vacation rental the other day that said your boyfriend helped with a maintenance issue even though he barely spoke English. That seemed odd, but I decided to be happy for you and go with it. I talked to Terry a few days ago and he said you guys had lunch and you ran off to meet somebody, but I thought surely that didn't mean anything. You were getting out and meeting people and thinking about your future."

Ashley cringed but thanked god Hannah hadn't talked to Terry within the last few days, when he would have told her of his new suspicions. Her hopes of an easy resolution to this phone call were quickly dashed, however, as Hannah continued.

"But now I've just had a call from the police out there asking if I knew my property might be housing an illegal migrant? What the fuck, Ashley?"

"Okay, hold on," Ashley said. Her voice wavered as she struggled to process all that Hannah had just said. "The thing with the police is just a misunderstanding about Thomas, really—"

"They seemed to understand perfectly well to me. Do you know what the climate around this is right now? Didn't you see the news the other day that there is a legitimate government proposal to put GPS trackers on asylum seekers?"

Ashley hadn't, but a quick search on her phone

brought the article up. She was silent as she scanned the article. "Can they do that? Treat people like endangered animals?"

"It doesn't matter what they can do, it doesn't matter whether it's a misunderstanding. What matters is what they are going to do."

"I'll talk to the police. I didn't mean for you to get dragged into this."

"*You* shouldn't have gotten dragged into this! Who is this guy anyway? Seriously, you are determined to ruin your life on both sides of the Atlantic, aren't you?"

"I—" Ashley started but couldn't find any words to fill in the blank space.

"I am leaving right now to drive out there to take care of this. I will throw that guy out myself if I have to."

"You don't have to do that."

"Yes, I do. Clearly." Hannah paused. "Where are you? It's awfully loud."

In a panic, Ashley hung up.

When Ashley tucked the phone back in her purse, her hands were shaking. Thomas's ID was now overdue by a day, and it was clear the police were taking action. They might have come by the flat that morning and realized she and Thomas weren't there. The police might have assumed they skipped town, which they had, technically. She was deep in this now, and she couldn't figure out a way to dig herself out of it. Another day or two wouldn't help. They had to act now.

Why had she ever agreed to help Thomas? If she had just worried about herself, none of this would have happened. Her emotions swung like a pendulum. She was suddenly angry at Thomas, that he had dragged her into this. That he had made her care for him just in time for him to leave. Her hopes of two minutes before laid shattered between their feet.

Thomas was gawping at the crowd, oblivious to the drama that had just unfolded.

Ashley whacked him on the chest.

His face snapped back to her, startled. "What?"

"Thanks for fucking everything up for me," she said.

His innocent expression made her resolve waver, but she plunged ahead nonetheless. "My cousin who owns my flat is headed to Salisbury right now. The police called her about you, and she's pissed."

"I'm sorry to cause problems with your family. What happened?"

He reached out a hand to her, but she shook him off. "Stop being so fucking nice!" she shouted. Ignoring the press of people around them, she threw her hands over her face and screamed.

Thomas stood over her in silence. He let her release her frustration.

When she calmed, she knew they had reached the end of whatever this relationship was. And she didn't want to leave it like this. "I'm sorry," she said. "I know it's not really your fault."

Thomas pulled her close to him, and she leaned her head on his shoulder. "I have to go, don't I?" he asked.

"Yes," she said. She surreptitiously wiped a tear from the corner of her eye, but another followed it, and she knew the game was up. She knew she looked awful, with her nose running and her face probably red and swollen. But she had to make her declaration anyway. If she didn't, she would always regret it. She peered into his eyes. "I don't want you to leave."

He perked up at this statement, his blue eyes

brightening. For an instant, Ashley thought he might decide to stay. But instead, he said, "I will miss you, too. I wish you could be with me."

She nodded slowly, absorbing the internal blow. "It has to happen today. I don't know how I'll explain it to Hannah, but I'll figure something out." She sighed and checked the time. "We have to get to the train station now so we can beat her there. We'll just go straight to the woods." They shared a grim glance before plunging through the crowd toward Waterloo.

When they arrived at the station, they had just missed a train to Salisbury and had to wait twenty minutes for the next. There hadn't been time to go back to the hotel to get their bags. Ashley figured she could retrieve them once she saw Thomas safely off and she dealt with Hannah—however she was going to manage that.

As she and Thomas sat down to wait, Hannah texted saying she was on her way and should be there in two and a half hours. Ashley calculated in her head: the train took an hour and a half, plus they had the twenty-minute wait. They should be able to make it home before Hannah arrived, although Ashley recalled that Hannah hadn't exactly driven in the slow lane when they made the trip to Salisbury together before.

Sitting on the train was torture. Even though they were moving, Ashley needed to feel like she was doing something. Her leg bounced up and down until Thomas set a hand on her knee to steady her. She was grateful for the distraction, but reality soon butted in. Her phone rang twice from the police station, then from another number she didn't recognize. She didn't answer any of them, instead letting them go to voicemail. A minute later, she braced herself to listen to the message from the unknown number. She held the phone slowly to her ear.

It was immigration. The case had been passed on. Thomas would need to register. Her heart picked up its pace. This was real now. There was no backup plan. If this didn't work—and, who was she kidding, the whole success of this enterprise rested on praying at a special rock—she would have to find a way to help Thomas escape from the authorities' clutches. Because where would they send him when he had no home here?

Thomas caught onto her distress. "Not good?"

She shoved her phone back into her jeans pocket. "It's fine," she lied. She squared her shoulders. What would the old Ashley do, the one who was so certain she could mold the events of the world to fit her will?

She would distract herself. Focus on the other person. Show she cared—and this time she actually did care, so, so much. "Do you know what you want to do?" she asked, remembering the instructions from the manuscript.

"Yes," he said firmly, "I do." He didn't elaborate, and she didn't push him. It was his secret if he wanted to keep it.

"Well, I'm glad. I'm sure whatever path you choose you'll do well in."

The conversation collapsed. She returned to watching out the window, though this time she was able to keep her leg and her emotions in check.

When they disembarked in Salisbury, she said, "We should go straight to the woods."

"No," Thomas said.

That was all she caught of his sentence through the din of the platform. He waved at his body instead, indicating his clothes.

"Right," she said. "You can't go back like that." She remembered the neat stack of his things he had left on her coffee table in preparation. Thank god he hadn't taken them to London where they would have been left behind. She checked her watch. "All right, but we have to hurry." She grabbed his hand, and they dashed through the streets of Salisbury.

She fumbled with the keypad on the street door but managed to let them in after a few attempts. At the top of the stairs, a middle-aged man emerged from the door opposite her flat.

"Excuse me," he said, "are you the young lady responsible for this flat? We're having an issue—"

"I'm sorry, I really can't talk now. It's an emergency. But I'll come back really soon, I promise." The door swung open, and she pulled Thomas inside.

While Thomas hurriedly got dressed, Ashley watched out the window that overlooked the street. After a moment, a familiar blue sedan moved slowly down the street while the driver searched for a parking space.

"Shit, she's here. We have to go."

Thomas grabbed his satchel, and they raced out of the flat without bothering to lock the door behind them. Across the way, the man had left the door open. Seeing Ashley reemerge, he moved to speak with her.

"I'll be right back, I promise!" Ashley yelled, her voice rising in surprise as Thomas lifted her up and carried her down the stairs. Her damn ankle was slowing them down. "You can go without me," she said as he set her down at the bottom of the stairs.

"No, you come," he said.

Outside, Hannah emerged from the car, now parked

a short distance down the street. Ashley pulled Thomas in the opposite direction. Behind her, Hannah yelled, "Ashley! Where are you going?"

Once they rounded the corner and were out of sight, Ashley paused to rip off her walking boot. She would just have to deal with the pain. There was no way they would make it without her being able to run. She leaned the boot up against a postbox. Maybe she could come get it, too, once Thomas was gone. She almost laughed at the absurd detritus she was leaving across the south of England, but she had to save her breath for their next mad dash through the streets.

A few minutes later they reached the edge of town. In the distance, she could see the copse of trees they needed to reach. They were almost there. As they waited to cross the final road before they reached the field, Hannah's car pulled around a curve. And behind her was a police vehicle.

"Run!" Ashley shouted. She and Thomas dashed across the road, hoping the cars would care enough to stop for them. After one set of screeching tires and a few good honks, they made it across. She heard her name yelled from behind them. A quick glance back showed Hannah standing beside her car, the police car pulled over behind it.

"What on earth are you doing?" Hannah shouted.

Resolving not to turn back again, Ashley followed Thomas in his dash across the field.

When they entered the protection of the trees, they paused, catching their breath. Ahead of them lay the moss-covered stone. Behind them, other feet scrambled up the hill, wheezing voices cursing her and Thomas. This was it.

Thomas knelt in front of the stone. Instead of clasping his hands in prayer, he looked up at her. "Are you ready?"

She took in a deep breath. This was goodbye. "Yes," she said.

"Good. Close your eyes."

She did as she was told. In the next instant, she felt his hand in hers. He became her only thought. She couldn't stand to let him go. She had no idea how she would clean up this mess when he was gone, but that was still not as dire as the thought of losing him forever. The approaching voices faded away, but she didn't dare open her eyes and look back.

She expected Thomas's hand to disappear, but a minute later she still felt its solidity in hers. Had it not worked?

She opened her eyes. There were no more shouts, no sound of Hannah and the police scrambling up the hill. Ashley was still surrounded by trees, but there was something different about the quality of the air, something off. After a moment, she recognized what it was: complete silence. No cars roared along the road a quarter of a mile away, no people shouted, no dogs barked.

She gazed around her. The trees were the same. The moss still straddled the stone.

Thomas was still beside her. He stood.

"Hurry," he said. "We have to make you presentable before anyone sees you."

Ignoring the awkward gait caused by the flaring pain in her ankle, Ashley dashed to where the edge of the wood should be. She carried on a few more yards past where she remembered the trees ending before emerging into the daylight.

There was nothing. No road, no signs, no buildings anywhere nearby. A mile or so off, the spire of Salisbury cathedral stuck out in the landscape, surrounded by low buildings. Along the edge of one field, a dirt track led toward the town. Farther in the distance, another village lined the horizon. There was green as far as she could see.

A stick snapped behind her. She half turned as Thomas joined her. He gave her a gentle smile. She stared out at the landscape, so different from anything she had ever seen.

They had both gotten what they wanted: to be together. Only they would be together here, in 1377. Where Thomas, at least, would be safe.

She grinned, flooded with relief. Whatever magic force inhabited this wood had known what she wanted better than she did. She threw her arms around Thomas's neck and kissed him for a long, long time.

A word about the author…

Beth Ford lives in the beautiful Shenandoah Valley of Virginia.

In addition to her novels, her work has appeared in a variety of literary journals.

https://bethfordauthor.com

Thank you for purchasing
this publication of The Wild Rose Press, Inc.

For questions or more information
contact us at
info@thewildrosepress.com.

The Wild Rose Press, Inc.

www.ingramcontent.com/pod-product-compliance
Lightning Source LLC
Chambersburg PA
CBHW052022020726
47501CB00004B/1189